Deli Chick

DELI CHICK

Discover a life beyond the counter.

PAULA NOBLE

First published in 2023 by Paula Noble.
Second edition 2025

ISBN 978 1 7643610 0 2

This is a work of fiction. Names, characters, places, and incidents are used fictitiously or are products of the authors imagination.

A catalogue record for this book is available from the National Library of Australia

Typesetting by Rack and Rune Publishing

info@rackandrune.com

Paula Noble acknowledges the Traditional Owners of the Country on which we live and work. She pays her respect to all Aboriginal and Torres Strait Islander-Elders, past and present.

This story was inspired by Beth Noble,
the original deli chick who co-wrote the play Deli Chick.

Thank you for your humour and wit,
which are etched in this story.

This book is dedicated to my mother Patricia.

Thank you for encouraging me to write.

Chapter One

Absentmindedly chewing his fingernails, Mr. Bader the supermarket manager was caught off guard when Lillian from the service desk entered his office.

'We have a new recruit,' she said, smiling back at Rachel. 'Sit over here dear.' She waved Rachel in and pointed to the chair on the other side of Mr. Bader's desk.

'I wasn't informed I had an interview today.' Mr. Bader frowned.

'Found it.' Lillian handed him Rachel's resume and patted his hand. 'We're all very busy. It's the Christmas rush.' She smiled at Rachel again and mouthed, *good luck*, as she left.

Rachel looked across the desk at Mr. Bader swallowed in his high back leather swivel chair. He scanned her resume while smoothing the thin strands of hair over the top of his shiny head—a mannerism she'd seen him do at least twice since entering his office.

'No checkout experience I see.' He pushed his steel rim glasses up the bridge of his nose.

'Oh no, I'm quite experienced with checkouts. It says there on my resume, Buy Right Fashion, the T-Shirt shop, Costless Shoes… ,' she trailed off. She'd had a lot of jobs.

Mr. Bader pushed his glasses up again. His balding head reflected the fluorescent light—so shiny she wondered if he polished it every morning.

'Why do you want this job?' His eyes looked even smaller through his lenses.

Rachel returned her attention from his shiny head and small eyes to the question every interviewer asked her. He'd scrunch her resume up in his nail-bitten fingers if she told him the truth: she was sacked from her last job and needed a new one.

But Mr. Bader continued, without waiting for her reply. 'What qualities can you bring to Goodsworth?'

'Qualities?' What sort of question was that? She thought about her last few jobs and how the only thing she added was frustration to her managers for being late, checking her Socials, and her girlfriends coming by to chat. 'I'm hard-working, honest, collaborative, self-motivated, efficient, and I treat customers with the respect they deserve,' she said, thinking about the customers who had told her she was hopeless, asked her what else she did with her life, and if she was single. She wanted to taser them.

'I see.' He looked at her seriously. 'Perhaps you might like to add the quality of humility.'

'Oh, of course.' Wasn't self-promotion the point of an interview?

'It's very important in this line of work to make scanning the produce look light, even the five-kilo box of washing powder. You need to ask your customer how their day is. And it goes without saying, but I'll say it anyway, disinfecting the counter after every customer is imperative. Now remember Renee,' he looked down at her resume, 'punctuality is key.'

'My name's Rachel. It's on my resume.'

Mr. Bader studied her resume. 'I hope you're sincere in your application for full-time work. Not just here for the holiday period, are we?' He raised his eyebrows.

'Definitely not. I think being the last friendly face the customer sees when they leave the store is a very important job. Checkouts is just what I'm after.' She cringed at this comment, *just what I'm after* sounded like she was buying a hair scrunchie rather than interviewing for a job. At least she wasn't interviewing for the deli. She wouldn't last a minute with dead pig and offal.

'Ah, hum,' he said, placing her application in the empty *Out-Tray* on his desk. 'We're very professional here at Goodsworth Renee. On time, clean uniform, and customer's always right.'

'Of course.' She thought about the customer at Costless Shoes who'd complained about her. She wore a skintight dress and stilettos, her heavy, caked-on foundation magnifying the lines around her eyes. She gave Rachel this line when she blamed her for selling a pair of shoes with a chipped heel. The fine dirt edged into the peeling heel left no doubt they'd been worn. The encounter had cost Rachel her job.

She glanced up at the black-framed certificates, hanging uneven and slightly crooked, on the wall behind him. *People Skills 101, Tier One* and *Tier Two People Management*, *Microsoft for Dummies*, and *Keys to Improving Workplace Productivity*; courses he'd attended.

'Goodworth gives professional development for their staff?' She eyed the certificates.

Mr. Bader frowned. 'What we have Renee is a supermarket, not McDonalds. We don't do development programs for our staff. We expect you to be developed enough already.'

'Oh, I just assumed… ' She gestured to the back wall.

'As the Goodsworth Manager courses are naturally offered to me.' He puffed out his chest slightly.

Wasn't this discrimination? But what did she care. It wasn't like she was going to make a career of this job.

'We don't waste good training on staff who are not committed long term, which seems to be most staff these days.' He pointed his finger to pause their conversation as his desk phone rang. 'Yes?' He swiveled around in his chair, facing his certificates.

Waiting for his call to finish, Rachel took in the details of his office. There was a dead palm in one corner and another struggling to stay alive, testament to the stuffy windowless office and perhaps his lack of care, or awareness.

On the wall beside the door was a whiteboard with a handwritten timetable and a chart called *Five-Year Strategic Plan.* The plan seemed to stop after two years, but it was hard to read as the writing was smudged. On his desk was a container of sharpened pencils, a laptop and monitor, and two black trays labelled *In-Tray* and *Out-Tray*. The *In-Tray* overflowed with paperwork. The *Out-Tray* held only her resume. Either he had a busy day ahead of him or he needed to review his *Workplace Productivity* course notes. At an arm's reach from his seat sat a glass-lidded, large jar of Smarties. A surprisingly colourful contrast to his uninspiring office.

Mr. Bader swiveled back to face her, clunking down the receiver. 'Now, where were we? Ah, yes, we're heading into the Christmas season, our busiest time of the year and we're currently understaffed… ' He looked up towards the doorway. 'What is it now Sandra?'

A short, stocky woman wearing a Goodsworth white shirt and black pants stormed into his office without even looking in Rachel's direction. Her name badge showed she was the Deli Team Leader. A ginger ponytail poked through the back of her cap. 'My chickens are off *again*!'

'I'm in the middle of an interview *Sandra*,' he said firmly.

Sandra, who looked like she was in her mid-thirties, rolled her eyes at Rachel. 'I don't care if Federer is sitting in your stupid office! I want this chicken problem solved.' She folded her arms, ready for a standoff.

Mr. Bader glanced awkwardly at Rachel over his glasses, as if trying to show he was in control and Sandra was a problem.

'You know what,' Rachel started, 'I can wait outside until you finish.' She began to rise from her chair but slowly sank back into it as a tall, fit looking, stand-out hottie strode up to the doorway.

'Bader! Need a word.'

Sandra put up her hand to halt him. 'Take a ticket Garth. I'm here first. Like I said Bades—'

'Sands, nothing in that deli is near important as checkouts,' the Hottie said.

Checkouts? Rachel's interest piqued. *Will I be working with standout hottie?*

'Yeah, well idiot, do you want off chickens going through your checkouts?' Sandra snapped.

'Can't manage your deli?' The hot guy smirked, then looked at Rachel. 'New?'

'H… hope to be.' She couldn't believe she stuttered.

Sandra rolled her eyes. 'Do yourself a favour new girl, leave now.'

Nice! What was up her arse? Rachel shook off her comment. She probably hated her job in the deli and was transferring her angst onto her.

'Sandra, I suggest you make an appointment,' Mr. Bader said, his tone dropping as if trying to sound assertive.

'And Sands, try to manage your staff better. How many left this month?' Hottie said.

'Shut up Garth.' Sandra's face was red. 'Bader, you either fix my chicken problems, or I'll be telling corporate about this,' she blasted, storming out of his office.

Rachel pretended to get something from her bag, feeling uncomfortable with this encounter. She made a mental note to avoid Sandra at all costs if she did get the job at checkouts.

'Like I said Bader, need a min.' Garth lingered in his office.

'Garth, this is Renee. A new Goodsworth employee for checkouts.'

New? Checkouts? She had the job then.

'Welcome to the team.' Garth smiled. 'I'm the Checkout Team Leader.' He said in a way that made it sound like the pinnacle of careers. He'd made it. He was proud of his job. Rachel smiled, liking his positivity, and his broad shoulders and pumped pecs that seemed to force the buttonholes on his shirt to stretch. His square jawline made his symmetrical face even more perfect. She guessed he was about twenty-five. A job at Goodsworth was looking awesome.

'Garth, come back in ten.' Mr. Bader checked the time on his watch.

'Renee?' Garth ignored him.

She smiled at him, conscious her teeth, though straightened with braces when she was thirteen, were no match for his perfect shining white veneers. 'Actually, my name's—'

'Deli huh?'

'What? God no! I don't eat ham. I'd be terrible in the deli. No, I'm here for checkouts.'

'Is that right? Terrible in the deli?' He pulled back his shoulders, forcefully expanding his pecs.

'Well not really,' she said, touching her necklace, pulling the silver circle back and forth across the chain. She stopped with a start when she nervously let out another giggle.

Garth redirected his gaze back to Mr. Bader. 'Need a word.'

'It can wait—'

'Only take a sec,' he said with force, then threw a wink at Rachel.

'Right, well, give us a minute Renee,' Mr. Bader said, trying to stifle his frustration as he followed Garth out of the office.

Rachel strained to hear their conversation but couldn't. She hoped Garth was telling Mr. Bader to put her on his shifts. After the way he looked at her it was possible. She couldn't believe her luck! She brushed her thumb over her painted nails, feeling relieved she'd followed the tutorial on dew-look makeup that morning. She wondered if he was single. Garth the Checkout Team Leader! It was going to be cool finally working with a hot looking guy. 'Let's just hope there's brains between the brawn,' she smiled to herself.

Mr. Bader returned, appearing even more frazzled than when she first met him. 'Now Renee,' he wiped his glasses on his shirt.

She leant in closer to the desk in anticipation of what he was about to say.

'As I mentioned, the job is yours.'

'That's great. Thank you.' *Great to have income, and great to be working with hot Garth.*

'However,' Mr. Bader tapped his desk and paused.

What was he about to say? A, *however*, was always a turning point of some consequence usually unexpected. Maybe the *however* was that she would need to be on Garth's shifts so he could train her. She smiled to herself at this idea.

He cleared his throat, 'as it turns out we are quite understaffed in the—'

'I'm more than happy to work extra shifts.' *With Garth.*

'Something we can organise in the—'

'Good and Garth will be training me then?' she blurted.

Mr. Bader looked at her over his glasses. 'Garth doesn't work in the deli? No Renee, it will be Sandra's job to train you.'

'The deli?' *Could this man please get her name and job description, right.* 'I think you accidentally said I'll be working in the deli.'

'Correct. You'll be working there,' he said dismissively, giving his glasses a push with his finger.

'Not checkouts?' *With hot Garth?*

'It's very clear this interview was for the delicatessen. However, if you'd prefer not to work there, here…' He let this last word linger.

'The interview was for checkouts,' she said, flustered. 'A few minutes ago, when Garth was here, you said the job at checkouts was mine. I can show you the email that the job was for checkouts.' She reached for her phone.

'I'm assuming you'd rather not take the job then.' He turned to study his computer monitor, the light beaming off his balding head.

This man was clearly incompetent; he didn't remember her name; took phone calls and let staff interrupt him during her interview; changed the job description, pretending he hadn't; and forgot he gave her the checkout position only a few minutes earlier. And now this. Fixating on his computer monitor like he had a problem to solve and ignoring her as if she wasn't there. She'd seen this often enough. Another manager promoted beyond their competency level.

'Mr. Bader, I think you were interviewing me for checkouts. You were saying greet the customer with 'How's your day—'

'How is your day,' he corrected.

'Um, yes. And you said to disinfect the counter after—'

'Qualities needed in the deli wouldn't you think?' he said bluntly.

'Well yes. But I thought I heard you say I was working at checkouts when hot… I mean Garth was here.'

Mr. Bader raised his eyebrows; she knew to be at her *hot* comment. 'Thought? Unfortunately, Renee you thought wrong. We need more staff in the deli so if you would like a job I suggest you take this opportunity.'

Rachel stared back at him, confused, but still trying to look amicable. She was tired of searching for jobs. She had five unsuccessful interviews already this week. She should have modified her resume. Nine jobs over two years was too many. She looked directly at Mr. Bader, trying to remain amicable. 'Can people transfer from the deli to checkouts?'

'I can't promise transfers. You're currently unemployed. Not snapping up this opportunity then?' He started to rise from his seat.

'I'll take it,' she blurted.

Mr. Bader sat back in his seat and glanced at her nails. 'I suggest you remove your nail polish. They'll be chipped by the end of your first shift. And since you are here, we can start your first shift now,' he said as if doing her a favour.

'Today?'

'You do want the job don't you?'

Clearly the course on *People Skills 101* didn't have an impact. 'I have plans.' *Like lying on the beach.* 'Isn't there training or an induction day?'

'We don't waste money on training uncommitted staff, which seems to be a societal problem these days. No instead, we let our team leaders, or managers as some of them still like to be called,' he rolled his eyes, 'train their staff on the go.'

'I'm not really dressed for working,' she said, thinking her white pants, new blush linen shirt, and mules, weren't suitable for the deli. 'I just don't think—'

'That's it then. Congratulations Renee. The job is yours.' He rose from his desk confident, as if he'd won a senate vote passing his new bill. 'Come with me and we'll get you sorted.'

There was little she could do. Mr. Bader just did not listen. He didn't listen to her, or even Sandra the deli manager. Sandra, who told her to 'leave now.' Sandra, who had no idea she was going to get a new staff member. Sandra, who'd seen Rachel guff over hot Garth. Sandra, who looked like she'd eat you for dinner if you got in her way. The thought of working with her was unpleasant for certain. But the thought of trying to find another job was worse. She'd just have to suck up this job and make it work, at least for the Christmas period. Finding a job was such an effort.

'Mr. Bader,' she called, scrambling out the door behind him.

'Ah hum?' He tapped busily at his phone while he walked.

'I get called Renee all the time.' She didn't. 'But my name is actually Rachel.'

Chapter Two

Lillian munched on a Krispy Kreme donut while reading a *New Idea.* The donut box, with two more donuts inside, lay open ready for further snacking.

'You can finish those later Lillian.' Mr. Bader rolled his eyes as if used to donuts on her desk. 'You can show Rachel the deli and tell Sandra she's starting today.'

'Sandra might need a bit more warning than this, don't you think?' Lillian swiftly wiped her hands.

'I'm the boss here and Sandra will do as I say.'

Lillian nodded and glanced kindly over at Rachel.

Mr. Bader turned to Rachel with barely a glance. 'Enjoy your time with us, Renee,' he mumbled, marching off quickly like he had some important meeting to attend.

'I wish he'd get my name right.'

Lillian packed up her donuts. 'He's a busy man with a lot on his mind dear. He'll remember your name soon enough.'

Rachel watched Mr. Bader head to a checkout where an older woman—who looked like she was ready to retire and drink G&Ts—was working. He flicked his hand in gesture to something he must have considered she did wrong. The older, ready-to-retire woman tilted her tussled grey head, giving him a look of indifference. He marched on, oblivious it seemed, to her disdain.

Oblivious too, to the fact he needed his glasses tightened and his hearing checked. *Renee*? Only she knew that to Mr. Bader she was just that girl, another replaceable minion in the store. She glanced over at checkouts. The customers busily offloaded their groceries onto the conveyer belts. The checkout operators were lucky—they didn't have to work with dead meat, offal, or Sandra.

Garth, the hottie, was at the end checkout chatting to a girl with dark hair and long lashes, giggling at him. Rachel felt a pang of a weird jealousy—because she wanted to be there, where hottie Garth would come past and hang out at her checkout. She watched them flirt with each other. If she'd got the checkout job, he'd be flirting with her. Because he already had in her interview, if that's what you'd call it.

'Now Rachel,' Lillian interrupted her thoughts. At least she could remember her name. 'Let's get you to your new home, the deli.'

According to Lillian, Goodsworth was in, 'Full swing operation Christmas.' It was busy, true, but poor old Goodsworth had nowhere near the number of customers which the large new Mega Mart at the other end of the mall attracted. How could it? With its dusty, caked, loose ceiling panels, peeling paint, turnstiles fresh from the 1960's, and only two self-service checkouts, it certainly lacked pizazz. Somehow Goodsworth had escaped upgrades, turnarounds, and innovation. It was still the same store that Rachel had shopped at with her mum. And even then, her mum told her, 'It looks just the same as when I was a little girl.'

Despite having fewer customers than its heavyweight competition, Goodsworth, like every supermarket across the country during the Christmas season, was frenetic. Christmas carols sang out across the store. Customers moronically stashed their trolleys full of food while negotiating their trolley driving, bumping into boxes dumped in aisles, waiting for packers to fill already stuffed shelves. They probably wished they'd shopped online.

Lillian needed to serve several customers at the counter before she could take Rachel to the deli. While she waited, a security guard, with muscle on muscle, wearing aviators, walked over to one of the checkouts.

'How're we t'day ladies?' he asked, leaning into the conveyor belt of the checkout closest to the service desk. 'How're you t'day Charlene?'

Charlene was attractive. With her long pink nails, messy blonde bun, ripped black jeans, and most likely, thought Rachel, a breast enlargement, she was the girl that guys like this security guard obviously obsessed over.

Charlene shot him a curt look through her thick lashes as she swiped a microwave pudding through the register. 'Same as I was five minutes ago Troy. Fine.'

Rachel was glad Lillian was getting a customer their cigarettes, so she could listen on. Troy had no idea he was outdated in dress and relationship cues, or that his interest in Charlene was not reciprocated.

'Good to see ya mood metre hasn't shifted,' he said, unperturbed at her obvious snub. 'I'll see ya later then Charls. Gotta head out for a ciggie.' Back at the entrance, he forgot his ciggie and pulled out his phone, scrolling away. She had to wonder what the point of a security guard was, let alone Troy, who by the look of him wouldn't detect an army tanker waltzing past.

Over at the fruit and vegie section a tall, lean grocer boy methodically stacked an apple pyramid. Next to it were three perfectly assembled varieties of apple and orange pyramids. He'd been busy. Rachel watched him stand back and admire the completed apple stack, just as a dark-haired little boy, who looked about five years old, took an apple from the bottom. Did he know what would happen? Was he checking the laws of gravity, in kid language: *let's watch them fall?*

The boy smiled as the apples toppled. The grocer boy, looking like his life's work was at stake, lunged forward with outstretched arms, attempting to save them from bruising and the bin.

'Happens most days,' Lillian said, as they watched him scramble across the floor to salvage them. 'He keeps making them. Poor luv'

Rachel felt sorry for him. But the kid's face, while his mother whisked him away, was good viewing.

'Sandra can come across a bit unfriendly at times,' Lillian said, as if trying to soften the blow. 'And what she did to Santa's beard last year certainly hasn't helped me with the Christmas planning this year.' She put her hand to her mouth to whisper, 'He declined to come to our regular event. Such a shame.'

Rachel wanted to ask what Sandra did to Santa's beard—burn it, cut it, plait it? Lillian moved on quickly, talking about the workings of the supermarket without drawing breath, while a store hand with his air pods in his ears and a trolley stacked full of boxes narrowly missed her.

A woman wearing a loose dress over swimmers, her hair wet from the beach or pool, bumped her bung-wheeled trolley into Rachel. Her toddler, perched in the trolley seat with a candy cane dangling like a lever from his nose, giggled loudly. His mum didn't even seem to notice, being fixed on the shelves of nuts.

Then Lillian paused and with a flourish of her hand, presented the deli to Rachel as if declaring the arrival of the Indian Pacific. There in the display fridge and covered in swathes of tinsel lay vacuum-sealed quarter pigs, glazed-eyed fish, ox tongues and sinewy chicken necks. However, neatly arranged in the white porcelain containers, they still screamed abattoir.

'Sandraaa,' Lillian called musically. Without waiting, she continued brightly. 'Meet Rachel, your new team member.'

Sandra clutched her clipboard and looked at Rachel with a dismissive, *you're pissing me off and wasting my time* face. 'This from Bader?'

'Yes,' Lillian held her smile.

'We haven't discussed this.' Sandra took the pencil resting on the top of her ear and shoved it between her teeth, studying Rachel like she was a mare for foaling.

'He oversees the supermarket, Sandra. He doesn't discuss who to hire, dear. Well then, I'll leave you to give Rachel her training.' She patted Rachel on the arm. 'See you later honey,' then whispered under her breath, 'you'll be fine.'

How could she possibly be fine? It was so cold and she wasn't sure why, but somehow she'd already pissed off Sandra, who could also do with a course on *Management Skills for Dummies*. She wondered if those books still existed. After all, were people still allowed to call each other *dummies*? Was it now an antiquated, cancelled, and shamed word? She couldn't keep up with the woke world. If you couldn't say it, you sure could think it.

Sandra clenched her teeth on her pencil with a look of disdain.

Rachel smiled awkwardly. This was awful. But she was going to be professional and suck this up. After all, it wasn't forever. She'd get to checkouts and away from this intolerable abattoir.

'Mules?' Sandra pointed to Rachel's shoes.

Rachel felt her neck go warm. 'I didn't plan on starting today.'

'Bader hired you then?'

'I thought I was interviewing for checkouts and then he decided—'

'He decided, did he?' she said, her face stony. 'Rachel, is it?'

'Yes, although Mr. Bader seems to call me Renee. He must've misheard or something.'

'Something alright.' She walked over to the backbench where she dropped her clipboard and turned on the tap. 'This deli's the hub of the store,' she said, washing her hands vigorously. 'Brings in twenty-five percent of the revenue. Without the deli and our fresh-cut meats, cured hams and gourmet pies, this supermarket would suffer. Everyone in this place knows the deli keeps the store afloat. Our targets are smashed every quarter.' She ripped the paper towel from its holder and cut a glance at Rachel with the confidence of a police officer directing traffic at peak hour. 'You're lucky, you know that?'

'Oh?'

'To be under my mentoring.'

'Of course.' Rachel viewed her new prison cell: white chicken pieces sandwiched into the glass cabinet glistened from the fluorescent light overhead; the overpowering smell of chickens cooked in the oven; and mounds of sliced ham overflowing white porcelain trays. She looked at the slicer, knives, tongs, and rubber gloves tossed in the bin—as if it had been a busy day in an operating theatre.

'You'll learn a lot from me,' Sandra said proudly. 'I'm on target for Employee of the Year, five years in a row. It's my staff management skills.'

She turned her head towards the coolroom and hollered, 'Valentina, get your arse out here and meet Rachel, she's new.'

Stepping out of the coolroom was a homely, kind looking woman, who Rachel guessed by her larger midline, pace of walking, and lines on her face, was in her mid-fifties. Her brown hair escaped from under her white hairnet. Her apron was smeared with assorted food stains, mainly red and brown. Rachel suspected a mix of marinades. What distinctly caught Rachel's eye though, were the bright red shoes that peaked under the cuffs of her black pants. How did she get away with this, especially around belligerent Sandra?

'Welcome dear,' the older woman said in thick accent. She turned to speak to Sandra. 'I thought you said you weren't hiring?'

'I'm not,' Sandra said, walking into the coolroom.

Valentina looked at Rachel. 'Sandra sacked Rhonda last week. A big mistake. I'm glad you are hired. We are desperate for another hand.'

Rachel felt more and more awkward.

Valentina lowered her voice so Sandra couldn't hear. 'I've worked here a long time. Don't let her fool you. She's a good person.' She squinted her eyes with a suggestion of sincerity. 'Anyway, she has me to thank for bringing peace into the deli. I shake my maracas every morning as a prayer ritual.' She re-adjusted her white meshed shower cap. 'Every morning,' she said loudly for Sandra's benefit.

'And they give me a bloody headache,' said Sandra walking out of the coolroom. 'Rachel, over here. Now.' Rachel did as she was told. 'She's my pro bono work,' she said quietly so Valentina couldn't hear.

'Pro bono?' Rachel was curious.

'Pro bono! Like Bono from U2 when he does something for nothing in return.' She tilted her head towards Valentina. 'Shakes those wretched maracas like it's Christmas every morning and wears them red shoes like a religious good luck charm. Tells me it's because the pope wears red shoes under his holy robe. Says it brings her good luck. Fat lot of luck it's brought the popes.'

Valentina lifted the two maracas from under the back counter for Rachel to see.

Rachel smiled, trying to look interested at her maracas. Valentina had made her feel even more confused about why she was in the deli. Sandra had sacked someone last week meant she could, and most likely by the way this introduction was going, would do it again. And why did Sandra have to oversee hiring? Sure, Rachel was new to how a supermarket operates, but even she knew a deli manager didn't normally get involved in hiring.

'Sandra, Valentina said you weren't hiring in the deli?'

'Nup.' Sandra picked up a pair of tongs lying in the cabinet and fiddled with the sausages. Lining them up and turning them, one at a time, like they were on a BBQ.

'So, not to seem ungrateful,' but she was, 'why did Mr. Bader place me in the deli and not checkouts, which I interviewed for?'

Sandra leant against the bench, her stony expression returning. 'Here's the problem.' She waved her tongs as she spoke. 'Bader thinks he operates this joint on his own. Well, he doesn't.'

'Hmm.' Rachel couldn't really give a shit. She just wanted to know why she was in this god-awful deli with two people who seemed out of touch with reality: one who shook maracas, and the other, an old-school workplace bully. 'Do you think I could transfer to checkouts then? Seeing as you're technically not hiring?'

'Who said I wasn't hiring?' She dropped her tongs and pulled her pencil from her ear and tapped it on her teeth. 'Bader doesn't run this deli. You bet I'm hiring.' She bit down on her pencil again. 'I couldn't give a stuff about you and bloody checkouts. All I care is that you pull your weight.' She shoved her pencil back behind her ear and straightened to her full height. 'And I don't need another Gen Z snowflake who can't hack the reality of the workforce. You need to have grit and drive to work here.'

'Of course.' Both would be hard to muster. All she felt right now was disappointment and a strong desire to walk out the door.

Sandra reached for a small box on the counter. 'Gloves,' she said, pulling two from the box and shoving them at Rachel. 'Coolroom,' she pointed to the steel door. 'Turn the knob when you close it, otherwise it won't shut tight.' She demonstrated how to turn the doorknob. 'And for God's sake, don't shut the door while you're in there. Broken latch, been telling Bader to fix it for months. If you get locked in you better hope someone knows you're there. Walls are fifteen centimetres thick of insulating foam and steel with a temperature of minus twelve degrees. Don't want no one dying on my watch. And let's address those shoes.' Rachel looked down at her mules. 'Damn stupid pair to wear in this place. Closed in black ones from now on.' She gave a tut with her tongue, then pointed at the chicken warming tray. 'Cooked chooks come out of the chicken oven after seventy-five minutes. They stay in the warming tray for three-and-a-half hours. After that we drop the price for thirty minutes. Then we chuck them.'

'You throw them away?'

'Yep. Health and Safety. Fact is these cooked chooks are made up mostly of unsold raw chickens about to expire. When we get them, they're only good for a day or two. My motto Rachel is—sell 'em or smell 'em. Supermarket's all about eliminating waste. Them premade chicken salads in the counter are made from non-sellers. Head honchos call it pre-purposing. I call it pre-poisoning. If I was manager of this supermarket, I'd do it better.'

Without waiting for an answer, Sandra hollered, 'Valentina, get Rachel an apron and show her the ropes. Rachel, I don't want to hear no pinging from your phone. Hit to silence. I'm off to my one-thirty-five meeting with Bades. Lots to be discussing, I tell you.' She hugged her clipboard, heading towards Bader's office.

Great, thought Rachel. *Not only are checkouts off limits but she's going to complain about me to Mr. Bader. And then she'll sack me.*

'Here, you can watch how I serve this customer,' said Valentina.

A customer, trying to ignore his two little girls giggling and scrambling through his legs, pulled a ticket. Rachel wished he'd managed to get a trolley before starting his shopping. Because if he had, he would not have plonked the poor, decapitated, vacuum-sealed quarter pig on the counter. As he read from his list, she felt a warm sensation in her mouth. No way, she couldn't gag, not here, not today. She turned to look at the backbench. There was a bin. As the warm mix of last night's spaghetti bolognaise, the morning's peanut butter on toast, and her double-shot cappuccino gurgled up through her stomach and into her throat, she had just enough time to dash to the bin, force it open and vomit. A feeling, she had to say, had been coming all morning.

Chapter Three

Sandra stormed into Bader's office, her clipboard in hand, ready for their regular shindig of disagreements about the daily specials. She expected him to be in his swivel chair, manning his computer in his typical obsessed manner. Only this morning he wasn't in his prize-possession—high-backed leather swivel chair—or his office. Not surprising really. The finicky little man was about as organised as a government transport bureaucrat. She stared at his timetable, scrawled across his grimy grey whiteboard. Great piece of use that was.

Moving to the other side of the desk, she droped into his chair, remembering the infamous tug-or-war he'd had with the previous store manager, Mac Sprink. Promoted to a position at Head Office, Mac wanted to take his prize chair, which had been given to him as a parting gift from his previous workplace. However, when Bader took up position in Mac's office he refused to give it up. Sandra still laughed at the memory of Mac clutching the headrest, Bader gripping the legs, both locked in combat at the top of the landing. The supermarket employees and shoppers watched with both amusement and concern. Not her. She thought it was epic when Mac let go of the chair and Bader fell down the stairs with the chair tumbling down on top of him. With a cut bloody lip and an instant lump on his head, Bader brushed himself off, grabbed the chair and wheeled it down to the service desk, and sat there in stubborn triumph until Mac left the store carrying his bag and cardboard box of pencils, pens, notepads and stained coffee mug.

She stretched out her legs, rested her feet on Bader's desk, and surveyed his office, scoffing to herself that he had not one Employee of the Year certificate. As she sat in his office, she felt triggered and enraged. *This office should be mine!*

Five years ago, when Mac Sprink told the Team Leaders he was leaving, Bader the balding little creep made sure her chance of promotion was zero. Mac told everyone in the meeting that Sandra was on the Big Boys' radar to take his job. Feeling pumped and validated for her efforts, grit, determination, and hard work, she felt elated that her dream job was finally going to land in her lap. All that changed when Mac turned up at the deli with a complaint from Bader that she'd been stealing groceries, which of course she hadn't. She agreed to walk out to her car to show them this was bullshit. Only—to her horror and rage—she found her car littered with more loose groceries than a MasterChef kitchen. It was obvious, to anyone with half a brain, Bader, the slimy little bastard, had planted the frozen pizzas, Maybelline makeup, packets of Burritos and other assortments of unrelatable grocery items. No matter how hard she tried to prove it, Sprink, wouldn't listen. He simply went from good guy advocate, to blinded unforgiving boss.

Up until that moment, Sandra had been proud of her career trajectory. She left school when she was sixteen. No one picked up that she was dyslexic. Coming from a family who thought literature was the latest gossip magazine, she'd never been one for academics. When she landed her first job at Goodsworth as a checkout operator, she knew this was the place for her. Highly motivated by her new environment, she mapped out her career path. And after one year on the job, she moved to the deli. Three years later, at nineteen, she was promoted to deli manager. Even though she enjoyed dominating her subordinates in this small pond, after ten years as the deli manager her next move was to leave the pond (where her influence could only go so far) and dominate the lake. Her plan was to be store manager. After this it was Head Office and then one day CEO.

Before Mac Sprink arrived as the new store manager, Sandra and Bader were good mates. She always thought he was a bit nerdy and socially inept, but he was harmless, good to say hello to and have the general bitch about deliveries, customers, and some of the new and younger staff.

He'd started working in the store six months before her and was one of the first to reach out and ask her if she needed help. As time went by and new staff came through, they smugly formed a natural alliance as more senior, knowledgeable members of the supermarket team. Both of their profiles stood taller, prouder, and more confident now that they were senior staff members. When Bader became produce manager and she deli manager, to celebrate they had a chardonnay, spring rolls, and a bowl of stir-fried prawns at the Chinese down the end of the mall.

'To us,' Sandra toasted Bader's glass, who awkwardly replied the same.

They would sit together in Mac's waste-of-time weekly meetings. Sandra would tell him about the new improvements she wanted to make, and what plans she had for the weekend. It was a safe, amicable, collegial friendship, or so she thought.

When Sandra heard Mac was leaving she told Bader she was going for his job. Bader had smiled and said, 'That's great,' but then quickly moved off to tell a store hand how the milk needed to be shelved with the most recent use-by date at the front. After that, Bader never stopped by the deli to even say hello, sat two seats away from her in Mac's meetings, and when she asked if he wanted to grab a bowl of stir-fried prawns at the Chinese, he always had an excuse. When he planted the goods in her car, she knew Bader was no longer her friend. He was now her enemy.

A smug smile crossed her face at the memory of finding Bader alone in aisle three where, barely able to restrain herself, she'd told him to consider himself lucky he only lost a few buttons when she grabbed him by his shirt and swore in his face until her voice was hoarse.

What she couldn't understand was why Sprink didn't check the CCTV footage to prove her innocence, even though she demanded him too. Instead, the incompetent lanky waste of space trashed her application for store manager and promoted Bader, the ugly little twerp. She'd threatened to tell everyone about Sprink's affair with Karen from The Coffee Hub at the end of the shopping centre if he didn't reverse his decision and make her the boss. An affair she'd turned a blind eye to since she spotted them a year earlier making out in his car like teenagers in a 1950's Drive In.

Unphased by her threat, Sprink made a deal. He'd make Bader drop the assault claims (which she hardly thought losing a few buttons warranted assault) if she dropped her threat against him and his Coffee Hub affair. Mac, red faced, frothing at the mouth, and thumping his fist on his desk, told her she should consider herself lucky he didn't report her theft to the police but let her remain deli manager. Sandra was livid. The job of her dream stolen by Bader.

She smirked at his *Five-Year Strategic Plan* on his whiteboard and reached into his Smarties jar, pouring a handful into her mouth. Several missed and landed on the floor. With satisfaction, she rolled over them with the wheel of his swivel chair.

She'd told Bader how clueless he was, making staff cuts across the store. Now her deli was understaffed, and under-skilled, especially in the Christmas period. Of course, the routine deflating of his tires was risky. Watching his contorted face as he yelled at his staff to fess up who did it was worth it. She grinned wider, thinking about him getting off the morning bus because he didn't know how to pump up his tires. Recently he'd started to park his car near hers again.

'Brave and stupid,' she said, as she crunched the Smarties in her mouth.

Bader walked abruptly into his office. 'Brave and stupid for what, having your feet on my desk?' His nostrils flared. 'Get out of my chair.'

Sandra sized him up. 'Why wasn't I part of the hiring process like I asked?'

'No one is part of the hiring process but me.'

'Good job you're doing. I had eleven staff on my books four years ago and now I only have three. One who's slower than a wet week, an actor who spends more time learning his lines than working,' she rolled her eyes at the thought of Justin, who was late again for his shift, 'and this new girl who looks allergic to work. I need more staff and to be part of the hiring process.'

Bader stood on the other side of his desk eyeing his chair. 'I've had a meeting with Corporate, who, as you know are visiting this week—'

'They're always impressed with the way I implement new strategies in the deli.'

'I hardly call rearranging where the slicer goes a new strategy. Besides, that's chicken feed compared to what I've done with this store.'

'What, nothing?'

'Corporate are very impressed with my management of this store.'

Sandra took her feet off his desk and dug her hand into the Smarties jar. She tilted back her head and dropped them one by one into her mouth. Bader's uselessness was jeopardising her reputation. How many times had she nagged him to fix the coolroom door, and now the timer on the oven? And how was it possible he still hadn't increased the number of self-service checkouts from a measly two, nor removed the archaic turn-style entry?

'You and those fossil managers don't even have the store set up for online trading. We're being left behind. Been warning you 'bout this for years. You don't listen.'

He frowned. 'It's come to my attention Sandra—'

'It's come to mine Bader that some boofhead is messing with my chicken deliveries. Ten boxes were delivered last week and half of them were off. This week I had three boxes go missing and another box with chickens as off as your mother's cooking. And if you'd fixed my oven timer, I wouldn't have Valentina pulling off blackened chickens every day. I suggest you get on the blower and order more chickens asap and work out what's going on down there at the Figgles bloody chicken plant. Their standards are slipping, I tell you.'

'Valentina's incompetent.' He glared at her from the other side of his desk.

Sandra gloated. She could see he was trying hard not to lose it. She'd watched him nibble more at his nails since he started as manager. The skin around his quicks looked horribly frayed and torn. Prior to taking the manager role, his hairline had only slightly receded. Now, the way it was going, he'd have no hair in a year or two.

'Face it Bades, you can't compete with that new Mega Mart.'

'Do I have to remind you of the assault charges—'

'Which you dropped.'

'You're bullying my staff. Nat's fruit pyramids are decimated every day.'

'You blame me?' Sandra retorted.

'We have CCTV footage.'

Sandra scoffed. 'Yeah, well Sprink, the incapable, should've used that when you loaded up my car with those goods, 'cause I know that's what you did,' she glared. 'Besides, it's resilience building. Nat needs some life skills.' Nat was overly nice to everyone. The day he found his backbone and told her off, would be the day she'd stop destroying his pyramids.

'Bruising my produce is hardly resilience building.' Bader pushed his glasses up the bridge of his nose, his eyes bulging. 'I suggest you get out of my chair.'

Sandra leaned into his desk. 'I have putrid chickens from the loading dock. I can't wait for replacements two days later. It's the Christmas period. And you still can't tell me why we have the quality control box for every chicken delivery, and why it has dick-brain Garth's name on it to check? He doesn't even work in the deli. And he knows nothing about food hygiene.' She wanted to scream. 'My off chickens started a month ago, same time he started checking those boxes. Explain that!'

What was it with the new bromance between Bader and Garth? It infuriated her, watching them walk around the supermarket together deep in conversation. Or worse, seeing Garth make his way to Bader's office. Like King of Checkouts needed more meetings.

Bader cleared his throat. 'I thought you blamed them on Rhonda?'

Sure, she'd taken the opportunity to get rid of Rhonda, the bad-breath opinionated woman who'd followed her loser taxi driver partner from Darwin to Sydney, only to discover he'd gambled his business and most of her small savings at the casino. Sandra felt sorry for Rhonda, for about a minute. When the off chickens started to emerge, Sandra blamed her for leaving them at the back dock for too long. Grouped in with her other offences: treading on Sandra's foot at the counter, shoving her into the oven door, and deliberately upending a cooked chicken to let the juice drip down Sandra's freshly washed apron (which even a double soak of stain remover didn't lift); getting Rhonda sacked was a no brainer.

'Point is Bades, we can't even use those chickens until after Garth's checked them. What's with that?' she snapped.

The deli was her domain and yet about a month ago Bader had decided to have a box of quality control chickens delivered to the coolroom with every chicken delivery. And Garth was the one to inspect them. She couldn't believe she was even complying with this stupid idea. At first, without Bader knowing, she checked the chickens inside the quality control boxes to see what the big deal was. After a while she could see how time-wasting and futile this was, so she stopped. Instead, she gave Garth, the entitled prince, her most pissed off look whenever he strutted into her deli to check the damn box.

'We have policies and procedures here,' Bader said.

'Policies have nothing to do with this. And you can't tell me why Garth's checking the boxes? He isn't even the produce manager. Oh, hang on, we don't have a produce manager since you sacked Mohammad.'

Sandra had liked Mohammad, a quiet, forty-year-old single man whom Bader dismissed when Garth had been promoted to Checkout Team Leader after only three months as a grocer boy. Mohammad had let on to Sandra that Garth was a snake in a chicken pen. She'd asked him if he thought she was a chicken in the pen? He'd laughed at her and told her she was the fox. 'Only trouble, Sands,' he said. 'Snakes eat foxes.'

She glared at Bader, tired of their meetings. He never listened to her suggestions for product placement and new food acquisitions. He didn't even care about the revenue her deli brought in. All he cared about was making himself look good. 'We need a new produce manager.'

Bader's left eye twitched. 'Add it to the agenda.'

'We don't have agendas,' she scoffed.

'Give me back my chair.'

She rose from his chair. She didn't take to being below his eye line anyway. Bader scurried around his desk in the opposite direction to her, taking possession of his swivel chair as if worried she'd change her mind and sit back down. She stared down at him from the other side of his desk. Bader sat upright, as high as he could in this chair, which seemed to swallow him, his frown fixed, trying to intimidate. This never worked on Sandra. She dug her hand in his Smarties jar and glared.

'Col and Andrew are visiting from Head Office this week,' Bader informed her as she dropped the Smarties into her mouth.

'Really?' This piqued her interest. She'd been counting on the Big Boys' visit. She loved the opportunity to show them how well she ran her staff and deli. Their input would give credibility to the final decision of Employee of the Year.

Bader cleared his throat. 'We've been in discussions and what we were thinking—'

'We?' Sandra crossed her arms.

'The deli needs a change of leadership.' He pulled the Smarties jar closer and replaced the lid.

'Change of leadership?'

'Fresh blood. New vision.'

'So, you're getting the sack?' She wished.

'You're not meeting target.'

'That's a lie. Besides, my deli's competing with that new Mega Mart and their flaming roast chickens and cappuccinos, which I've been telling you about for months.'

'Not telling Sandra, nagging. Besides, may I remind you our store prides itself on being a cheaper option for consumers.'

'You're losing customers because you're lazy.'

'I'm the boss Sandra, and I'll have you know your employment here—'

'Don't you even think about moving me from the deli, you incompetent fool.'

'You need to watch the way you're talking—'

'See that dead tree in the corner?'

Bader darted a glance at the dead plant he'd been given for his birthday by Cindy the accounts manager.

'That tree represents the way you run this place. Neglect.'

'Listen here Sandra, I've put up with your insubordination for long enough.' He cleared his throat. 'You've been on my delinquent list for a while now for the way you speak to me and treat the staff.'

'Delinquent list?' Sandra scoffed, staring down at the red-faced Bader.

'You're sacked,' he said.

'What?' She hadn't seen this coming. True, they argued every meeting, she talked about him behind his back to the other staff, and insulted his management style on a regular basis, but apart from her regular threats, abusive comments, and name-calling, she figured she was doing a profoundly superior job at managing her staff and the customer service. 'You can't do this,' she fumed. 'This is illegal.'

'I can make this very legal.' Bader's left eye twitched again.

'You may have gotten away with stashing my car full of groceries, but you won't get away with this! You don't move staff during the holiday period. Big Boys know that. Besides, I'm a member of the union. They'll help me fight this unfair dismissal, you incompetent baboon.'

Bader wiped his comb-over and then tapped his fingers on the desk as if trying to regain his composure. 'You can't speak to me—'

'Listen you useless, incompetent excuse for a manager, sack me without reason and you'll be the one answering to the Big Boys. Like I said, my targets are the best in the store. Get rid of me and you're gonna look like you don't know how to manage your staff—which you don't.'

'Sandra, this is your warning.'

'Warning? I thought I was sacked?'

'It's now a warning.' He wiped his hair, his hand shaking.

Sandra wondered if Bader, who had a pea for a brain, had someone in mind to replace her. She couldn't think straight. 'You'll never get rid of me. One day I'll be sitting where you are. In your chair!'

Abruptly, Bader picked up the phone receiver as if making a call would get Sandra out of his office. 'This is not the end of this conversation Sandra.' He pointed his finger firmly at her in rage. 'Now leave.'

Sandra left his office, not because he ordered her out, but because she couldn't stand the sight of him any longer. 'You're right, she mumbled to herself. 'The end is when I'm sitting in your leather swivel chair, manning the fort and you're out on your arse for incompetence.'

How dare he put this much pressure on her. Her, the award winner. She knew he could do it though. She'd had enough warnings from Head Office about her behaviour towards him. It would be difficult to go to HR with an unfair dismissal complaint.

Damn Bader. He's never going to get rid of me. I'm gonna make damn sure of that.

Chapter Four

Sandra marched back into the deli brandishing her clipboard. She glared at Valentina and Rachel, chatting at the back bench; they quickly dispersed, pretending to be busy. Valentina wiped the sink with a wad of paper towel. Rachel walked over to tidy the carton of eggs on top of the front bench, trying to figure out what she needed to be doing.

'You have no clue what to do, right?' Sandra glanced at her apronless attire.

How was it Sandra could make her feel guilty, even though it wasn't Rachel's fault she didn't have an apron or knew a skerrick what to do? She could tell what was coming next. After chatting with Bader, Sandra would tell her they'd made a mistake. She was fired. See you later. On your way. Au revoir. Kaput. Rachel opened her mouth to explain how she was waiting for Valentina to show her the ropes. But Sandra got in first.

'Useless.'

Rachel closed her mouth. Was Sandra saying she was *useless*? What sort of manager was this lady? No, *lady* was a bit strong. Sandra, with her heavy Blundstones, fluffy ginger mo—which she really needed to wax—and monotone deep voice that talked at her like she was spoiling for a fight, was more like a rugby coach before the big game than a retail manager.

'Every day I give her the same instructions,' Sandra complained. 'Needs to be micromanaged. Damn near exhausts me.'

'Oh.' Rachel felt somewhat relieved it was Valentina she was referring to. Bad for Val, but good for her. Okay, so she didn't need to quit. Not yet anyway. Sandra was never going to be the boss she would like, let alone respect. Her first impression of Sandra might never change. She was bossy, belligerent, and stroppy. Oh, the joy of working under her management.

Sandra ordered Rachel to follow her around the deli. She gave instructions in a clipped, fast voice while stacking the pressed chicken ham in a Herringbone pattern. Firmly, Sandra told Rachel she'd need to work her ass off. Sandra didn't want any slackers in her deli. She was on her way to getting Employee of the Year fifth year in a row, and no one was going to ruin this for her. Sandra told her how she could run the supermarket better than 'old Badey,' who got the job out of deceit. Rachel was curious to know what she meant. Sandra didn't elaborate. She stopped arranging the pressed chicken. 'You got your roster?'

'Yes, I'm, ah, on tomorrow an… and the rest of the week, from nine till nine. But I wanted to check this. It's like twelve hours.' It had to be illegal to make someone work that long. And why was this place making her stutter?

'Not "like" Rachel. Is! Twelve-hour shifts over the Christmas rush. Rosters come out fortnightly. After Christmas, your hours will be reduced.' She said it like it was a punishment. 'And none of this late Zoomer bullshit.'

Rachel pondered. Most of her "Zoomer" friends, as Sandra put it, weren't irresponsible but the exact opposite—worried where they'd be in twelve months, some working their butts off in jobs driving them to psychologists, their anxiety was spiking so high. How much more obvious could Sandra be? She didn't want her there. By the end of the week she'd be sacked. And if she wasn't, Sandra would micro-manage and belittled her until she quit. She could never understand mean bosses who thought they were superior just because of their job title and pay. Maybe she should quit and not bother with training.

'Sandra,' she began, 'I think –'

'You're an hour late,' Sandra barked over her shoulder, holding up the tongs in her hand, ignoring Rachel.

Rachel followed Sandra's gaze. A guy, about her age, with a motorbike helmet under one arm and a leather jacket in the other, ambled into the deli as if it was an afterthought in his day.

'Good to see you too Sands,' he said, eyeing Rachel.

Sandra snapped her tongs. 'Don't Sands me. You're late.'

'Late night on the stage.' He placed his messenger bag on the bench and pulled out his ear-pods.

'Yeah well, I don't care if your house was hit by a meteorite. How many times do I have to tell you, be on time? And tuck your shirt in,' she ordered. 'Running an iron over it wouldn't hurt either.'

Sandra was right, his shirt was badly creased, like it had spent the night under a cement roller. His black jeans were ripped everywhere; she guessed his apron would hide most of them.

'So,' he turned his attention to Rachel. 'New?'

'Just started. I'm Rachel. Rachel Fellings,' she said her last name out of habit and feeling a little taken off guard and nervous by his entry into the deli. It hadn't even crossed her mind about who else might work there.

'I'm Justin. Justin Walker,' he said with a slight smile, wiping his fringe from his eyes.

Rachel felt relieved he would be working here too. 'What was it you were saying, Rachel?' Sandra called across the deli.

'Oh,' she thought about her decision to quit and the fact that Sandra didn't miss a beat. Justin was a breath of fresh air in this place, and seemed relatively normal, whatever that was defined as, in this not-so-normal setting. Maybe working in the deli might be a little bit more tolerable with him here. And if she did stay, she would at least have a chance to get to checkouts. Sandra, who was hostile and pugnacious, would never be tolerable, but she could just take one day at a time.

'I… I was just going to say I think… that I can um, quickly get the hang of it… it being the deli of course.'

'Hang of it? Quickly?' Sandra quipped. 'This isn't the shortcut to the hospitality trade. This is the foundation of hospitality.' She put her tongs in her apron pocket, forgetting Rachel's induction, and served the waiting customer.

Justin smiled at her. 'Secret to surviving in this place is leaving your brain at the entrance.'

'You left yours there on the way in then?' She joked, keeping a straight face.

'Yep.' She liked the cheeky glint in his eyes. 'Just here for the Chrissy period then?' he asked.

'Oh ah, nup, here for, um, a bit longer.'

'Sure.' He gave her a look suggesting she wasn't.

'I actually thought I was interviewing for checkouts. I mean I *was* interviewing for checkouts, 'cause that's what the email about the interview said. After Mr. Bader offered me the job, and I had accepted, he told me it was for the deli, for real. Then he tells me to start today. Tells, not ask.' She looked at Justin as if for explanation. Maybe he could help shed light on the strange interview and job location.

'Doesn't surprise me,' he laughed slightly. 'Bader is such an odd, officious man. You've probably noticed this place isn't exactly organised.'

'Completely dysfunctional.'

'Agree,' he smiled. 'Disappointed to land in the deli then?'

'Ye-ah!' *Was it that obvious?*

'And Sandra, she's not exactly—'

'Friendly?'

He laughed. 'So, you're planning a transfer to checkouts?'

'What do you mean?'

He eyed her carefully. 'No desire to get to checkouts?'

'Well, yes, I mean yeah… of course.'

'Good luck then. Management isn't exactly fast-moving on transfers. Guess you've seen Bader's in-tray. A tsunami going nowhere.' They both smiled.

'Are you a musician?' she asked. 'You said, stage?'

'Actor. Work here between gigs. Our show finished a month ago.'

'No late night on the stage then?'

'No,' he said, self-assured. 'I'm learning a script for an audition at the end of the week.' He pulled out several crushed pieces of paper from his bag and placed them on the bench. 'My lines. Learn them whenever Sands is out of the deli, which is often.' He ran his fingers through his hair, giving her his attention.

'Justin, get Rachel a cap, Valentina forgot,' Sandra hollered across the deli as she dished stuffed peppers into a container without looking in Justin's direction.

'Not forget,' Valentina defended. 'You only said to get her an apron.'

'Yeah, and you couldn't even manage that,' Sandra said. 'And Rachel, don't lose your cap. Only get one a quarter. That's if you're lucky.' She placed the container on the weigh scale and looked back at them both. 'And no fraternising or flirting with customers or employees.' She rolled her eyes at Justin, who raised his hands in protest with a grin. 'We're here to serve, not perv,' she said sternly, handing the customer their container of peppers.

'Okay, let's get you an apron and,' Justin rummaged through a box under the counter, 'yes we have one—lucky you—a cap.' He lifted a pen off the back bench and scribbled on the inside. 'Here.'

She stared at her name written inside the cap. 'You wrote my name?'

'Trust me, you don't want to lose it. Because that's the alternative.' He darted a glance at Valentina's hair net. 'Imagine wearing that all day?'

'Ghastly,' she said.

'Exactly,' he smiled.

She put on her new cap and apron, thinking about the sticky floor and her mules? Tomorrow she was going to wear her old black school shoes, which she could not believe she still had shoved in the back of her cupboard.

Sandra called across the deli. 'I'm stepping out for my break. Valentina, keep an eye on the chooks. Need to be out of the oven in seven and a half minutes, remember. Justin, get the chooks from the receiving dock. Delivery's down on chickens for some lame arse reason—at Christmas too. I've had words with Bades 'bout it, but nothing changes. And Justin, show Rachel the ropes. And Rachel remind Justin to get them chooks from the receiving dock. He never remembers.' She pulled off her apron and with a meticulous fold placed it under the counter.

'Sands,' he faked a hurt expression.

'Don't Sands me. If we have another order of off chooks, there'll be heads rolling. Now top up the containers and serve.'

Was she serious about heads rolling? Rachel watched Sandra disappear up the aisle. She certainly liked her breaks, or meetings, or slackening off. Whatever it was, Rachel was glad Sandra out of the deli. But why make her responsible for reminding Justin to get the chickens from the loading dock? Like, don't they have a storeman?

'She was pretty pissed about the chickens last week. Whole delivery off. Blamed Rhonda. She'd been looking for an opportunity to get rid of her. Don't worry, she won't sack you,' Justin said.

'Oh, I wasn't wondering.' But she was. 'How can you be so sure she won't *sack* me?'

'Because if she didn't like you, she'd have you cleaning out the ham hock container already.'

'Oh!' It was a relief to think she'd escaped this obvious sign of dislike. Only she could tell by Sandra's distinct look of disdain, and the fact Mr. Bader had hired her, that she'd find a reason to get rid of her.

Justin hit the ticket machine. 'Come on, I'll show you how to perv, I mean serve,' he joked.

A grey-haired man stood at the counter, waiting patiently for them to serve him. He chatted about the weather, the busy shopping centre, and how challenging it was to find a car park. He was pleasant, forgiving of the hectic Christmas pace, retired, happy to stroll through the supermarket he'd frequented since the sixties when he was a child and Goodsworth was state-of-the-art.

Justin placed the wrapped sausages on the digital weigh scale. 'An idiot could use this.' He printed the price tag. 'Not suggesting you are.' They laughed with the man, still holding his ticket. 'So, Rach,' Justin said, 'think you have the hang of this place?'

Rachel tilted her head thoughtfully. Mr. Bader, it seemed, was not the only boss of the supermarket. Sandra was a belligerent, inconsistent taskmaster who hated Mr. Bader. Valentina believed her maracas created a peaceful atmosphere. And the only thing Justin took seriously was learning his lines.

'Yeah, I think I have the hang of it,' she said, beginning to also think, that maybe if Sandra was absent from the deli as often as Justin said, then she just might be able to handle working in this crazy place.

Chapter Five

Justin's induction was elementary, but she was okay with that. He seemed to enjoy showing her how to slice a salami, chuck the slices on the digital weigh scale, and how to manipulate the chicken oven with its broken timer. The worst part of her induction was when Justin made her serve the guy with straggly, long wet hair, who rocked up to the counter right when Justin was busy collecting 2.5 grams of nearly every type of ham for his customer. Justin called over to Rachel to serve the guy. 'It's easy,' he said. 'I'll help you with the weigh scale.'

She put on her professional face, 'How can I help you?'

'Just me weekly order thanks. A kilo of necks,' he said from the other side of the counter. 'Dogs love 'em.'

She darted a glance at Justin, who shrugged and smiled cheekily. He knew straggly haired man would order these, his weekly order! *Not funny*, she mouthed.

'Justin is there something to get the necks out with?' she asked, noticing the absence of tongs. She could have sworn she'd seen Sandra wielding some earlier when fussing with sausages Why weren't there more around?

'Yep, tongs, or hands.' Justin smiled to himself. 'Wash some of those tongs in the sink.'

She looked over at the sink, crowded with dirty trays, ladles, and tongs. She eyed the tongs in his hands, which he was using to lift out his customer's shaved ham. Valentina was using tongs too. Her only option was to dig one out of the sink but that looked too overwhelming. 'So, I just—'

'Put your hands in and grab.'

She angled her head away, half-squinting at the limp, decapitated, sinewy spines. Suppessing a groan, she lifted out a handful of purply necks. They were cold and slippery through her gloves, they nearly made her gag. Still, she weighed and wrapped them, and passed the package across the counter.

'Not so bad?' Justin asked.

'Terrible,' she replied.

As the morning moved in a painfully slow trajectory, she observed that customers assumed the deli staff were experts on all things deli. They'd ask her which chicken was the most suitable for curry. What to do with marinated peppers. *Why buy when you don't know*? And what bacon was best value for money—rashes or short cut. She didn't even know what a rash was. She was grateful for Valentina, who came to her rescue, relishing the opportunity to share her cooking prowess.

Holding an uncooked chicken ready for the oven, Valentina gave Rachel a lowdown on her technique at lifting the chickens from the oven. The chicken slipped from her hands onto the hard grey, tiled floor. Without missing a beat, she bent down, picked it up, and spit wiped it with her apron. 'Heat kills germs,' she said, as she stashed it in the oven. Rachel thought it was a miracle none of the five customers in the queue had noticed.

Justin, on the other hand, caught her eye and smiled. 'Happens.' He didn't seem to care.

She'd never buy a chicken from this place.

After serving her next three customers, she pulled out her phone and took a video of the deli, zooming in on the chicken necks.

'Videoing necks?' Justin queried.

'Don't know why but I want to prove to my friends I wasn't kidding where I was working.' She tapped on her phone, sending the video to her girlfriend Liz, who didn't think she'd take a job selling ham and animal parts.

'Here, give me your phone.'

'No.' She didn't trust him.

'Trust me. I'll take a photo of you in your get-up. A memory for you.' She handed him the phone, thinking it was a dumb idea. Why would she want to remember this place?

'Love your screen. It looks like mine,' he joked at her cracked and splintered screen. Something she had been meaning to fix since last year. He snapped one, then standing next to her, said, 'Look up.' And without comment she smiled with him into the camera. 'Cute,' he said looking at the photo. She gave him a half-smile, not full—she wanted to give him a hint she thought it wasn't cool taking a photo of them together, even though she liked it. She glanced again at the photo.

'Good huh?' he smiled.

She rolled her eyes and swiped up her Instagram, toying with the idea of posting the photo of her and Justin. Why not? He wouldn't mind. Without checking with him she posted it, then quickly flicked through the latest Stories.

Josie, who always had a holiday destination to share, was at Bologna in Italy. Her story was several frames of food on plates with the cobbled, paved streets and lined yellow and orange buildings in the background. Her long-haired boyfriend Kieran at the table, wearing a white shirt, a vino in his hand, looking like a movie star. Sharaya, who recently bought her first apartment, posted a story showing white walls and long flowing drapes, framing a raw timber sideboard with a charcoal Mud bowl. Dante, a friend from school with a fashion start-up, created a storyboard of her one sleeved black top and white pants in bulrushes near the beach. Rachel sent heart emojis to them all, wishing she hadn't posted herself in the deli. A latest bestseller casually resting on her towel with the surf in the background would have been better.

'Are you getting some love?' Justin almost teased. 'You posted the photo, right?'

'Oh, I… '

Justin had his phone in his hand. 'Accept my follow request.'

She checked her phone.

'Rachel Fellings is pretty easy to find,' he teased.

Why did she post that stupid photo? Who cared about her new job at the deli anyway? It was embarrassing compared to her friends' lives. She accepted his request and watched him *love* her photo.

'I need to get a water bottle. Forgot mine,' she said. 'If Sandra comes back and wonders where I am—'

'I'll tell her you needed a water bottle.'

'Thanks.' She grabbed her wallet, ignoring the water bottle in her bag.

Maybe she should just curate her life on her Socials a bit better. She was so annoyingly honest. She checked the photo again. Eighteen likes already. A comment from Sharaya, of course she would. *Hey babe, great to see you got another job.* What was she saying? That she changed jobs too much, or that she needed work? A message on Socials could be so cryptic. Her mood dropped. She swiped through her photos and found the beach, towel, and book photo from last week. She loaded it up on her Insta, tagging the beach. That would shut up Sharaya, who lived half a day away from the water.

Lillian gave her a friendly wave as she picked out sparkling water from the display fridge. She raised her water bottle as if needing to explain why she wasn't in the deli. With the absence of self-serve checkouts—like why?—she wandered towards the checkout of Charlene, where Troy had been hanging out only a few hours earlier. Charlene was heavily made-up with eyeliner making her own attempt at cat's eyes seem feeble.

A heavy-set guy with black, slicked hair, rolled sleeves above his thick biceps, and a blood-covered apron wrapped around his stomach, strode past her, directly to Charlene's checkout. He had to be the resident butcher. And Charlene, it was becoming more apparent, was the in-house queen bee of checkouts. The girl that guys like Troy and butcher dude here, made an idiot of themselves for.

The butcher dude moved from one foot to the other, eager for the man in front with two kids hanging off the trolley to move on. Rachel contemplated changing aisles; his apron was so off-putting. He glanced back at her and grinned. She smiled back, quickly picking up the closest magazine. With that apron, she didn't want to make small talk.

Charlene, with her long nails and platinum blonde hair, mechanically swiped the items, printed out the receipt, and gave a curt, 'have a nice day.' The man wearing blue shorts, faded T-shirt and Birkenstocks, took his receipt and lifted the little girl, who looked about three and wearing a long sleeve swimsuit, into the trolley.

The butcher dude watched as the other little girl hopped onto the back of the trolley, giggling. Eagerly, he moved along.

'You swipe them groceries real smooth Charls.'

Charlene gave him a bored look. 'Buyin' somefin?' She took a swig from her water bottle. 'It's really hard lookin' at that.' She gestured to his apron.

'Buying something?' he repeated, as if thinking what to buy.

'Yeah, like, what else you doin' hoggin' my counter? I got customers to serve, you know.' She darted her gaze at Rachel.

He reached for a packet of chewing gum and threw it on the conveyor belt with a broad smile.

'Two dollars eighty,' she demanded, chomping on her own gum.

'Oh, wait. Discount card.' He handed his card to her.

She swiped the card. 'A dollar sixty-five.' She pumped sanitiser over her hands.

'A dollar sixty-five,' he repeated, while counting the exact money from the coins he pulled out of his back pocket.

She dropped the coins into the till, giving her hands another pump of sanitiser. 'Next,' she called.

Rachel enjoyed watching the two of them. He liked her. Charlene didn't reciprocate the same feelings. Rachel could hardly blame her. The apron was a major turn off.

The butcher dude spied the magazine in Rachel's hand. 'Brad and Jen caught kissing again huh! Why don't they do us all a favour and get back together?'

'Yeah.' She didn't care.

He eyed her cap. 'New?'

'Yep. Started in the deli today. I'm Rachel,' she said, placing her water bottle on the conveyor belt.

'Mario, 2IC of the butchery. And this is—'

'Charlene,' she said matter-of-factly.

Rachel tapped her card on the card reader.

'Needing a break huh?' He eyed her water bottle.

'Yup.'

'Okay Mario, back to your butcher's den,' Charlene groaned at him. 'That apron stinks.'

Charlene was right, Mario's bloody caked apron, which looked like he'd mopped up an entire abattoir, was difficult to look at. With his long boning knife in its leather sheath, dangling from his hip belt, he could pass for an underworld figure who worked in a dark basement torturing his victims.

He beamed at Charlene, as if she'd given him a compliment. 'See you round beau'ful.'

'Probably, since we work in the same place,' she said, dryly.

With a hip swagger Mario fell in step with Rachel, following her to the deli. 'She's a great gal ain't she?' He opened the packet of gum and offered her a piece. 'You gonna enjoy working here,' he said confidently. 'Aldi was gonna do a deal with Goodsworth. Changed their mind last minute. Probs saw the writing on the wall with the new Mega Mart goin' in. Only been open a few months and sales here,' he pointed his finger to the ground, 'plummeted. Pissed off Bades big time. Reckon he's under the pump with corporate, who were real upset after Aldi rejected it. Gotta perform right? They seem to forget we're just a mum-and-pop grocery store. Can't compete with the biggies. Hey, we've got our jobs. So that's all that matters, right?' He didn't wait for her to respond. 'You know Roger, me manager, who's on leave with a slipped disc, says I'm in line for his job when he retires end of the year.' He beamed. 'We're smaller than Mega Fart but a cut above the rest,' he smile at his joke. 'Rog says I'm the best worker he's ever had. Master of the five Ps. Preparation, which prevents piss-poor performance. Get here the crack of dawn, Styrofoam and seal the meat, whack it on the shelves, then chill for the day.' He looked proud.

She could see Mario liked to talk. In their short walk to the deli, she learnt he was thirty-three and had worked at Goodsworth for ten years. He didn't hold back on telling her that since Charlene arrived six months ago, he'd been chatting her up—although—he was happy to tell her, he might be ready to move on. Rachel ignored the look he gave her and quickly entered the deli, leaving him on the other side of the counter.

'Dude,' he said to Justin while pushing his hands on the glass cabinet, causing his biceps to flex, 'this supermarket's bringing in some hot chicks these days, ay?'

Justin looked at Rachel and winked as he handed his customer their order and hit the ticket machine, calling another number. She tried to suppress her smile. She liked it when Justin winked at her.

'Sandra not here?' Mario asked.

'Nup,' Justin said.

Rachel was surprised how long Sandra took for her break. It was more than an hour since she left.

Mario strutted into the deli and picked at the antipasto. 'So, babe, you and me?' He grinned at her, as if expecting her to jump at the chance. Rachel pretended not to hear, fussing in her bag at the backbench, hoping he'd go back to the butchery for the day. He dropped an olive into his mouth, looking her way. 'Babe,' he got straight to the point. 'I'm looking for a plus one for me cuz's weddin'. You free Saturday two weeks?'

Rachel shoved her bag back under the bench. This guy had the self-confidence of a lux-listing real estate agent. He truly believed, bloody apron and all, that she would say yes. However, there was something friendly about him, he wasn't arrogant, just stupid maybe, in a naïve, self-absorbed kind of way.

'I have something on that day, um with my boyfriend,' she blurted, hating that she had to lie to make him feel less rejected. Why did she care about his feelings? The way he looked at her with his big brown puppy dog eyes, she wanted to let him down easily and definitively.

'Boyfriend huh?' Mario sucked the juicy flesh off the olive. 'Guess I'll have to let Charls come with me after all. Can't keep her eyes off me.'

'Sure, she can't,' Justin stirred, while serving a customer, 'but you still asked out Rach, even though you've been hovering over Charls since she arrived?'

'Gotta keep all options open buddy.' He looked at Rachel. 'I mean babes, youse number one, but boyfriend, huh. Makes Charls back to top contender.'

Was this guy for real? She tried to notice a hint of something jokey between the two guys. Mario looked serious. Rachel reckoned he'd been watching too many MAFS. She liked how Justin shortened her name—Rach. He was beginning to feel like an old friend already.

Mario spat the sucked-clean olive pip towards the bin a metre away. 'But here's the problemo. Charls plays this hard-to-get stuff. She's ignoring me in the lunchroom, watching all them makeup tutorials, and then pretends to diss me at the checkout. You've seen her?'

Rachel had. If only he could realise, his apron was a major turn off.

'Just to clarify, you were asking out Rach to make Charls jealous?' Justin questioned.

'Aw yeah, but also because,' he looked at Rachel seriously, 'you're hot babe.'

'Thanks for the compliment, I think,' Rachel gave a slight smile, and made herself busy fiddling with the food in the counter. She didn't want Sandra to come back and see her talking again. She needed to make a good impression. 'Anyway, I don't eat ham or pigs for that matter. So we wouldn't exactly be a good match.'

'Babe, no pig? Don't know how you do it!'

'It's surprisingly easy,' she said, thinking if he stood there any longer with his bloody apron, she'd become a vegetarian too.

He finished sucking his olives, sending their pips spraying into the bin. 'Well, my meat isn't gonna slice itself. See you 'round beau'ful.' He clicked his finger and pointed it affectionately at her, then ambled up the aisle.

Justin raised his eyebrows, amused, as Rachel stared after Mario in disbelief.

'What's that guy's deal?'

'He's been obsessed with Charlene since she got here.'

Mario's only reason for asking her out was to make Charlene jealous. 'He's kinda rude.'

Justin nodded. 'Ignore him. I usually do.'

She wanted to but she felt kind of stupid. She should have told him to get lost, although he was too friendly for that. She was glad she said she had a boyfriend. At least Mario didn't diss her before she dissed him. This was a relief. 'I actually don't have a boyfriend. I was just trying to make him go away,' she said.

Justin wrapped chicken breasts for a customer. 'Rach, you don't have to explain yourself to me,' he said, handing the breasts to a customer.

Now she was feeling awkward. How did her social life suddenly come into her work? Mario, who had no boundaries. It was becoming more and more obvious that she was going to have to work hard on her boundaries in this place, to make people treat her respectfully.

'Besides,' Justin added, 'even if you did have a thing for Mario, would you really want to date someone you worked with?'

'No, course not! Never a good idea,' she said, spotting Garth strutting past the orange pyramid and towards them.

Garth stopped at the cheese display and checked himself in the glass reflection of the cabinet. His eyes locked on himself as he moved his head to check different angles of his face and hair. He looked over at her and caught her eye. He smiled, his teeth glowing. She smiled back.

'Don't even think about him,' Justin said, scooping olives into a small container.

'Excuse me?'

'He's checking you out.'

'Who is?' She acted naïve, suddenly interested in cleaning down a perpetually sticky countertop.

'Santa Claus. Whom do you think?' He flicked his head in the direction of Garth, who gave him a smug look as he walked into the deli.

'Justin.'

'Garth.'

Their interaction was noticeably as cold as the freezer.

'Enjoying the job?' Garth ran his eyes down to her mules.

'Oh… ah… yes.' She felt strangely awkward. Garth, with his pearly white straight teeth, framed with his square jaw and evenly tanned skin, was just so gob-smackingly attractive.

'Sucks they've chucked you back here in the old deli. Told Bader to keep you at checkouts. Wouldn't listen. Said they needed you down here.' His eyes settled on her face. 'Waste.'

She felt relieved. Saying she was wasting her talent, which was of course what he was suggesting, felt nice.

'I can get you to checkouts,' he went on.

'You could?' she asked.

'Yep,' his reply brazen. 'Sandra 'round?' He looked past her.

'Nup.' Justin had finished serving a customer and had been leaning against the counter listening to their conversation.

Rachel didn't care what Justin thought. She was wondering if Garth was here to tell Sandra he was organising her transfer to checkouts. 'She'll be back soon. So, you're going to get me a job at checkouts?'

'I have a lot of power in this store,' he bragged. 'Leave it to me.' He looked at her confidently, his eyes narrowed, suggesting he could nail the job for her easily. 'Just need to check something,' he said, strutting into the coolroom.

Rachel couldn't believe it. Garth wanted her at checkouts. She was going to get out of this prison cell and be up at the front with him.

Justin looked at her. 'Hope you didn't really think that douche just came to see you.'

She felt her neck go warm. *Dah, that's exactly what he came for.*

'And he's bullshitting about checkouts. You know that don't you? The dick comes in here to check one stupid box called *quality control.* I'm amazed Sandra hasn't chucked it at him. Pisses her off big time.'

'Oh,' she said dismissively. Uninterested. Garth came to see Sandra to tell her that Rachel was going to be transferred to checkouts. Justin was being unkind.

Garth came out of the coolroom rubbing his upper arms to warm up. 'Qual' control chooks are good to go deli dick.' He smirked at Justin.

Justin lifted his gloved index finger in reply.

Garth smiled at Rachel while walking back to checkouts, his shoulders shifting in line with his strutting legs. She tried to suppress the smile that was crinkling at her lips, conscious Justin was watching.

'There's something seriously off about that guy.'

She ignored his comment. She didn't care what Justin had against Garth: probably jealous because Garth was the full package. Hot, charming, and Checkout Team Leader. She called for the next customer. Garth's visit had made her feel hopeful. He could get her out of the deli and up to checkouts where she wanted. This place was crazier than the Bachelor mansion, with way too many roosters roaming around. Garth seemed like he was actually interested in her in a serious dating way. He was the chief rooster. And her ticket to checkouts.

Chapter Six

Sandra sat on the bench at the edge of the car park, with a meat pie and can of Coke from The Coffee Hub. She didn't want to sit in the lunchroom today. She'd take the fumes of the car park over that suffocating room.

How could Bader threaten to take away her job? She knew he could get rid of her, the slimy bastard. She'd seen what he'd done to Mohammad, getting rid of him without a reason. She thought about Mohammad and his high staff turnover. 'Night fillers don't hang 'round long in this joint,' he'd told her. 'Most of my time's wasted on pointless inductions.'

She'd have zero tolerance doing Mohammad's job—training a revolving door of casual night fillers. Who would enjoy telling those opinionated Zoomers how to shelve the milk, position eggs, and where the lesser-known products like Dukkha lived? As for the stoners they employed, she'd seen them place the toilet paper in the plastic container section.

Sandra tore open the brown paper bag and smeared a thick layer of tomato sauce over the top of her pie. Biting into the lukewarm pie, she stared across the car park at Bader's car, contemplating donning a balaclava and egging the scrap heap. She'd heard him brag about getting a new car. She snorted at the idea, taking another bite of her pie. The gooey brown meat dripped down her chin. She wiped it with the back of her hand and chewed. Maybe keying his car was a better option.

She wouldn't do that—she was better than that, than him. *How could such an idiot be the supermarket manager? Over her, the award winner?* She'd worked her arse off since she was 15 to be where she was.

How could she be such an idiot to go along with his quality control box idea? What was with that? Who cared about chickens and quality control? It was never an issue with the Big Boys before. She wanted to throw the damn box at Bader. He was like hemorrhoids to a cyclist, unbearable.

She popped open her can of Coke, gulping down the fizzy dark liquid while squinting at the blazing sun. What was it about hiring Rachel without consulting her, the deli manager? She didn't need another teenager in the deli, trying to save up for their next Contiki tour. She'd had enough of girls like Rachel staying for the Christmas period then moving on. Waste of time training them. Think they know everything anyway. *Bet she doesn't know the difference between a chicken's head and butthole.* She laughed to herself at this thought.

She shoved the remaining pie into her mouth, washing it down with a long scull of Coke. She burped, tossing the brown paper bag and can into the bin. She thought about Bader and his growing infatuation with Garth. She needed to keep an eye on those two boneheads. It felt as if Garth had something on Bades.

Garth had been promoted suspiciously fast. He'd gone from pimply grocer boy—always running late and hanging shit on the other workers—to Checkout Team Leader in less than a year. Sandra scoffed at his new nose and chin, and those ridiculously white perfect teeth. *He must have paid a pretty price to clean up that pimply skin of his*, she thought.

Garth was always chatting up Trudy, Lucy, and Charlene—the three stooges who were employed after he became Checkout Team Leader. No surprises there. Sandra knew Garth influenced the employment of the pretty, vacant young women. They'd think him chatting them up was the highlight of their day. Garth, the self-absorbed egotistical gym junky, was always checking his phone—too busy to serve any customers. *How the hell did he get that role?*

When Sandra brought up Garth's behaviour to Bader, he told her to mind her own business and "stay in her lane!" Stay in her lane? Sandra would make Bader stay in his lane. As for Garth, he never stayed in his lane.

Sandra knew Bader was threatening her and she didn't want to lose her job. She also didn't want to lose any of her staff. Sure, she'd threatened to get rid of Justin, but he was a good worker—late, but on top of his game. And Valentina jumped to her every command—now that was hard to find these days in an employee. As for the new girl Rachel, she might not stay for long like the rest of the girls her age, but there was nothing really wrong with her besides being naïve, possibly lazy, and obviously disorganised. But she seemed like a nice kid who wouldn't answer back or challenge her authority. She would be easy to boss around.

Bader was up to something. He was behaving more weirdly than usual. And it had to do with Garth—ego-man, whose self-infatuation didn't leave room in his brain to think about work, or much else.

She tugged at her cap, making sure it was snug over her short auburn fringe. She needed to get back to the deli to check her staff were on their game. Never know when the Big Boys might appear. She didn't want to lose Employee of the Year. She needed to up her game and get their attention. Her job could be at risk. Heck, the supermarket could be at risk with those cavemen running the show. It was up to her and her deli chicks to make sure the supermarket stayed strong.

On her way back to the store she stopped outside Angelo Catalina's Real Estate. He stared down at her from a large poster filling the front window. His neatly parted black hair and toothy 'trust me' smile told shoppers in the mall that he was the man to trust when it came to selling their most precious possession. She'd heard from Lillian that these overbearing photos, which had appeared around the centre and in the local paper, had seen Angelo's sales soar.

This is what I need to do to keep myself in the game for Employee of the Year, she thought as she picked at the stuck piece of fine meat between her teeth with her finger. Posters of her, the deli manager, around the supermarket. Awesome! She'd be front and centre of everyone's attention—Big Boys, shoppers, Garth, and loser Bader. Brilliant. Bader wouldn't be able to sack a deli manager who was proactive and ahead of her game.

She pulled out her phone and scrolled through her photos looking for the perfect snap. *With my photo hanging across the store like a professional I'll show Bades how smart and skilled I am. He's gonna regret trying to make my life hell.*

Chapter Seven

Rachel had lived in the 1960's three-bedroom red brick house for all of her 20 years. The lawn out front, green from summer sun and rain, was short, mowed weekly by her father, Ian. White hydrangeas planted under the front living room window, their tiny mass of white petals formed into big flowering balls. Holding her bag on her shoulder so it wouldn't slip, she bent to pick several stems. A kookaburra laughed at her from the power lines. The sharp scent of eucalyptus drifted from the large gum tree shedding its bark near the fence. She never tired of the smell of this gumtree.

She checked the incoming message on her phone. A thumbs down emoji from her friend Liz was pretty much what she'd expected when she got the job in the deli.

Liz, a bid writer for large construction companies, wouldn't hesitate to remind Rachel the supermarket would just be another short-lived job.

Showing on her fractured screen were five texts from some guy she barely knew called Nick. She hadn't been in the mood to go to the pub last Friday night with Liz and a few of the girls from school. Liz had driven over, saying she wouldn't leave until Rachel got in the car.

'I'm menstruating,' she'd said, in the tone she used to exaggerate how much she hated getting her period with its monthly big bleeds, bloating, and cramps.

'That was your excuse last week.'

'I can't help it if I have super long, painful periods.'

'You my friend haven't dated anyone for at least a year.' Liz opened Rachel's wardrobe, then looked back at the clothes on the floor.

'That's not true,' Rachel defended.

'One-night stands aren't dating.'

Rachel sat on her bed and hugged her pillow. 'Last time we went out with Stephanie I woke up with a penis drawn on my hand in indelible ink—remember?'

'Don't get so drunk then! Besides, you're lucky Steph only drew it on your hand.'

Rachel had never found this joke funny. Steph, a freelance photographer, with strong political views. When drunk, she carried an indelible marker and drew penises anywhere she could. Some kind of juvenile regression from being so woke all the time, Rachel guessed.

Rachel had given in. She'd gone to the pub at the wharf, and kissed a guy called Nick. Somehow, she'd managed to give him her number, and had no recollection of him the next day, or even now.

She ignored his messages—too eager—and taking off her mules that were ruined with grease from the chickens, she opened the front door. 'Hey,' she sang out into the house.

'In the kitchen,' Ian called out.

He stood grating cheese, wearing an apron with the slogan, *"I love to cook with wine. I sometimes even put it in the food.* A gift to her mum from him. The test match broadcast from the living room. Whenever the cricket was on, so was the TV.

'Yum,' she said, the smell of spaghetti nudging her hunger. She dumped her bag on the floor and opened a cupboard, looking for a vase. 'It's after nine. Dinner is late! What's up?' Usually, Ian ate dinner the same time every night, at seven.

'Got carried away in the garden and knew you'd be hungry, so I waited.' He smiled at her, then added thoughtfully, 'Not the job you wanted huh?'

'It's never the job I want,' she said, arranging the flowers into the vase. 'Pretty.' She looked at the flowers, placing them on the dining room table.

Ian moved over to the stove, taking the wooden spoon to stir the spaghetti. His dark hair had subtle beginnings of grey at the side. His lean physique, from daily runs and fastidious healthy eating, made him look younger than his fifty-two years. Rachel was pleased he'd kept cycling with the same group from his university days. They made sure he got out and about and kept social after her mum died.

'Your mum's favourites,' he referred to flowers.

'Still are,' Rachel said quietly to herself.

'Did you tell the supermarket manager you don't eat ham?'

'Wouldn't make any difference in that stupid place.' She opened the fridge, and surveyed the shelves, not looking for any food in particular. 'I've been thinking about becoming a beautician,' she said, lifting a floppy carrot out of the vegetable tray and carrying it to the small compost bin under the sink.

'Missed that one.' He followed the carrot with his eyes.

'You don't believe me?'

'About what?' He resumed grating the cheese.

'About becoming a beautician.'

'I believed you when you said you were going to be a teacher, then work in daycare, and reception work…'

'So, it takes time to decide what to do with your life.'

'Thought the last job was going well.'

She opened the fridge again, feeling annoyed. She was tired of their *debates* about her *job jumping*, as her dad called them.

'There's a package for you.' He motioned with his eyes to the package at the end of the kitchen bench, which was, as usual, clean of any junk.

Ian had taken over the *running of the household*, as he called it, when her mum had first become sick. He'd developed a strict cleaning routine, which largely left her off the hook. The only thing she had to do was wash her clothes and cook a meal occasionally. She was grateful he enjoyed cleaning.

Mondays were sheets and towels, vacuuming and bathrooms. Tuesdays he dusted and did his washing, not hers, which lay in a compost mound on her floor. On Wednesdays he ordered online groceries and spent the rest of the day in the garden, wearing his floppy beige hat. Even though he'd complain about the effort it took, weeding, watering, digging, trimming, and mowing the lawn, she could tell by his whistling that he found gardening therapeutic. She often wondered what he was thinking when at the end of the day in the garden, he'd sit on the back deck drinking a cold beer in silence. He still hadn't returned to work himself. A topic he was keen to avoid while nagging Rachel about her own.

She picked up the express post package from the kitchen bench.

'Clothes?' he asked.

'Nah, just some make-up. It was cheap.' She rummaged in the drawer for scissors. *Why did she always feel the need to say things were 'cheap'?*

She slid the scissors through the tape sealing the box. It was the hair colour kit she'd ordered after watching a tutorial on how to colour your own hair. Her dark roots were really starting to show. She shut the box, not wanting Ian to see her purchase. He'd think she was crazy dyeing her own hair. When you had no money, what else could you expect?

Ian dished out spaghetti, a fresh salad already on the table. With red wine in hand, he flicked the TV to Australian Story. Sometimes Rachel imagined she and Ian being interviewed around their rustic ash dining table, talking about her mum's death and the inspiring life they'd built since. The second part was only ever going to be fantasy. Sometimes she imagined she'd become an oncologist who had discovered a cure or started a foundation which raised millions for those who couldn't afford cancer treatment not on the PBS list.

She sipped her wine. 'The deli is psycho. Look at my pants.' Oil dotted her white pants. 'Chicken bags are designed to leak and the apron doesn't remotely protect your clothes.' She mourned her new white pants. She'd promised herself no new clothes until she had $500 in the bank. That never seemed to happen.

'I'm sure you'll get used to the smell after a while,' Ian said gently.

'I'll never get used to the smell. I'll probably get bird flu with all those raw chickens.'

'That's what gloves are for.'

'It's cold, colourless and boring.' She twirled the spaghetti.

'Wear a jumper. And get stain remover on those pants tonight.' Ian changed the subject. 'Michelle next door called across the driveway this morning, "I worry about you Ian." And then accidentally knocked over the bin as she drove off.'

Rachel laughed. 'She had no idea?'

'None.'

'Tell her when she says she's "worried" about you, that next time she can pick up the rubbish.'

Rachel could tell Michelle had her eyes on Ian. When she came to visit the house with a hummingbird cake the week after her mum died, she blatantly said, "Your dad's a catch." Catch? Rachel wanted to hurl the cake at her–to catch. Instead, she faked a smile, thanked her, and shut the door as Michelle tried to take a step forward. She'd stood for several minutes on the front porch, probably expecting Rachel to reopen the door and ask her to come in and eat the cake with her dad. Like that was ever going to happen.

'I've had a look at some university courses you might be interested in,' Ian said, flicking back to the cricket.

'Thanks, but I have everything under control.' She sprinkled more grated cheese onto her spaghetti.

'You're having difficulty making a decision.'

'I'm not.' She twirled the spaghetti onto her fork.

'Look at how many jobs you've had.'

'Not many.' She frowned. 'And besides, they prove I'm making decisions, right? I'm not sitting in my room watching Netflix.'

'You've complained about all of them.'

'Everyone does that,' she shrugged, taking a large mouthful. 'I'm trying my hand at different things. I know you want me to go to uni. I get it. You and mum both. Maybe I don't have the brains. I mean, my HSC was brutal'

'Your mum was sick.'

'That's an excuse.'

'It's a reason. It was a difficult time.'

They ate in silence, broken only by cheers from the cricket. Ian stood up and moved closer to the screen to catch the replay, cheering, and commenting how good the hit was. Rachel never could get into the game. He sat back at the table, circling back to where he left off.

'Women a hundred years ago, and less, would give their eye-teeth to have the opportunities around university that you have today. Remember Rach, no one can take away that piece of paper.

'I'm fine in the deli, for now. And besides, the Checkout Team Leader is going to help me get a transfer to checkouts. Then I'll get more experience.' She ignored his raised eyebrows suggesting she'd had enough experience already. 'And then who knows,' she said, trying to get him off her case about university. 'I might jump from job to job but at least I have one.' She hated these conversations. Her dad worried too much about her jobs, while avoiding talking about his own. He'd worked in pathology, but when her mum's cancer returned a second time, he chose to work part-time. At first it was so he could look after her mum, but now she wondered if it was because he didn't want to be too close to anything medical. 'Anyway, you can talk, its time you got another job mister!'

'Just so happened that Joh rang me yesterday to see if I wanted to come back full-time. My old job basically.' He looked pleased.

'Wish someone would ring me up and offer me a job,' she said with a tone of truth while trying to sound upbeat. 'But that's great dad. Guess you were going to tell me when it was official?'

'Haven't seen you a lot lately. Seem busy.'

Busy? She'd hardly call sitting at her computer applying for jobs, or late-night benders out with Liz, busy. However, she was relieved he was going back to full-time work. Because speaking of busy, it was exactly what he needed. Maybe now was a good time to tell him about her plan to move out.

'Dad, Liz has a couple of friends, girls, who said I could move in with them, after Christmas. The other girl's moving back to the country, so they have a spare room. It's in Surry Hills.'

'Move out? With what money?'

'I'll save, now I have a job.'

'Well just make sure you can afford it.' He stood up and wiped the table with his paper napkin, dropping it into his empty bowl. She could tell he would miss her.

Afford it? Well at least he didn't say the B word. Budget! There was nothing she could afford, let alone move out. But she wanted to. Somehow the thought of moving into a shared house in an old terrace in Surry Hills, with cockroaches sneaking across the floor at night, mold on the bathroom ceiling, and torn and threaded carpet, appealed to her. The only people her age still at home were saving for a house; which would take a lifetime! Some were studying or just had too much of a good thing going on in the appliance and home services department, aka: dinner made, clothes drier on the ready, and when they opened the fridge—there was food!

Ian sank into the lounge chair and turned up the volume on the cricket. She picked up the hair kit and headed to her room. She finally took off her deli stinky clothes and flung them on the floor.

She turned on the bath tap, steam curling upward. She thought about the deli. The stench of chickens, the offal, the grease. Impressed she'd survived one shift, she made herself a deal: if Garth didn't get her transferred by the end of the week, she was quitting for sure.

Chapter Eight

How hard could it be dying your own hair? Rachel skimmed through the tutorial on foiling by Stacey Pacey. She twisted her hair in her fingers, weighing the challenge. On screen, Stacey Pacey sparkled like a QVC fairy godmother. "Ladies," she chirped, her shiny blonde mane catching the ring light, 'are you ready to change your life?'

Yes, thought Rachel. If Garth noticed her with roots growing out, then he'd notice her even more once her hair was touched up to its original blonde.

'So, what are you waiting for?' beamed Stacey Pacey. 'Buy these five bottles and get the blonde hot look you deserve!' Rachel paused the video. She was ready. Stacey Pacey's motivational spiel made her feel empowered. She wished she could be like this girl—confidently making money through selling online products.

Rachel lifted the bottles of toner and colours from the box.

'No labels? Okay, this is weird.'

All the bottles were the same shape, size and colour.

'There has to be instructions here,' she said, feeling less confident at the pending task, and in Stacey Pacey.

In all the finely shredded strips of brown paper, there was not an instruction to be found. She flicked on the YouTube video, beginning to feel frustrated at Stacey Pacey, the so-called makeup and hair vlogger guru. Smiling Stacey told her how to apply the products, fold the foils, and how to rinse them out. But that was it. Not one instruction telling her what was in each bottle. And wait time? 'Around thirty minutes should do it!' Translation: flip a coin and hope for the best.

Rachel called Liz. She'd know what to do. After all Liz had recommended Stacey Pacey, having heard Emily, her work colleague, brag about this money-saving hack of $60.00 to dye your own hair, and the fact Stacey had over 20,000 likes.

'No labels?' Liz gasped. 'Maybe you shouldn't try it Rach. Your hair always looks fine to me.'

'Fine?'

'Looks great.'

'You said great because I prompted you.'

'Your regrowth looks shit and yeah, you should dye it without knowing what's in each bottle. What could possibly go wrong? Better?'

'No, because now I don't know what you think.'

'There's nothing wrong with your hair. Wait until you can do this properly, like at a salon.'

'You said Emily does it all the time and swears by it. And her hair looks good right?'

'Yeah, but she does touch ups, not a whole head.'

'I'm going to trust the process. You always say, "YouTube is your friend."'

'Maybe on this occasion it's dubious. Clearly.'

'I need Garth's attention.'

'Sounds like you've got enough of it without resorting to self-sabotage?'

'Have you seen my regrowth? I need to get his undivided attention. He's my ticket to checkouts remember.'

'Yeah, well make sure this ticket is worth it.'

Liz had no idea how it felt to be in this dilemma. She had never dyed her brown hair, which seemed to enhance her dark eyes. Her hair was cut into a perfect line, sitting neatly on her shoulders. She never had to bother with regrowth and the only makeup she wore was lip-gloss. With her high cheekbones, long dark eyelashes, and neatly plucked, full eyebrows, she didn't need to enhance her features. Rachel was certain she'd have to know how naturally beautiful she was.

'How's the deli anyway? It can't be that bad?' Liz asked.

'Yes, it is. You should see my nails.' Rachel glanced at her chipped nail thinking how right Bader was; polished nails and the deli were not compatible!

'Not the lazy girl job like you wanted,' Liz stirred.

'Hardly,' Rachel sighed.

'It's an interim job,' Liz encouraged.

'Like all my other jobs?'

'Right,' Liz said, a little too seriously for Rachel's liking.

'What I'd give to have a lazy girl job like you.'

'I hardly call bid writing lazy.'

'Please. You could do it in Bali with a cocktail. You even bought that mouse jiggler to fake being online. Meanwhile, I'm out here scrubbing roast chicken trays.'

She secretly envied her friends interning overseas or finishing Masters degrees. Rachel's resume read like a speed-dating profile for retail.

'Maybe I'm over thinking this,' said Rachel.

'Maybe you're under-thinking this,' Liz replied, and hung up.

Rachel eyed the bottles. What could possibly go wrong? The box said 'hot blonde.' Not 'accidental goth,' not 'surprise bald.' Hot blonde.

Stacey Pacey's voice echoed once more from the screen, as Rachel poured what she guessed was the correct amount of colour into separate bowls. The liquid toner was easy to figure out as it was runny, not goupy like the contents in the other bottles.

'Right Rach, you've got this!' she told herself, half pep-talk, half prayer.

Half an hour later, having made what she thought was a pretty good, concerted guessing effort of what mixture was what, she smiled back at herself in the mirror feeling like a real pro.

'Not so tricky after all,' she said, admiring the neat little rows of foils on her head.

She clicked thumbs up for Stacey's video and went back to her room to watch another episode of Selling Sunset. She couldn't wait to see how good her hair would look without its dark roots.

'First thing I'll do tomorrow is make a non-obvious bee line to Garth. Checkouts, here I come.'

Chapter Nine

'Shit! Sandra's going to kill me. Shit. Shit. Shit.' Rachel lunged out of bed. 'I should have been at work twenty minutes ago.'

She yanked her jeans and clean-ish white shirt off the floor. With a quick smell and spray of Chanel (a gift from her girlfriends for her birthday), her clothes would be good for another day—just. And then there, staring back at her from the bathroom mirror, was the terrible mistake. If only it could have been a bad dream. And was that a pimple on her chin?

'Maybe I should pull a sicky.' But Sandra would sack her.

She dabbed her pimple with foundation hoping to make it less obvious. Rushing, the bottle of foundation slipped from her fingers, dotting her shirt in luminous silk natural glow.

'Great.' Scrubbing just made it worse. And no spare shirt. Brilliant. Nothing like wearing a buttoned up cardigan to work on the 42-degree day.

Thanks to Stacey bloody Pacey's YouTube 'blonde bombshell' tutorial, her hair had to remain out of sight and under her cap. Hard to do, but a must.

She dug through her bag for her Goodsworth cap. Not there. Not in the car.

'Is this where my cashmere jumper went?' she muttered, pulling clothes off the seat. Her car was less 'vehicle' and more 'lost property office.'

'This is going to be the worst day,' she said, putting her hoodie on over her cardigan, wishing she had more common sense and had taken Liz's sound advice and ignored Stacey Pacey's.

Last night, after she'd rinsed her hair, the outcome was unlike anything she could have imagined. Fanta-orange roots. Her stomach hit her mouth, or was it her mouth hit her stomach? Either way, she felt a rush of panic in her gut. Clicking back on YouTube, she ran through Stacey's video again. What had she done wrong? What step had she left out? She rang Liz.

'Did you use toner?'

'Yes.'

'Well maybe you do the toner again. To get the orange down. I think toner does that.'

'Think?'

'Guessing.'

Rachel tried toning her hair again. After all, this hair deal was now all about guessing. After what felt like hours of a science experiment, her Fanta-orange roots were exchanged for a tint of berry-blue. She now looked like a Smurf who'd lost a bet.

Rachel wanted to throw the five bottles at Stacey Pacey. Instead, she gave her a thumbs down and wrote a review. *Who is Stacey Pacey? A fake! She sucks you into buying her products with no labels or instructions. Want blue hair? Try Stacey Fakey Pacey!*

And now she had to face Sandra and ask for another cap.

At work, Sandra didn't disappoint. She stabbed the oyster tray into the ice like it owed her money. 'You're late,' she snapped. 'Strolling in here like work's an afterthought. And where's your cap? And what's up with your hair? This ain't bloody Newtown, we don't get creative types here.'

'Sorry, it won't happen again.' Rachel peeled off her hoodie and placed it under the bench.

Sandra's eyes zeroed in. 'What's that brown stain on your shirt?' Sandra snapped as Rachel fumbled with the buttons, attempting to cover her shirt. From her peripheral vision, she could see Justin looking. Was he smirking?

'I suggest you keep your cardigan buttoned all day. As for your cap.' Sandra marched over to a box under the counter.

Rachel started to explain. 'Well, the thing is—'

'Here.' Sandra handed her a white rectangular object.

'What do you want me to do with that?' Rachel had no idea what she was looking at.

'I want you to walk your dog with it. What do you think I want you to do with it?' she said, stretching the object apart, then flinging it at Rachel. 'Caps are a one-off free item. Ain't no more in stock 'til after Christmas and then it'll be docked from your pay.'

Rachel stretched the white floppy rectangular object contemplating which was worse. Blue hair or this attractive hair piece? *I'm going to love serving hot guys coming in for their party antipasto, wearing this.* 'So, no more free caps?'

'Correct.'

'I have to pay—'

'After Christmas, yes.' Sandra was clearly pissed off.

'I have to wear this?'

'I love to wear it,' said Valentina, taking the netting from Rachel's hand. 'It better than the cap, which flattens my hair like a pancake.' She pulled the object open with her fingers. 'It goes like this.' She demonstrated with the flair of someone auditioning for a low-budget hairnet commercial.

Reluctantly, Rachel took the hairnet, ignoring Justin's smirk and Sandra's obvious enjoyment in her suffering. Carefully tucking under the blue strands of hair, she smiled at Valentina, appreciating she was trying to make her feel better. From her reflection in the stainless-steel rim of the chicken oven she could see the blue, portentously visible, through the hair net.

'New trend?' Justin joked.

'Yep. Latest fashion coming out of Europe,' Rachel said dismissively, tying up her apron.

'Haven't seen much of it yet but you seem like a trend setter.'

'I like this colour coming out of Europe,' Valentina gestured at her hair.

'Oh here.' Rachel dug into her bag, retrieving several magazines. 'Because you like cooking. My dad, Ian, was going to ch… ,' she caught herself. *Chucking* made it sound like Valentina was getting leftovers. 'Change his cooking magazines around.' *Really?* 'So, he… we, wanted you to have these.' She sounded awkward. How hard was it to gift secondhand mags?

'Oh, thank you dear!' Valentina looked thrilled. 'It's a good day already. I shake my maracas extra hard today.'

'And given me another bloody headache,' complained Sandra. 'If I wasn't such a saint there'd be no maraca shaking in this deli, I tell you.'

Valentina gave Rachel a comforting smile and touched her arm. 'What are you doing for Christmas this year?'

Rachel hadn't expected this question. Even though yesterday, when Valentina had asked her about her family, she'd mentioned offhandedly that her mum had passed away. Valentina's kindness and tears forming in the corner of her eyes were a bit jarring. She was relieved when a guy whistled at her to take his order for marinara mix, while he resumed his Teams meeting on his phone.

'I'm, ah, having Christmas dinner with my dad,' she said quickly, hoping Valentina wouldn't ask anything else, but also wishing Christmas could be different.

Last Christmas had been with her dad's sister Meg and partner, anger-disordered Rick, the over-sixties self-inflated beach volleyball champion. He'd ruined the day with his bragging about his trophies, while telling Meg she couldn't cook and flicking a spoonful of gravy at her in the kitchen when he thought no one was looking. From her side eye Rachel saw it land on Meg's new cream dress. A "little mishap when tasting my gravy," she'd said. Later at home, Ian reassured her they'd give Christmas with Rick a miss next year.

Valentina gently tapped her on the arm. 'Why don't you and your father come to my house for Christmas dinner this year? Sandra and Katie are coming."

Rachel thought she saw a hint of a smile from Sandra. But it was short lived.

'That's enough of Christmas hogwash,' she snapped. 'I'm heading out for a jiff. I need you lot to keep this place—'

'Singing,' Justin said with a knowing grin.

'Correct.' She grabbed her clipboard. 'Rachel, remind Valentina to get those chooks off at 10.15!' she bellowed, as she left.

Valentina, looking like she'd accomplished something good for the day, placed the magazines carefully under the bench and went to serve an elderly man. Without a basket, Rachel guessed he was rushing to fill his deli order and get out of the supermarket as fast as he could. Lucky him. Before Valentina relinquished the wrapped package of fish from her hand to his, she told him how he should marinate the fish in lemon and chili to make fish Ceviche. 'Lemon breaks down the protein you see. It makes the fish firm and clear. It's a fishy citrus cocktail,' she declared to the man, who looked relieved when the package was finally released into his hand.

Valentina loved nothing more than lecturing customers on how to cook. Regulars had already figured out the trick—wave their ticket at Rachel or Justin like they were flagging a taxi. If you wanted to get out of the deli before retirement, you didn't let Valentina catch you.

'What's that smell?' Rachel asked, wrinkling her nose.

Justin bolted to the oven like a man who'd rehearsed this exact disaster. He yanked the door open, releasing a cloud of grey smoke thick enough to fumigate the cheese cabinet.

'Ah, not again!' Valentina cried.

Rachel gawked at the twelve charcoaled chickens as Justin helped Valentina fan away the smoke.

'I forgot again.' Valentina shook her head in frustration.

'Yeah, you did.' Justin coughed. 'But you shouldn't have to remember. Maybe Bader could, I don't know, fix the oven timer?'

'It's Bader's fault!' Valentina instantly agreed.

'Remembering to take them off at the right time wouldn't hurt either V,' said Justin. He shot a look at Rachel. 'This happens a lot.'

'I get so absorbed in my work,' Valentina protested. 'Rachel, you were meant to remind me.'

Rachel blinked. Oh, so the chickens were her fault now? She'd been there five minutes. What did she know?

'Rach, oven mitts,' Justin ordered, handing her a pair of frayed and burnt mitts.

'What exactly are you suggesting?' Rachel asked, eyeing the blackened birds.

'We get rid of the evidence before Sandra comes walks in.' He grabbed one with tongs and plopped it into a giant garbage bag.

'Good idea. I'll clear the energy,' Valentina said, rummaging under the counter for her maracas.

Rachel held her breath against the greasy smoke, hauling out burnt chicken after burnt chicken. Why was she the one elbow-deep in chicken corpses? She walked with Justin to the loading dock where he heaved the bag into the bin with a thud.

'What a waste.'

'Yeah. Really bothers me how much waste there is here,' Justin said, dragging a trolley. 'Come on, let's grab the new boxes.'

'The ones you were supposed to get yesterday?'

'The ones you were supposed to remind me to get,' he said with a wink.

'Why does she do that?'

'What?'

'Order, me to remind you guys to do your job?'

'She likes scaring the newbies. Testing you.'

'Yeah? Well, it works. And I've clearly failed.'

Justin chuckled. 'Relax. Her bark's worse than her bite.'

'I doubt it,' she said seriously. 'Why doesn't Mr. Bader—'

'Just Bader,' he said, loading several fresh boxes into the trolley.

'Only person who calls him Mr. Bader is Lillian.'

She appreciated his suggestion, having in fact wondered when she was going to start dropping *Mr.* like everyone else. 'Why doesn't Bader fix the oven? Seems so anomalous for a supermarket manager.'

'I'd agree if I knew what you just said.'

Rachel often tried out big words in conversation. Something Ian had done with her since she was a kid. 'Oh, you know, it's dumb. He's not following standards that are expected of a supermarket. I mean, you fix an oven timer, right?'

'What I've learnt about Bader and fixing shit is that he nods and agrees but nothing happens. Sandra's been waiting for the coolroom door to be fixed for over a year.' He looked at the boxes in the trolley. 'Chooks take seventy-five minutes to cook. These ladies won't be ready for the next rush hour.'

'What time is rush hour?'

'Eleven, three and seven.'

'Very accurate,' she said, starting to realise Justin wasn't really as slack as he seemed. 'Didn't you say Sandra blamed Rhonda for the off chickens last week and sacked her?'

'Yep.'

'Then she'll pin this on me.'

'Nah, she knows V's in charge of the chooks. And she'll never fire her. Let's just hope she overlooks the eleven o'clock rush though.'

'What about we buy some chickens from Mega Mart? We could put them in the warming tray. Sandra never needs to know.'

He eyed her thoughtfully.

'You agree, she'd pin it on me even though she knows it's the broken timer and it's Val's job to watch them, right?' She didn't wait for his reply. 'We need to get chickens.' She calculated the cost in her mind. 'We could split it; you, me and Val.'

'Might work,' he said thoughtfully.

Rachel felt heartened, he didn't hesitate to agree. He could easily have said he didn't have the money. 'You don't want to lose your job either?' she teased.

'Ah yeah. It would be a shame to see you go since you just got the job.'

Did he just admit he liked having her around?

'Let's get the chickens before Sandra gets back,' he said.

She took that as a definite yes.

Chapter Ten

Sandra could always rely on Wilma and Jen from checkouts, and of course Lillian, to keep her up to date with what was going on in the supermarket. Together they stood huddled, talking over each other, wearing serious expressions, relishing the daily gossip: who was new, who'd left, and who was hooking up.

Boring Jen, as Sandra quietly referred to her, had worked in the store for thirty years. Her lid was off her takeaway coffee, and she was using one finger to scoop out the cappuccino froth and lick it. Jen mostly complained about her varicose veins, how hard standing at checkouts was getting now she was a 'woman of a certain age', and her incurable sleep apnoea. It wasn't riveting conversation, until there was gossip.

'Garth's trying to cut my hours,' Jen complained. 'How am I gonna pay my bills if he only gives me two shifts a week?' She looked stinking cross.

'Two shifts?' Sandra couldn't believe firstly anyone would cut Jen's shifts, and second, Garth the ex-pimple head would have the authority to do this. Jen was an institution at the supermarket. Despite her whining about her veins, she was as speedy as they come, swiping, and packing groceries. 'How can he cut your hours?' Sandra fumed.

'Have you seen how often he's in Bader's office? Little shit thinks he owns the joint,' Wilma said indignantly.

Sandra glanced at Lillian, who nodded back, her eyes wide with concern. The three women were the old hens of the store. They'd each been there at least 30 years.

'If they reduce my hours, who knows how long it'll be till I'm out completely,' Jen worried.

Wilma shook her head. 'Only people who think he's okay are those new young girls.'

'Brainless idiots,' Sandra said.

'Hired by Garth,' Wilma added.

The Hens looked serious.

'Garths got his finger into everyone's business,' Lillian said. 'I don't think Mr. Bader is himself lately.'

'That might be an improvement,' Wilma said. 'Never was much of a manager anyway.'

They all agreed, even Lillian, who usually defended her boss when the girls rubbished him.

Sandra glanced at the time. Jen and Wilma had five minutes left of their break, but they'd take ten more. One advantage of years at checkouts. The young staff never argued with them about their long breaks. Sandra liked that Wilma had this power over the 'underlings,' as she liked to call them. Jen and Wilma made sure their morning break was always together. Off they'd go, gossiping and complaining all the way to Mick's café outside the supermarket, which served reheated burnt coffee and the best cream buns with large hunks of raspberry jam. Even Garth's threat of reducing Jen's hours didn't deter the two hens from taking longer breaks.

'Leave it to me ladies.' Sandra would take care of these old hens.

Something had to be done about Garth and Bader's idiot reign in the supermarket. You couldn't turf out the women who'd been there since she was just a young kid coming in with her parents. She remembered Jen and Wilma handing her a free chocolate with mint centre, wrapped in green foil, every time she visited. Those visits had felt like treats: filling a trolley with food, choosing chips, ice-cream, and Coco Pops, and topping it off with the warm greeting of these old hens—of course they weren't so old at the time. They were kind, thoughtful, and saw her. A young girl with an eye-patch for her lazy eye, a lisp (corrected with her father giving her an intensive week of tongue twisters and saving a packet from speech therapy), and several broken arms from age five to ten because when she'd fall off her bike she'd land with outstretched arms and her radius and ulnar would take the full force of impact. Something her physio corrected, "Sandra, you need to roll when you fall of your bike." She never broke an arm again.

The conversation about Garth unnerved her. Something was going on. He had no business meddling with staffing. It was Bader's job, the supermarket manager, to determine workers' hours. Not Garth! She'd had enough of Bader. And with Rachel being late for work, she'd let him know what a bad decision he'd made. Hiring Rachel without consulting her was plain stupid.

Nearing his office, she heard him clear his throat several times, a clear indicator he was stressed. She grinned, ready to enter, when she heard him talking to someone. She paused, holding back from entering the doorway.

'Way I see it, Bader, is you're either in charge of this place or not,' it was Garth. She backed up against the wall clear of the doorway, straining to listen.

'Perhaps you can stop eating my Smarties. You've had quite a few handfuls already,' Bader said. 'I got rid of Stephanie so you could have the Checkout Team Leader job, and Mohammad so you had more control of produce.' He sounded defensive. 'I let you have your job here because your friend Clive at Head Office wanted a favour. He talked you up like the next best thing. Obviously, another fabricated resume, Garth.'

Bader got rid of Stephanie and Mohammad for Garth? Sandra felt outraged. If Bader did this for Garth, Jen would have buckleys of saving her job.

'I won't let you and Clive bully me. I'm in charge of this supermarket,' Bader quibbled.

'Really. Then why'd you get rid of Stephanie and Mohammad like I asked?'

Sandra thought the same.

'She was incompetent,' Bader squeaked. 'No great loss there.'

It was true, Stephanie, the previous Checkout Team Leader wasn't great. She spent a lot of time checking Instagram, but she was well-liked by her colleagues. Losing her job had been a surprise to the staff. One day she was there, the next she was gone. And Garth, as opportunistic as an Australian politician, had taken over her position.

When Mohammad told her his job had been made redundant, she'd smelt a rat. Now she knew there was not one rat, but two. Without a produce manager regularly inspecting merchandise, checking expiration dates, and maintaining displays, things were going downhill fast—like the regular delivery of bad chooks from Figgles Chickens.

'I agreed to put Renee in the deli at your demand even without experience,' she heard Bader. 'I've given away another prize position. Like the others she'll only last till the end of the summer then most likely leave for university or a job requiring experience, which she'll have because I gave it to her besides my better judgment.

Better judgment?

'That blonde chick is into me,' Garth said. 'No missing the way she checked me out when I came into your office last week.'

She couldn't believe what she was hearing. Bader really was letting Garth decide who was employed? No doubt based on looks. And he thinks Renee, who is obviously Rachel, is clueless. The two bone heads couldn't even get her name right.

Sandra thought otherwise about Rachel. She could tell she was a deep thinker. She hadn't rambled about how 'icky' the food smelled or looked, even though Sandra knew that's what she was thinking. Nor had she complained about the air conditioning like the last hundred young girls she'd trained and said goodbye to. She could tell Rachel wouldn't be as stupid as Valentina, who she'd seen drop chickens on the floor and clean them with her spit and polish. Rachel seemed to be the sort of girl who'd hate to eat contaminated food, let alone sell it.

'Don't forget who's boss around here,' Garth said.

Boss?

'No, please no… there's no need to—' Bader protested.

'You need a warning ya pussy,' Garth threatened.

It was hard to restrain herself from looking around the door as the sound of smashing objects hit the wall and Bader hollered for Garth to stop. She couldn't wait to get in there and see what was going on. Quickly, she stepped away to make it look like she was just coming down the hallway. Garth flew through the door. His face, dark and angry. He glared at her and shoved her shoulder as he passed.

'Piss off dick,' she called out to him as he kept walking, then under her breath said, 'misogynist pig.' She wiped her shoulder, as if to get rid of contamination. How dare he nudge her. And how dare he call the shots over who was hired in the store. Who was this Clive from Head Office? And why did he want Garth in the supermarket as Checkout Team Leader?

Bader's office was a mess: potting mix had been flung on the wall behind his chair; his palm tree was snapped in two; and crushed masticated flecks of Smarties—like hundreds and thousands—decorated his specs. The Smarties jar lay on the floor empty.

Not only was his office in disarray, but she was acutely aware of a distinct putrid smell. Had someone peed on the dead plant? She remembered Bader asking Garth not to do something. She raised her hand to her nose.

Bader gave his comb-over several quick wipes. 'What seems to be the problem now Sandra?' he sighed. 'Oh, and that smell,' he tutted, waving towards the plant as if the smell was nothing, 'Seasol, plant fertiliser. Did it this morning.'

Sandra knew very well the smell was not the seaweed spray so common among plant lovers. No doubt Garth had massively overreacted and lost it.

'Well, be quick then.' He looked through the flecks of Smarties on his glasses, as if ignoring them and the carnage in his room might make the mess invisible.

Unable to hide her astonishment at the sight of his office, she looked down at him in his chair. She almost felt sorry for him. The specs of Smarties, she concluded, could only arrive on his glasses via Garth's projective spit while chewing said Smarties.

'I told you I should be part of the hiring process,' she said firmly. 'Rachel can't even be on time. First week!'

'Well then, your induction was obviously ineffective,' he said, wiping his glasses with his handkerchief, then blowing his breath on the lenses for a second polish. He placed the glasses back on the bridge of his nose. 'Is that it then?'

'Good question Bader,' she said coldly. 'What's with Garth and his meetings?' She gestured towards the dirt on his wall.

Bader darted a sideways uncertain glance and cleared his throat. 'Yes, well it seems Garth has a bit of a temper.' He tapped his fingers on the desk looking cross. 'Something you might be familiar with.' He picked up his phone receiver. 'Is that all then, Sandra?'

'Yeah,' she said curtly, then under her breath, 'for now.'

She walked out of his office. She could hear him on the phone to Lillian asking for Sylvie, the cleaner to come to his office. Sylvie had one hell of a mess to clean up. She'd look forward to hearing about it in the lunchroom later. As for Garth, he was up to something. She didn't like his increasing power in Goodsworth. Something she needed to put an end to.

Chapter Eleven

The deli at Mega Mart was swamped with customers. This worked in their favour: as no one would notice Rachel and Justin clearing out the warming oven of its plump, golden-roasted chickens. As she hurried alongside Justin with the trolley full of chickens, she noticed how much more appealing Mega Mart, with its warmer lights and wide-open aisles. Justin pushed the trolley through the checkout manned by a guy named Alexis.

'You guys work at Goodsworth deli, right?' He eyed Rachel's hair net, which she'd forgotten she was still wearing. A dead giveaway. But then again, so was Justin's deli cap with Goodsworth Deli on it, and their name badges. Rachel wished they'd been a bit more organised and got rid of this evidence.

'Yep,' said Justin, helping Rachel load the chickens on the conveyor belt.

'Right.' Alexis raised his eyebrows.

Justin's poker face gave nothing away. Rachel felt stronger, or was it cooler, with him around? Who cared what Alexis thought.

'Thanks,' she said, snatching the receipt from his hand, ignoring the weird look he gave them.

'You know what he's thinking, don't you?' Rachel said to Justin who pushed the trolley.

'That we're going to sell Mega Mart chickens?' Justin found it funny.

'Yes. What if he tells someone?''

'Nah, he's like us Rach. In for the dollar. Probably thinks it's funny too. Bet he comes down later to check.'

'Do you worry about anything?'

'Only when I need to.' He turned to her and smiled.

A woman, carrying more shopping bags than she had hands to hold, knocked into Rachel, bumping her into the trolley. Justin stopped. 'You okay?'

'Yes.' She hopped on the end of the trolley. 'I need a free ride.'

He laughed. 'Of course.'

Several minutes later, with Rachel standing on the end of the trolley and both still laughing at the craziness of the moment, Justin whizzed the Mega Mart trolley into the deli and up to the warming rack ready to unload the chickens. Rachel was relieved to find Sandra was nowhere in sight. As usual.

They exchanged the Mega Mart chickens from their foil packets to the Goodsworth heat-proof plastic bags and placed them onto the warming rack just as the customers started flooding in for the 11am rush hour (it really was like clockwork!). Sandra was still nowhere to be seen.

Justin collected a box of raw chickens from the coolroom. Pulling on a fresh pair of latex gloves, Rachel stood ready to help him unload them into the empty oven. A job Valentina could have done while they were gone but hadn't.

An awful smell of off chicken wafted from the box.

'What's that smell?' Rachel lifted her hand to her nose.

'Can you believe it?' Justin sounded like he was going to laugh. 'The chickens are off again.'

Rachel held her nose. 'Doesn't this store have systems in place to stop chickens going bad—like refrigeration?'

'Nup.' He opened another box.

'Off?' Rachel asked rhetorically, waving her hand against the smell.

'We're going to be sacked,' Valentina cried.

'No one gets sacked over off chickens.' Rachel tried to reassure Valentina and herself. 'This isn't our fault.'

'Unless you're Rhonda,' Justin reminded.

Valentina looked worried. 'Sandra's going to eat us alive.'

Rachel pulled her perfume from her bag and doused herself with it, trying to stay positive. 'Are you sure there aren't any more boxes?'

'That's it. Another fabulous dodgy delivery.'

Rachel watched Justin close the box. 'Sandra knows it's not our fault. Just tell her.'

'Tell her what?' Mario from the Butchery stood on the other side of the counter beaming at Rachel. 'Saw you guys messing around with a Mega Mart trolley. Slow in the deli today, huh?' he said with a twinkle in his eye, then noticed her hair. 'Woah beau'ful.' Tilting his head, he tried to peer past the net. 'Your hair—it's blue!' He pointed both fingers at her like an umpire declaring a goal.

'Thanks Captain Obvious,' Rachel shot back.

'It's the latest fashion in Europe,' Valentina declared with authority.

Mario stuck out his lip thoughtfully, suggesting he knew this was the case. 'Course, 'course. Looks good babe, real cool.'

He was unconvincing, but Rachel appreciated that he was at least trying to be nice. She avoided looking at his blood-caked apron. 'We have off chickens again Mario. Do you know anything about this?'

'Nah. Geez, bad luck hey. Sand's gonna be pissed. Seen her storm around the supermarket today. Came out of Bader's office looking feisty.' He eyed the glass cabinet for nibbles.

Rachel focused on the chickens. Sandra would use this stuff-up as an excuse to sack her. She saw how much Sandra despised Bader. She'd love nothing more than to tell him he was wrong in hiring her and the off chickens were exhibit A of her incompetence. She pulled out her lip gloss and ran it over her lips several times. *This isn't our problem. And it certainly isn't mine. It's Bader's for not fixing the oven.* She consoled herself. *And the fridge!*

'We're all in big trouble,' Valentina moaned.

'Yeah,' Mario agreed. 'And you guys ain't got another delivery till tomorrow, maybe the next. Chicken delivs are all over the place. Used to be Smooks Chooks—great juicy birds they were. About a month ago

Figgles took over. Ain't cuttin' it.' He wandered off to the marinated olives. 'Big Boys visit any day. No chooks in the oven. Sands's gonna crack it.' He popped several olives into his mouth.

Justin ran his latex fingers through his hair. 'Don't worry, she'll kill us before they get here.'

'And use our flesh instead of the chickens to fill the counter. I've seen *Fried Green Tomatoes*. It's do-able,' Valentina whined.

'Those Big Boys don't check Health and Safety, right?' Rachel had no idea what *Fried Green Tomatoes* was. But she did have an idea that might solve the one hell of a mess they were in.

Mario licked his fingers. 'Nup. And Sandra don't put much value in Health and Safety either. All she cares about is Employee of the Year. And she's got competition this year. I've sharpened my knives, polished my benches, and chucked in a new assortment of stuffed roasts. Big Boys aren't gonna pass me up for Employee of the Year this time.' He stuffed more olives into his mouth.

'Bet this doesn't happen at Mega Mart,' Rachel muttered, kicking herself for not applying for a job there.

'Nup. Dimitri their deli manager is a stickler for Health and Safety,' Mario said, sucking his fingers clean.

What a chaotic, disorganised place, Rachel thought, chewing her thumbnail. If anyone got the blame, it would be her. After all, it was becoming more obvious Justin and Valentina were Sandra's favourites and would never get the sack, even though she gave them beef. Rhonda, with her attitude was an easy target. And she was bound to get fired because Dadei hired her, and Sandra didn't. She needed to come up with a solution to this mess before Sandra returned. *What was the cleaning product her dad used to get rid of the mold smell from the shower?*

'I have it,' she announced, turning dramatically to the others—who were now ignoring the lone customer patiently holding a ticket. 'I know exactly what to do. We wash the chickens in bleach, White King, and mark up the prices so no one buys them.'

'Clever girl!' Valentina declared.

Justin looked at her like she'd sprouted another head. 'And then we can all go to prison for poisoning the customers. It's borderline criminal.'

'Nah, mate. You should see what we do to the meat,' Mario said, supporting Rachel's decision.

'It's a great idea,' Valentina gushed. 'We kill the fermentation and get rid of the odour.'

'No one will ever know,' Rachel insisted, giving the male customer in his faded Nike singlet a wave, suggesting he'd be served eventually.

Justin's jaw dropped. 'Are you stupid?'

Rachel bristled. 'No. You are—for not helping. And you don't call someone stupid when they're trying to help.' She glanced at Nike-singlet man, who finally gave up and walked away.

Mario bit into a twiggy stick. 'Guys, I wish I'd thought of this last week when I had surplus ox tongue two weeks outta date.'

Justin sighed. 'Rach, it's dodgy. You can't do it.'

'I disagree. It's Goodsworth's fault we have this effluent drama and we're just trying to—'

'Get the sack?'

She could tell he thought she'd back down and come to her senses. No chance. 'No one will know. We're washing them in the bleach, not soaking them in it. And have you seen how these chooks are handled? They probably need disinfecting.'

'Mate, they bleach 'em already in those chicken farms,' Mario said, nodding in solidarity.

Over at the chicken warming tray stood a frazzled mother contemplating which chicken to choose. Her two little boys aged about five and seven with sun-kissed red faces pushed each other off the back of the trolley, whining for ice cream. The little girl, about two years old, sat in the trolley seat giggling at her brothers. Their mother threatened, 'There's no ice-cream if you're silly.' The boys stopped fighting for the back of the trolley and stood quietly, waiting for mum to make her choice. She picked off two Mega Mart plump roast chickens. There were now only three remaining. Rachel could hear Valentina in the coolroom with her maracas, praying for protection from Sandra. They'd need it. The chickens were selling fast.

A woman, waiting with her over-loaded basket, with what appeared to be a failed attempt at a small shop, flashed her ticket in her direction. Rachel reached for her purse. 'Mario, where's Sandra?'

'In the lunchroom, chatting with Wilms. Probs getting the goss.'

'I've got time.'

Mario nodded confidently.

Minutes later, after a race to the household cleaning aisle, she returned, armed with White King, grateful there were no customers at the counter.

Mario grinned. 'Had to see this,'

Justin looked up from his phone. 'I'm googling White King poisoning.'

Rachel pulled on her latex gloves watching his expression. 'What's it say?'

'That it breaks down into harmless substances—'

'There, see. It's innocuous.'

'For washing. Not eating,' Justin corrected.

'It still says harmless,' she tried to sound convincing both to Justin and herself. 'Bring the boxes over here to the sink. We need to hurry before Sandra comes back.'

Mario looked impressed. 'You sure got the smarts. Use big words too.' He crammed more prosciuttos into his mouth.

'You reckon?' Justin muttered, reluctantly lifting a box.

'I heard that.' Rachel shot him a look.

'Rach, you're washing the chickens in bleach.'

'Well, someone has to save our jobs!'

Justin plonked the box on the sink, 'I'm going to serve customers.'

She wished she hadn't snapped. The stress was getting to her. Mario gave her a friendly thump on the arm. She forced a smile thinking about the absolute mess they were getting themselves into. But she needed to get moving.

'Val, let's hurry.' She filled a bucket with water and tipped in the bleach. The smell, sharp like a public pool, stung her nostrils. She scrubbed the chickens and handed them to Valentina to pat dry with paper towels before loading them into the oven. 'You're doing a good job,' Valentina affirmed.

'We are.' Rachel could not believe what she was doing.

'Sandra will never know,' Justin remarked sarcastically.

'Sandra will never know, right Val?' Rachel checked.

'Cross my heart.'

The next decision Rachel made even surprised her. She was sinking low, but someone had to make the hard decisions to save everyone's jobs. Ignoring Justin, who was not short on a negative comment or two, she made an executive decision to lower the price of all the chicken pieces to encourage shoppers to buy the 'specials' instead of ready cooked chooks, at least until they were cooked.

'This is getting worse by the minute,' Justin shook his head. 'Why not tell Sandra the truth? All she'll do is yell at us for a while. Or better—blame Bader. Because Rach, your plan is going to get us charged with poisoning the customers. And I don't know about you, but I'm not a fan of ending up in prison.' Still, he headed into the coolroom to get the plastic container of chicken breasts, as if knowing his argument was well and truly lost. 'Just tell me you're not planning on cooking them.'

'There are enough chemicals in chooks already. Who cares?' Valentina said flustered.

'True.' Rachel thought about news reports on hormone-injected poultry. Still, she needed to ensure the chickens didn't end up on dinner plates. 'We could cook them, then turn off the oven and leave them for the day and make sure no one buys them.'

'Okay crazy! And what are you going to do with this lot if you don't change over the chickens? Sandra's going to find out for sure.' He pointed to the remaining chickens on the sink.

'We'll figure it out. Val, since we can't fit all the chickens in the oven put these,' she gestured to the four chickens left on the sink, 'back into the box and hide them on the shelf.'

Valentina scooped the chickens into her apron. 'Sandra will never know.' She dashed away into the coolroom.

Rachel took a deep breath. They couldn't let Sandra find out about the chickens. Sandra would complain to Bader that this was her fault. After all, she'd done it to Rhonda, whoever she was. She sighed, feeling sick to her guts. She just hoped the Big Boys didn't show up before they ditched the toxic chickens.

Chapter Twelve

The customers asked such unanswerable questions. Where were the prawns sourced? How much pancetta did it take to stuff two turkeys? And where, exactly, did the copha and turkey basters live? Rachel didn't even know what copha was, and as far as she knew, turkey basters were only used for inseminating sperm. Did they assume that because she worked in the deli, she was an expert on all things food? Why didn't they just Google it?

The stench of the deli was everywhere. Even on breaks, she could still smell the place. Justin pretended to choke each time she sprayed herself with her perfume to cover the smell. She eyed him standing at the back bench, an air pod in one ear, reading from a sheet of paper.

He caught her gaze. 'Learning my lines. Audition.' He looked back at the page.

'Auditioning for what?'

'Bit part in a movie. Who knows?' He shrugged his shoulders. 'Gotta be in it to win it, right?'

'Guess so.' She grabbed for her water bottle and took a sip. 'Can't believe how much stress those chickens cause.' She tested his reaction, checking to see if he was still pissed with her over them.

'Haven't you noticed this place isn't normal?' he said.

'Far from normal,' she laughed. 'Have you been acting long?'

'You haven't seen any of my work?' he joked.

'No, can't say I have,' she smiled, taking a sip of water.

'I've been doing acting gigs for a year. Started a degree in Economics but life's too short for something I hated.'

'You didn't like uni?'

'I didn't like Economics.'

She studied him. If she started Economics her dad would be

thrilled. If she dropped out, he'd be devastated, although he'd try to hide it. 'My dad really wants me to go to uni. He means well with all his encouragement, but you know, it's pressure.' She wondered if Justin's parents cared about his choices.

'What does your mum think?' he asked.

'She wants me to study. Or rather wanted. She died three years ago.' Rachel grabbed a fresh pair of gloves, wishing she hadn't said anything. She'd been determined not to bring her personal life into her next job. Good job she was doing so far—blue hair and now her mum. *Great.*

Justin came over to the counter. 'Must suck losing your mum.'

'Yeah.' Her hands felt clammy as she fiddled with her gloves, managing to partially stretch them over her fingers while the rest wobbled freely. She tugged at them and finally gave up, using them half on, half off. He chuckled at her expression, which suggested she was over trying to get on her gloves. 'Mum died of cancer,' she said, figuring he'd be wondering how she died but was considerate enough not to ask. She liked this about him. He looked thoughtful, giving her space if she wanted to say more. Feeling awkward with silence, she said, 'I got the marks you know.'

'For what?' he asked, looking surprised as he called for ticket fifty-five.

'Uni.' She called for ticket fifty-six and served mixed olives. 'People assume I'm not at uni because I—'

'Didn't get in?' he said. 'But you chose not to go? Cool.'

She bit her lip. 'See, if you go and drop out, people still think you're smart. But if you don't go at all, they think you couldn't.'

'Complicated way of looking at it.' He seemed more interested in his customer's order than her line of logic.

'It's the unconscious bias,' she said.

'I didn't ask if you were studying.'

'Everyone else does.'

'Everyone?'

'Yes—family, friends, strangers. And those bureaucrats and academics plugging uni as the only ticket to success. You know who really has skin in the game?'

'Sandra?' He smirked.

"Exactly. And people like you and me. Us here in the supermarket, selling stuff and feeding humanity. This,' she waved her latex floppy fingered hand out toward the supermarket, 'is the door to the real world. Half the grads don't even need their degrees.'

'Sure, it's not for everyone. If you've got the brains, then go for it.' He looked at her. 'You're happy working here then, "feeding the human race"?'

'Are you?'

He smiled at her, deflecting his comment. 'Sure. Easy money and no pressure.'

When Sandra walked back into the deli sporting a long face and slamming them all for slackening off, Rachel questioned Justin's comment about no pressure. For a slow, small grocery store there was an incongruent amount of pressure, mostly coming from Sandra.

'You feeling okay about the chooks?' Rachel whispered.

'I'm feeling irresponsible,' Justin replied.

She felt the same but didn't want to let on. 'Speaking of irresponsible… ' She darted her eyes at Mario, swaggering in with a pig carcass across his shoulder. Between his low-slung apron, boning knife, and butcher swagger, he looked more like a medieval warrior than a supermarket employee. 'What are you carrying?' she said, almost dry retching, trying to avoid the pig on his shoulder. 'Don't you have a delivery person for that sort of thing?'

'Nah, Bader sacked 'em. Just me and Rog, who's off work with his slipped disc from too much heavy lifting.' He patted the pig leg as if affirming how tough it was collecting the meat from the loading dock.

Rachel looked around, checking to see why Sandra and her hawk-eye hadn't seen Mario and his pig. Sandra stood at the back bench, the tap on, water streaming over the pile of containers in the sink.

'Babe, think Charl's gonna say yes to my cousin's wedding. Told her I asked you and you said yes.'

'You what?'

'Made her jealous.' He pushed out his mouth, suggesting his plan worked. Then looking like he was setting up camp for a while, he casually dumped the pig on the counter.

Rachel picked up the tongs and fiddled with the antipasto, trying to avoid Mario, the dead animal, and her urge to vomit. Customers stared like he'd lost his mind.

'Mario! Get that pig off my counter!' Sandra bellowed.

'Sure thing Sands.' Mario slung it back on his shoulder and trailed Rachel as she moved further down the counter attempting to avoid his apron and pig combo.

'Babe, I need some advice.'

'Advice?' she said, adjusting the olive containers, avoiding eye contact.

'I'm over Charls playing hard-to-get. You chicks get each other, right? So, what I gotta do to get her attention?'

As hard as it was she rested her gaze on Mario's apron. 'Ditch the *Rambo* apron, Mario.'

Mario studied his apron. 'Nah, this is a trademark. A visual of butchery excellence. Proof of hard work.'

'It's a sign of grossness.'

'A bloody apron's tradition.'

'And key to solitude.'

'Vince, me cousin, reckons it shows you're working hard. You know, you've dedicated yourself to the craft of the carcass.'

Rachel looked directly at him. 'You want Charlene?'

Mario nodded seriously.

'Ditch the bloody apron Mario.'

Mario tilted his head, considering. 'Funny thing—animal blood's fine, but human blood makes me chunder. Go figure.'

'Weird,' Rachel forced a polite fake interested smile. Confused how there could be a difference and who cared right now.

Sandra cut across. 'Mario, I've enough problems with Garth using his so-called managerial status, acting like he owns the joint. I don't need you disrespecting me with that decapitated carcass on show.'

Mario looked like a toddler who'd just been told his mud pie creation was absolutely not allowed inside. 'Sandy, I'm on the other side, free world over here. So don't diss my carcass,' he whined. 'But I know what you mean 'bout Garth the tosser.' He looked at her as if registering her comment. 'Caught him checking my mincer a while back. Said he was checking it for OH&S. Pulled out my knife and told the douche if he set foot in my butchery again, I'd chop off his clanga.'

Rachel had never seen Mario look serious until then.

'Well, I have aut'omy,' Sandra grumbled, 'and Garth knows it.'

'Who's Ort Tommy?' Mario looked curious.

'Control, stupid!' She rolled her eyes. 'Now get that pig outta here. You're scaring my customers.'

'Babe, pass me some twiggies, quick,' Mario said.

A woman, wearing a delicate string of pearls that met at the rim of her linen jacket, stretched out her ticket in Rachel's direction. Her greying hair was teased and set into a neat smooth bob. Her appearance suggested she should be sipping bubbles at a fundraiser for the local theatre rather than shopping at the cheapest line of grocery stores in the suburbs. She smiled warmly as if sensing the difficulty of Rachel's day.

'Hang on a sec Mario,' Rachel replied, going to serve the customer, hoping Mario would take the hint and leave. Instead, he waited to the side. Rachel wondered if he just wanted to show off his pig or turn off Sandra's customers. Either way, it was unusual.

The woman in pearls was courteous and well-mannered. As Rachel collected her pancetta and olives, she told her that she once worked in the deli when she was a teenager. 'Some things never change,' she smiled at Rachel, then continued her shopping.

'Thinks you're a teenager,' Mario cajoled.

'She needs glasses. Here, take your twiggies.' She passed him a handful.

As Mario took hold of the twiggies, Sandra marched out of the coolroom looking more upset than usual. In a fleeting instant Rachel had a sick feeling this had something to do with the chickens.

'What the bloody hell is this?' Sandra bellowed, holding a large bucket.

Rachel darted a questioning look at Valentina. These were the four washed chickens that she'd asked her to put back in the box and hide. Why were they still in the bucket? Valentina ripped off a ream of paper towels and started cleaning the back bench, avoiding Sandra, while Justin busied himself at the counter by tidying up the shaved ham mound, something Rachel had never seen him do before. This was it. She was about to get her head chopped.

'Why are these uncooked chickens in a bucket? And what the hell is this smell?' Sandra's face was red.

'It's the washed floors.' Valentina gestured at the ground.

'Do I work with a minefield of idiots?' Sandra glared at them. 'Okay morons, who have half a brain between you, more if Mario wasn't here, why do these chicken breasts smell like my washed futsal shorts?'

Mario patted the hoof of his pig like he was carrying a three-year-old on a day trip around Dream World. 'Best be off.' He dropped his volume. 'Babe, I could ask for a transfer to the meat department for you?'

'I'd rather chew off my arm', Rachel said, pondering how to lie her way out of this dilemma.

'Please explain.' Sandra waited for an answer.

'Calling us morons is workplace harassment,' Rachel said.

'And what's this? Cooking?' Sandra raised her voice. 'Unless you all want the sack, someone tell me what you mor… idiots have been up to. What the blazers is going on?' Sandra dropped the bucket and glared at them.

Valentina crumbled under the strain and told the whole story while Justin and Rachel both avoided her glare. When Valentina finished, she reached for her maracas and gave them a gentle shake. 'God forgive Rachel for almost poisoning the customers,' she said under her breath.

'I don't believe this.' Sandra stared at them. 'Justin mate... Rachel and Valentina, it makes sense... but you?'

Rachel gawked at Sandra's comment. Justin held up his hands and gave her look as if to say *he couldn't help being perfect.* She rolled her eyes at him, thinking how she needed to come up with a decent explanation for the White King chickens.

'Sandra, I know it's the Christmas season, but it's no one's fault, as the timer's broken. Besides, Justin googled and White King breaks-down into harmless substances... '

'Christmas? It's the Big Boys I care about. Imagine if they see empty ovens.'

'I'll get rid of them,' Rachel offered.

'No. No, leave them.' Sandra put up her hand to stop her.

'What?' Rachel blinked.

'You're kidding, right?' Justin looked more surprised.

'You know I don't make jokes.' Sandra paced the deli. 'We need cooked chickens in the warming oven because the Big Boys could be here today. And if it's empty and there's no reason, well it ain't gonna look good on me.' She stared at the oven. 'There aren't any more chickens at the loading dock. And Rachel, what was it you said,' she dropped her eyes to look at the bucket, 'White King—I can't believe it—breaks down into harmless substances?'

'Yes,' replied Rachel at the same time as Justin responded 'No.'

'Damn it. Don't any of you know what's going on around here?' Sandra snapped. 'Chickens are our most popular selling item. Our bread and bloody butter. We have no choice but to use those goddamn poisonous chooks.'

Did this mean she wasn't getting the sack? Rachel raised her eyebrows at Justin—*see, I told you so.*

'I don't think this is a good idea,' Justin said.

Sandra glared at the back wall as if trying to gain her composure before she spoke. 'You washed them, right?'

Rachel nodded. She was on her game. They had Mega Mart flame roasted chickens ready for sale in the warming racks. They had the White King chickens in the oven, but they couldn't let the customers buy them. 'We need to keep the bleached chickens in the oven to show we have stock. If we run out of those in the warming shelf—'

'We'll run out of them shortly,' Justin said matter-of-factly.

'Then,' Rachel put on her most serious, intelligent ideas face, 'we tell the customers we've been swamped by demand for the best chickens in the centre and sold out and the next batch won't be ready for another hour. They aren't going to wait for chickens to cook. They'll go to Mega Mart instead.' Rachel hoped she could convince Sandra.

Sandra bit her pencil. 'Damn Bader. It's his fault for not fixing the oven.' She shoved her pencil behind her ear. 'So, like I said. We keep them chickens in the oven and tell the customers they're cooking. We do this until the next batch of chickens arrive. Let's just hope them Big Boys don't come by. You idiots are risking my job by your monumental stuff-up.' Sandra picked up her clipboard and clutched it, as if this would make her look more important and boss-like. She stared at the deli staff silently carrying out her orders. She sighed, muttering, 'Bet Maggie Beer never had to put up with this bullshit.'

Chapter Thirteen

Later that day Nat, the lanky grocer boy, who looked twenty, but she'd discovered was thirty three and married with a kid, came by the deli to chat with Justin. She'd come to learn that Justin was pretty much on good terms with everyone who worked in the store. Nat and Mario often stopped to crack a few jokes with him.

'Hey, Rach, get this,' Justin called, as she leaned against the back bench, filing her nails, basking in the calm after the morning rush. 'Guess what Nat found in the storeroom?'

'If it's Mario's pig carcass I don't want to know.'

'It's better.' Justin laughed.

It turned out Mario had actually taken on board Rachel's advice that his apron was a major turn off. When no one was looking he snuck into the storeroom where the aprons were kept. Why he didn't just take the apron, no one knew? He had his reasons she guessed, or maybe he really did think differently to most people. She'd heard Sandra mouth off *he wasn't the sharpest pencil in the tin.*

The not-so-sharp pencil took the clean white apron from its place on the shelf and replaced it with his visible sign of the "craft of the carcass". When Dom, an employee she hadn't met yet, went to get a new apron, he pulled Mario's straight off the pile. The sight gave him such a shock that he fainted, hit his head on the shelf on the way down, and knocked out a tooth.

Justin and Nat were nearly crying with laughter. Rachel wasn't impressed. To her, it was horrific and plain stupid. All she could put it down to was… nothing really…other than Mario wasn't just a really blunt pencil—he was the broken stub you found at the bottom of the pencil case. What bothered her most was: why hadn't Mario grabbed her a new cap while he was in there?

'Reckon he just forgot he'd left it there on the shelf,' said Nat.

'Looks like Mario took up your suggestion Rach.' Justin, looking relaxed with his arms crossed, laughed at how vague Mario could be.

Well at least he has a clean apron, she thought, loading a large bratwurst onto the slicer, letting her mind wander to imagine the guy of her dreams smiling back at her on the other side of the counter. It was silly really, but after a string of mind-numbing jobs, this was her thing. She imagined him with a twinkle in his eyes, looking at her as if he'd fallen for her, even with blue hair and a hair net. She practiced the *you had me when you ordered cabanossi* look.

Lately, the dream guy had been Garth. But today, she was relieved he hadn't seen her. Between the chicken fiasco and worrying about him catching a glimpse of her hair, she was wrecked. She needed to get her hair dyed—professionally this time. The only question was when… and how was she going to afford it?

'Rach, Earth to Mars.'

She turned to look at Justin.

'The brat?' He nodded towards the slicing machine.

'We were low,' she said flippantly, scooping up the mountain of bratwurst.

'Not anymore,' he smiled.

Not only was the deli small but so was the mindset. Who cared how much bratwurst she'd sliced? She tried to act like she didn't mind Justin's comment, but she did. In most of her jobs someone eventually called her out for daydreaming or slacking off. What? Did she have to be on, busy, and perfect every minute of the day?

She packed the bratwurst slices into the counter, careful to keep the paper wrap between her rubber gloved hands and the ham. She ran her lip gloss over her lips, checking her reflection in the stainless-steel. What a long day.

Daydreaming gave her reprieve from the customers who treated her like she was a vacuous unfeeling servant behind the counter. The last customer, a tall, wiry woman wearing a black business skirt and jacket, had waved her ticket in Rachel's direction, and called out, 'Yoo whoo.'

Spitting out her order all in one go, she told Rachel to be quick as she was in a hurry. Her toddler, with a friendlier face than his mother, sucked on his candy cane. He pulled it from out of his mouth and held it in Rachel's direction. 'Thuck?'

'No thank you,' Rachel smiled at him. 'It's all yours.'

While Rachel collected all the items, the customer announced she once worked at checkouts. 'Thank God it was only while I studied,' she added. 'I was studying Law, you know. Law,' she repeated, making sure Rachel heard. 'And what are you studying?'

The toddler began to bang the handle of the trolley with his wet sticky candy cane hands, saving Rachel from answering. What would she say? That this job was all she did. Wasn't that good enough?

The toddler's mum dug into her bag to find a wet wipe. 'Oh, such a gooey mess Beau,' she said, abruptly taking the candy cane and folding it in the wet wipe, declaring it was 'all gone'.

'Stoopid mummeee!' Beau wailed, bouncing on the seat, arms flailing, legs kicking. His mum tried to wipe him down, tossing the used wipe into the grocery-laden trolley. Beau retaliated, clawing at the plastic bread bag and flinging it to the ground. Flustered, his mum bent down to pick it up. Rachel cringed as Beau's pudgy fingers clasped the large jar of peanut butter sending it sailing, smacking the *I once worked at checkouts* lady on the head.

'You little shit,' she shouted.

Rachel tried to think of something sad to distract her from the compulsive urge to giggle. The thought of the vacuumed sealed pigs did it.

'Are you okay?' Rachel asked, collecting ice from around the olive containers, her face showing concern at the red mark on the side of the lady's face.

'Stop it, Beau.' She grabbed him by the pants and pushed him back into the seat, without responding to Rachel. 'Stay there. What about we get a choccy at the checkout? Mummy will just get the fucking ham first.' Her anger now directed at Rachel.

The toddler, taking in several big sighs, stuck his thumb in his mouth and looked at Rachel through his big, innocent blue eyes. She offered the lady the ice as she handed her the wrapped ham. Snatching the ham, ignoring the ice, she whipped around the trolley and left.

'You're welcome,' Rachel muttered to herself, then turned to look at Justin who gave her a knowing look. 'That lady asked if this was all I do.'

'I heard. Can't take it personally. Customers try to work us out.'

'Meaning?'

'We fall into categories.'

'Categories?'

'There are the senior workers who'll retire here. This is their life's work.' He flicked his eyes to Valentina. 'The Nat's, who make any job their passion. The students, who most shoppers assume we are. And then us, not totally into our other careers yet but needing money.'

Rachel thought about this. 'You missed one. Sandra. The one who actually wants to work here because she's going all the way. You've heard her.'

Sandra had no shame in telling them she was after Bader's job, and she could one day see herself as CEO of Goodsworth. Already on Rachel's first day Sandra emphasised she had "the guts, sweat and the desire and nothing was going to get in her way."

'True.' Justin nodded. 'You holding onto your new look?' he referred to her hair.

'No,' she said flatly, feeling disappointed he had to bring it up again.

'Great, because Garth only likes blondes.'

'Like I care what he likes.' But she did.

'Then you won't care he's halfway down the aisle?'

Rachel glanced towards the meat section. Garth was checking the Styrofoam plastic wrapped meat looking like he was making his way down the aisle. 'I need to grab stuff from the coolroom,' she said hastily.

'The... ah... hocks are low.' She snatched her cardigan, which she had taken off after rushing around during the chicken dilemma. Oddly, Sandra seemed to have forgotten the stain on her white shirt. Perhaps the chicken drama gave her more to worry about than a simple white stained shirt. She hurried into the coolroom, hoping Garth wouldn't check the weird quality control box.

'Hey deli chick,' she heard Garth call out to Justin.

'Gazman,' Justin replied. 'After something, someone?'

'Renee in today?'

She listened from the coolroom. *Renee? Really?*

'You mean Rachel?' Justin's tone dripped with sarcasm.

'Ah... yeah. That's what I said, didn't I?'

After a pause, clearly Justin not responding, at least not loud enough for her to hear, she finally heard Garth say, 'So she's not in?'

'So, you're after Rachel not Renee?'

'I'm just checking up on my staff.'

'Well, technically she's not your staff.' Justin said. 'How're the checkout chicks going? Through them yet?'

Rachel cringed. Justin could be such an arse.

'You need to watch your attitude deli chick.' She could hear Garth's warning. 'Tell Ren... Rachel I came by,' he said brashly.

She peered around the door, making sure Garth was well up the aisle.

'Real quality guy there,' Justin said. 'How're the ham hocks by the way?

'Weren't any left.'

'Sure,' Justin smirked to himself.

'That was a healthy conversation.' She hit the ticket machine and called the next number.

'You were listening?' he pretended to be surprised.

'He's not that bad.'

'You're deluded about him.'

'He's just doing his job—'

'Like I said, deluded.'

Not deluded. The fact Garth had come to check on her suggested he wanted her at checkouts, or better still, wanted to ask her out. She smiled to herself, this was great, even if he couldn't remember her name. Some people just weren't good at remembering names. She really had to fix her hair colour if she wanted to keep his interest. She didn't want to admit it, but Justin was right, he seemed like the type that wouldn't go for psychedelic blue hair.

'I need to make a call,' she said. And without waiting for Justin's reply, she ducked out of the deli and headed towards the hair salon at the other end of the shopping centre.

It was awkward explaining her hair dilemma to the girl at the counter with the stylish blonde bob.

'I've seen this kind of thing only once. Very rare,' the girl said brusquely, her eyes wandering across the screen, checking availability.

Rare? Seen this kind of thing only once before? Rachel touched her hair net self-consciously.

The girl with the perfect hair looked up from the online calendar. 'So, I have an appointment in two days at ten. Want it?'

She'd have to use her credit card—something she'd sworn off after her last $5,000 debt—but she blurted, 'I'll take it,' as if she would lose the opportunity if she hesitated.

'I'm sure you will,' the girl replied, resting her gaze on Rachel's hair.

Two more days with blue hair. As shallow as it sounded, she'd just have to make sure she avoided Garth.

Chapter Fourteen

Passing through the archaic turnstile, Rachel glanced across at checkouts where Charlene swiped her groceries with stiff fingers, favouring her long acrylic nails. Trudy, at checkout two, looked past Rachel as if something had grabbed her attention.

'Hey, Rach.'

Rachel turned. Justin was behind her, coffee in hand.

'I think Trudy's looking at you,' she said.

'And I think you're imagining things.' He popped off the lid and took a sip.

Rachel pointed at the cup, hinting at another break. He mimed a phone against his ear, reminding her she'd snuck off to make a call. Rachel pretended to be annoyed, but in fact she was pleased he didn't show interest in Trudy.

'Speaking of someone looking at you—there's your friend.' Justin nodded toward the fruit and veg section, where Garth was talking to Nat.

In an attempt to avoid Garth, Rachel spun around hoping to walk back through a checkout and down another aisle, not thinking how close Justin was behind her.

'Shit!' She crashed into him and his lidless coffee.

'You okay?' He looked as startled as she was.

'Why'd you take off your lid?' She yanked her wet shirt away from her chest. 'My shirt!' She made a vain attempt at wiping the coffee from her already stained shirt. 'Can you walk any closer?'

'Sure, if you want,' he joked, ignoring his own white shirt dripping with coffee.

'It's not funny,' she said, glancing back towards Garth, who was thankfully out of sight.

'Didn't want Garth to see your new hair colour huh?' He drank what was left of his coffee.

'Shut up.' She marched toward the deli.

Justin fell in step beside her. 'You shouldn't care what he thinks.'

'I don't.' She felt annoyed with him. 'Sandra's going to be pissed at this.' She brushed at her shirt and quickened her pace.

Justin kept up with her. 'Your shirts already stained. Don't stress. Anyway, if a guy's into you, he doesn't care what colour your hair is.'

'I don't know what you're talking about!'

'You're worried Garth'll see you looking like a Smurf.'

'I'm not worried,' she defended. 'And I don't look like a Smur—'

Garth stepped out from the other side of the cheese display.

'Okay, that's creepy,' Justin muttered.

Rachel froze. This was the worst luck imaginable. Here she was. Standing in front of Garth, drenched, blue-haired, and mortified. She remembered her pimple. Could he see that too? She forced a smile, trying to act cool, like absolutely nothing was different to the day he met her in Bader's office.

'Woah!' Garth's eyes swept from her hair to her chest. 'New take on a wet shirt contest?' He winked.

She crossed her arms. Yep, all was lost. Garth would now see her as nothing but a deli chick who was getting more unappealing by the second. He'd never come by the deli again.

'It just happened. Justin's coffee. I, we… '

'Bumped into each other,' Justin said flatly, crushing the empty cup in his hand.

'Yeah, an accident. Gotta get to work.' She tried to edge past, but Garth stepped closer.

'Oh hey, don't get too close to Rach. She has nits,' Justin eyed her hair net.

'I do not,' she shot back.

'Mate, you need a bigger shirt, your buttons are popping. Justin shoved the crumpled cup between two blocks of cheese and walked off.

Garth expanded his chest. 'Told Bader you should be at checkouts.' He ran his eyes over her again.

'You did?' She ignored the awkward feeling his eye scanning gave her. She was just relieved he didn't comment on her hair. Justin had him all wrong, and she had to acknowledge, so had she. Garth clearly didn't care about superficial stuff like appearances—or maybe just his.

'Said you got what it takes for front of house.'

'Front of house?' She smiled. 'And Bader agreed?'

'Give me time and you'll be there. You single?'

'Uh… yes.' The question felt both invasive and thrilling.

'Me too.' He grinned, then sauntered off.

Absentmindedly she twisted a strand of blue hair that had fallen from her hair net, while she stared at his muscular tight arse. She was floating. He'd almost asked her out!

'Interesting chat?' Justin teased when she walked into the deli.

'It's called conversation.'

'Conversation? Come on, Rach, what is it about dickhead that makes you like this?' He waved his hands at her in jest.

'Like what?'

'You know.'

'No, I don't know. And not that it's any of your business, but Garth is nothing but a transactional professional relationship.' She pushed her palm toward him, signalling the discussion was over.

'You're right, Rach. Only Garth's transactional relationships are probably not the ones you're used to.'

She reached for her apron, ignoring Justin. She was relieved Sandra was still out of the deli so she didn't have to face another berating. Garth had told Bader she should be at checkouts. He was the only one trying to help her. She tied up her apron, hoping it would hide her stained shirt, reminding herself to get her cardigan from the coolroom where she left it when Garth came by earlier. Pulling on her gloves, she pondered his question, "Are you single?"

She glanced at Justin; his fringe fell across his face. What was it with his constant digs about Garth? And why try to sour her mood. The fact Garth had shown interest in her should be making her feel hopeful. Instead, as she watched Justin wipe his fringe back with his gloved hand, she felt an odd sense of loss. And she couldn't explain why.

Chapter Fifteen

Sandra walked up to Trudy's checkout, exasperated at how slowly she passed the groceries under the scanner. 'Garth wants you to do a price check on Snow Bright dishwashing liquid.'

Trudy looked puzzled. Sandra gave her dagger eyes. 'Oh, okay,' she mumbled, and hurried off to carry out the price check.

Sandra loved how easy Trudy was to push around. She glanced across at Wilma and Jen, who were engrossed in their grocery scanning and making small talk to their customers. Charlene caught her eye.

'Trudy rushed off and left her register open,' she said aloud for Charlene's benefit. Charlene shrugged her shoulders as if she didn't care.

When no one was looking, Sandra slipped several fifty-dollar bills from the till and shoved them in her pocket. *That should cover the cost of bloody Mega Mart chickens.* She felt annoyed, she was deep in this stupid dilemma.

The Mega Mart entrance was lush with flowers overflowing in buckets. Instead of Goodsworth's endless Christmas carols, Seal's Kiss from a Rose (or whatever the song was called) floated through the store. For a moment she imagined clouds parting, golden rays shining down on her. This was it—supermarket heaven.

The Living Lettuce corner with hydroponic setup enticed her. Pickup lockers at the entrance and the ready-to-go food section made her anxious with FOMO. She'd read up on this new store with the LED lights and carbon efficient refrigeration and air-conditioning. She hated that it had a designer deli with cappuccinos and cured meats. And to top it off, there was an olive bar and a cheese cave stashed with about two hundred different kinds of cheeses.

Her fists clenched. The golden rays vanished. *What I could do with Goodsworth. The vision I have for the store.* She felt a surge of anger mounting.

Instead of sitting in Bader's high back leather swivel chair controlling the supermarket, she was here buying chickens from the enemy. Begrudgingly, she cleared the warming bain-marie of their juicy plump flame-roasted chickens and pushed the trolley with perfect wheel alignment to the self-serve checkouts. This was a real low point. She was going to kick the arses of the 'children' she had to manage in her deli.

She strode back into the deli with the juicy chickens and transferred them from the security of their warm-foil Mega Mart bags into the Goodsworth's flimsy plastic ones and placed them in the cooked chicken display. At least they would save her neck for the next few hours. Without a word to the deli chicks, she drove to Officeworks to collect the posters she'd ordered.

She wasn't about to let Bader's mismanagement and threats of moving her affect her winning Employee of the Year. She used the photo Mohammad had taken with her arms folded across her chest, staring down the camera, looking like the in-charge deli manager she was. She ignored the smug grin of the prepubescent infantile Officeworks employee when she collected her them.

She gloated to herself, impressed with her idea. *Those Big Boys and worker bees will know who I am. Sandra, boss of the deli. A standout. Proactive, determined, loyal worker. I'll win Employee of the Year for sure. And soon enough, the supermarket will be mine.*

'These, subordinates,' she declared, dropping the posters on the back bench and peeling off the rubber band so they unfurled like architectural blueprints, 'are proof of my excellence in this place.'

Justin, Valentina, and Rachel stared at the photo of Sandra. Her face stern, wearing her deli uniform, the headlined font on the poster reading, *Sandra Saunders for Employee of the Year.*

'This is to remind everyone at Goodsworth I'm the best manager this supermarket's ever seen.' She reached under the bench and pulled out a shopping bag, triumphantly producing several sporting trophies.

'Impressive,' Justin said.

'Damn straight this is impressive,' Sandra arranged the trophies on the counter. 'These trophies represent my determination, fortitude, and winning ability.' She thought how brilliant her idea was to bring in the trophies from home. 'Them Big Boys are gonna be begging me to take Employee of the Year,' she gloated. 'Justin, take these posters and put them up around the store will you. And here,' she handed him a ten dollar note. 'Get me two Red Bulls. It's been a long day.'

'Me too,' Rachel said, fishing in her bag for money.

'I think we all need an energy hit.' Justin raised his eyebrows in jest as he headed off on his mission, declining Rachel's cash.

Sandra set to work, Blu-Tacking the posters on the cheese display and the back wall of the deli. 'Impressive,' she said to herself.

After she downed the cold fizzy energy boost drink from Justin, she headed up towards Bader's office knowing he would be on his usual late-afternoon lunch run to Subway. She had to know why he wanted to sack her. She was certain he didn't know it was her who repeatedly let the air out of his tires. He was jealous because she was so damn good at her job. That's why he hated her.

The palm tree from Bader's office now stood in the hallway, with a sticky note on one leaf stating, 'Dead, please dispose of.'

If only it was this easy to get rid of this idiot at the helm, sinking the ship.

She could hear him tapping at his computer. He was late for his routine Subway snack. His phone rang. She remained still against the wall outside his office, cupping her ear to listen.

'At Subway now? I can't… text next time. Don't keep calling me, Garth… Alright, alright… Fine! I'm coming.'

Garth? Meeting at Subway? What were the two deadbeats up to? Sandra stepped behind the fake palm, which, unlike the dead one waiting for the cleaner to collect, had enough fronds to hide behind. She watched Bader march pass, staring directly ahead, his face furrowed in concern.

She snuck into his office and pulled open several drawers hoping to find a clue to their alliance. She sniggered at the magnifying mirror and tweezers in his top draw. She pushed the mirror to the side of the drawer, surprised to find a variety of medications. She sifted through them, eager to know what the psycho was taking, thinking about the story she'd read in the paper about a pharmacist sprinkling a cocktail of medications into the drink of some chick he'd met at a bar. She pocketed a few pills from each packet. *Never know when they might come in handy.*

She opened Bader's laptop and smirked at his inefficiency. *Am I the only competent person in this place? Idiot doesn't even lock his computer.* Despite being frustrated at Bader, she was pleased with how easy it was to search through his computer desktop. She clicked on Outlook, searching for any emails from Garth. Just as she expected there was an email from the snake.

> *To: Ferdinand Bader*
> *From: Garth Lincoln*
> *Subject: Deli*
>
> *Bader, Sandra's gotta go if you wanta save on expenses.*
> *G*

What the hell? She read Bader's response, her eyes wide as saucepans.

> *To: Garth Lincoln*
> *From: Ferdinand Bader*
> *Subject: Deli*
>
> *Garth,*
> *I've told you already, getting rid of Sandra is like getting rid of herpes. Impossible!*

She wanted to hurl Bader's computer through the door. What were they up to? How dare they talk about her and her job like a commodity. She read on.

I've placed Renee where you asked. Don't come into my office and interrupt an interview again.

Ferdinand Bader
Store Manager
Goodsworth

Sandra leant back in his chair. *Why was Garth telling Bader what to do? And if Garth thinks Rachel is so perfect, why doesn't he let Bader put her in checkouts where she wanted? And for God's sake, at least remember her name.*

Garth knew the deli pulled in a high revenue and she was Employee of the Year, every year. He had to be planning on taking over her job and combining it with produce manager and checkouts so he could be the star of the store. She'd seen him hover around the deli enough to know he was jealous of her status in Goodsworth. And Bader, the piss-weak pushover with a melon for a brain, was helping him. Why did the guy from Head Office insist Bader hire Garth? There was nothing special about him.

That's it. She hit her hand on his desk. The quality control boxes were Bader's way to get Garth ingratiated in the deli. Next, he'd have the snake check the ham and cheeses, and the seasoning on the chickens before roasting. Slowly, right under her nose he'd show her up, and Bader would fake a reason to get rid of her. Then Garth would take over the deli. She bet he wanted Rachel in the deli for eye candy when he took over. *Bastard.*

She could feel her rage building. She opened Bader's Smarties jar and threw a handful into her mouth. She gave the remaining Smarties in her hand a lick and dropped them back into the jar. She thought about how Bader loaded her car with groceries and accused her of stealing. She searched for emails sent to Glen Smyth.

To: Glen Smyth
From: Ferdinand Bader
Subject: Deli Manager

Dear Glen,
As you know the supermarket has been struggling with productivity for the past year. After thorough and careful review of the management team it's become apparent the best option is to downsize the deli staff as this will not affect the main areas where produce is bringing in good revenue. Sandra, the deli manager is regularly not meeting targets and with the economic downturn I suggest we let her go. At your approval I can give her one month's notice and have Garth, the current Checkout Team Leader—who excels in his position—manage the deli, produce and checkouts for the short term until one of the current deli staff is trained to fill this role.

Sincerely
Ferdinand Bader
Store Manager
Goodsworth

She stared at the screen; her eyes almost hanging from their sockets. Not meeting targets? Was he messing with the books? How was this chain of emails even possible? Bader had sunk to a new low. He left her no choice. She cracked her knuckles and began to compose an email to Glen Smyth. *You're gonna feel like a headless chook when this comes out Bades.*

Chapter Sixteen

Sandra tugged an orange from the bottom of one of Nat's carefully stacked pyramids. The whole thing collapsed in a glorious avalanche of citrus rolling across the floor. Mean, yes—but deeply cathartic. Especially when you had to deal with boofheads like Garth and Bader.

She lingered at aisle three, watching bumbling Bader walk to his office, his regular weak cappuccino and Subway sandwich in hand. A little opportunity was presenting itself. Bader in his office alone.

She stayed out of his sight at the side of his doorway and pulled out a small compact makeup mirror, which she'd nicked from the beauty aisle. She angled it just right to spy on Bader at his desk. There he was, perched in his swivel chair, taking measured bites of his chicken-and-mayo sub, nodding to himself like it was fine dining. Same lunch every single day. Just like everything else about him; same, boring, predictable. When he finished, he balled up the wrapper and lobbed it toward the bin. By his smug grin, Sandra guessed the stupid lunch wrap landed in the bin. After spending a few minutes fussing over the papers on his desk he picked up his phone and barked several orders at Lillian. He hung up the receiver with aplomb, a smug expression on his face.

'I keep the staff in line,' he muttered proudly.

Do you Badey? Really? Hardly think your conversation with Garth kept him in line. She wished he'd hurry up and read his emails before someone came along and saw her holding the mirror.

He leant back in his swivel chair and tapped his mouse.

Good, now where talking business. She held the mirror steady.

He moved the mouse, studying his screen. She watched on. A store hand walked past, whistling loudly. Quickly she pulled the mirror away and slapped her phone up to her ear, pretending to look deep in conversation, frowning at the grocer boy walking past to stop him from even thinking about saying hello. He kept walking. She slipped the mirror back into place.

Bader hummed to himself, moving his mouse around, sipping his coffee, oblivious to what he was about to come across. To Sandra's delight, Bader sat bolt upright, spraying coffee across the screen.

'No, no, no!' he exclaimed. 'Why would Glen send me this?'

He rose off his seat and pulled out his hanky from his back pocket, frantically wiping the spray off his screen. Through the mirror Sandra watched on as he tapped at his keyboard. 'What? I didn't send this.'

Bader picked up his desk phone and, fortunately for Sandra, he put it on the loudspeaker. She lowered the mirror and listened.

'It's Bader here,' he said abruptly. 'I have a spam email. What's going on with your system?'

'What exactly seems to be the problem?' the IT guy responded.

'Problem? I have spam, that's the problem,' his voice shook.

'You say you have spam?' The IT guy asked.

'I have a virus in my email!'

'Was the email specifically addressed to you?'

'Yes, it was directed to me.'

'And have you opened and read it?'

'Why would I be calling you if I hadn't opened it?'

'Sure, sure,' the IT guy said coolly. 'And has your computer been invaded with this virus?'

'Invaded? I have an email in front of me, which apparently is in response to an email I sent earlier, which I haven't sent because I didn't write it. I can assure you this is not a virus!' Bader spat into the phone.

'Did you try turning your computer off and on? Like rebooting it?'

'Listen you idiot! An email has been sent from my address that I DID NOT SEND'.

This was fantastic.

'What time was the other email sent sir?' The IT guy was clearly used to people yelling at him.

'Twelve-oh-five. What the hell's time got to do with it?'

'Sir, were you at your desk at this time?'

'At my desk?' Bader sounded hesitant.

Sandra held her breath.

'Is there anything else I can help you with… ?' The IT guy's voice trailed off as if he was distracted by something else.

'You haven't helped me with this problem so no, there's nothing else. You tech heads are useless.' Bader slammed the receiver.

Sandra positioned her mirror back at the edge of the door. Bader sat looking frazzled, rubbing his face in his hands. She watched as he read his emails. Letting out what seemed an involuntary scream. He sculled the rest of his coffee and reached for his Smarties, pouring a handful into his mouth. Munching mindlessly, she could see him flick up another email.

She wanted to push him off his high back swivel chair and read it herself. She watched as he sat motionless, frozen at his desk, his mouth agape. Then as if waking in fright, he picked up the phone and dialed.

This time a warm friendly voice answered. 'Hello Glen Smyth's office, Marjorie speaking.'

Sandra was pleased he used the loudspeaker again.

'Yes, ah… hello Marjorie. I need to speak to Glen… please.'

'And who shall I say is speaking?'

'It's Ferdinand Bader, from the Frenchs Forest store.'

'Mr. Bader,' her friendly tone lapsed. 'Glen is out of the office at present.'

'You just said, "who shall I say is speaking?" Meaning you were preparing to put through my call.' His voice shook.

Sandra wanted to high five herself. One, she'd messed up his day—job even—and two, she'd managed to see it all. She only wished she'd thought of videoing it to show Katie later.

'Yes, well we know how busy Glen is. It's the Christmas period after all.'

'You're lying,' Bader's tone was desperate.

'I beg your pardon Mr. Bader, but you are out of line.'

'I have an email in front of me that has been sent to Glen.'

'I'm aware,' she said, smug.

Bader cleared his throat. 'Yes, well I didn't write or send it.'

'Ah hum.' Marjorie's tone sounded condescending. Clearly Sandra's emails had caused a major upset in Head Office. Marjorie, in her 40's, had a Bachelor of Arts degree, a memory like an elephant, and was clever and sophisticated. Sandra could not fathom why she'd settle for being Glen's EA when she could practically run the show and be CEO.

Bader's voice was shaky, 'I need to speak to Glen and explain it wasn't me, it was ah, um, a cleaner. His paranoid. You know, affected by too many drugs.'

'I suggest you put this in an email to Glen, and he'll get back to you shortly.'

'Listen here Marjorie, if you did your job properly, you'd put me through.'

'I'm sorry—'

'Well Marjorie, it's obvious you can't do your job properly then isn't it!' He slammed the receiver.

Sandra watched him lower his head on the desk with several bangs, pounding his fists in unison. Wonderful. She'd seen enough, only she couldn't help but disturb his peace further. 'Rough day Bades,' she said, shoving the small mirror in her back pocket as she entered his office.

'What do you want?' He hastily sat up straight.

'Reflux?' She referenced the packet of Zoton on his desk, a drug she'd seen her mother take for her inflamed gastroesophageal reflux. 'Painful stuff.' She couldn't care less.

'I'm in the middle of something,' he said, picking up the packet and throwing it in his top drawer. He wiped his strands of hair, his hands shaking, beads of sweat forming on his brow. 'I've had enough of you coming into my office whenever it fancies you. Make a meeting.'

'Sure,' she said, faking her compliance. She'd seen enough. He was already pissing his pants. *Now to stop Garth the egomaniac from taking over the supermarket.*

Chapter Seventeen

Who knew you could work so many toilet breaks into a shift? Aside from smoking, going to the bathroom was unlimited. Justin was an expert at taking breaks, as Valentina reminded him often when he came back into the deli. 'All you do is take breaks, breaks, breaks.' She'd roll her head in annoyance.

The day, as usual, was long. Rachel followed Justin's lead out to the car park bench for fresh air and a pseudo toilet break. Troy was there having a smoko. His aviator sunnies, a regular feature on his face.

He blew several smoke rings. 'You guys have an accident or something?' He looked at their shirts, then continued without waiting for their explanation. 'Heard about Mario's fail.'

'Which one?' Rachel asked, glad he changed the subject, and she didn't have to explain their shirt saga to another staff member.

Troy chuckled at her comment. 'Which one's right. The chicken one!' He raised his eyebrows.

Valentina was alone again, in the deli when Mario rocked up ready for a chat and some antipasto. Valentina, desperate for a toilet break herself, took the opportunity and asked him to mind the deli, just for a second. Mario was always happy to mind the deli with its antipasto. The trouble was, it slipped his mind that the chickens he sold were the marinated White King disasters.

'How was I supposed to know?' He genuinely looked surprised.

'Ah, I don't know—maybe because you saw us wash and put them there. And they smell!' Rachel said crossly. 'Do you know what this means?'

'Yeah, that I got rid of the chicken problemo. You can start fresh now.'

'Are you non compos mentis?'

Mario looked at Justin for an explanation. Was she giving him a compliment? By the look on her face, he guessed not. 'Geez, babe, I just thought they'd be gone by now.'

She wished they were. The Big Boys hadn't been through the supermarket and Sandra was determined to have her deli looking fully stocked. Valentina let it slip that several years back, Sandra was on track for Employee of the Year, until Isla, a 17-year-old school leaver, told a customer to, 'Calm the fuck down,' or she'd throw their feta in their face. Turned out the customer deliberately being difficult for Isla was a secret shopper, planted by corporate. Valentina reported that Sandra was so cross at Isla for jeopardising her chance of Employee of the Year that the 'fucks' that came out of her mouth could be heard right across the store. Not only that, Bader ignored Sandra's complaint and moved Isla to checkouts, but she lasted a day. At checkouts, she couldn't hide in a coolroom and slacken off.

'Thought it was odd they were cold.' Mario had his confused look on.

'Didn't you smell them?' Rachel asked in frustration.

'I don't normally smell stuff before I sell it.'

'You, a stupid boy.' Valentina gave him a slap across the back of the head.

'Ouch, Val.' He rubbed his head with a grimace. 'What do you suggest we do?' he asked, trying to help.

'Sandra's going to kill us,' Rachel said, still amazed they had been able to hide their stained shirts from Sandra and that she hadn't noticed them when she returned earlier with the chickens from Mega Mart. 'Do you think the people who bought them will notice?'

'I don't know about you, but the chickens I buy don't normally smell like the bathroom floor.' Justin swept his tussled hair off his forehead with both his hands and sighed.

'We're all going to get sacked,' Valentina moaned.

'I wouldn't worry about getting sacked, Val—it's going to prison that I'm worried about.' Justin frowned.

Without another word Mario disappeared. She guessed he'd gone back to work, dissing the problem as theirs, not his. Fifteen minutes later, wearing a broad smile, he returned with the chickens.

'As luck would have it,' he beamed, 'the people who bought them were still in the store. All I had to do was reach into their trolleys when they were distracted and walla! Here.' He plonked the chickens on the back bench. 'Charls is the real hero, though.' Mario looked like he'd discovered a cure for a rare disease. 'There was this one package in this girl's trolley, but there was no way I could get my hands on it. That's when I raced to Charls's checkout, told her our problemo. Got her to wave the girl through her checkout, and then I distracted her by chatting. That's when Charls dropped the chook under the counter. Regular 007.' He grinned.

'Yeah,' Rachel said, guessing it wouldn't hurt to let Mario think he and Charlene were geniuses right now, as all the chickens were safely back in the oven—cooked, cold and poisonous.

'Mario thinks he saved the day, you know,' Troy chuckled.

'Of course he does,' Justin said kicking a stone on the pavement.

'You can't tell anyone, Troy,' Rachel said, wishing Mario could learn to shut his big mouth.

'Secret's safe with me,' Troy said, walking back into the mall.

She wondered: did Troy take as many breaks as Justin? Well, he did smoke, so technically he'd probably take more.

'Justin, why does Goodsworth have a security guard when Mega Mart doesn't even have one?'

Justin explained how Troy came to work at Goodsworth a couple of years earlier due to an increase in shoplifting. Goodsworth was the only store in the mall affected as they didn't have CCTV throughout the store but only in a few sections, making it an easy target for shoplifters.

Corporate decided a security guard was cheaper than installing more cameras. *Clearly*, thought Rachel, *they hadn't done their maths*.

'Do you think Troy will keep quiet?' Rachel asked as they walked into the supermarket.

'Who knows? Everyone has a big mouth in this place. Charls is in on it and no doubt she'd tell Luce and Trudes,' Justin said pragmatically.

'Mario assured us that Charlene was going to keep it quiet.'

'Let's hope.' Justin didn't look hopeful.

When they walked back into the deli, Sandra stepped out of the coolroom. 'Shirts?' she blasted, waving her hand at Rachel and Justin's coffee-stained shirts. 'The Big Boys are here any day and you two think you're on bloody Schoolies, pouring drinks all over your shirts and taking breaks whenever you feel like it. I leave for forty minutes, and this is what I come back to. Rachel, cardigan? Justin,' Sandra looked flustered at his shirt, 'hide if the Big Boys come today.' She shook her head in disgust. 'And Rachel, fill the green olives. Justin work! If you know what that even means. And Val, keep an eye on the oven. God, imagine if any of them were sold!' She stormed over to the counter, grabbed a salami and bit off the end. 'I tell ya. The bloody pressure you all put me under.'

Chapter Eighteen

Lillian's voice echoed through the speakers. 'Sandra to the service desk. Sandra.'

An hour earlier, Lillian had raced down to the deli to tell Sandra that Marjorie from Head Office called to tell her the Big Boys were on their way. Sandra demanded her staff spruce up the deli by cleaning the back bench, mopping the floor, filling up the produce, and serving every customer like their life depended on it. 'Otherwise,' she threatened, 'heads will roll.'

She could feel Rachel and Justin's gaze at her, no doubt wondering why she was summoned by Lillian. As she whipped off her apron and dusted down the thighs of her black pants, biting the inside of her lip to hold back a grin, she knew exactly why Lillian called her. It was obvious. Her email had worked.

She gave her deli chicks final orders and strode proudly up the aisle. There was no doubt in her mind—she was being summoned to take over Bader's job, and the Big Boys were here to hand it to her. They'd probably tell her Bader had to take urgent leave. She'd know what that meant.

As she neared Lillian's counter, she could see two men wearing swanky uncrushable suits —one charcoal, one navy. There was no Bader. It was, she thought, a fabulous day.

'I'm Sandra Saunders, manager of the deli where we've been meeting above target every quarter.'

The Big Boys swapped looks.

Lillian looked flustered. 'Mr. Bader's indisposed briefly.'

Sandra raised her eyebrows. It was this easy. It was happening already. Bader was indisposed. Sandra tried not to smile. She'd never smiled at Lillian before. She didn't want to give anything away.

'Sandra, in Mr. Bader's brief absence can you please show Mr.... ' Lillian paused.

The businessman in the charcoal grey suit extended his hand to Sandra. 'Col Manning. And this,' he turned to the businessman in the navy suit with waxed eyebrows and a smooth bridge to his nose, too perfect for natural selection, 'is Andrew Moore.'

Sandra shook their hands and looked smugly at Lillian, suggesting she get their names next time. 'Pleased to meet you both.' If only they knew how pleased she was to see them. Her spine lengthened a good two millimetres. 'Let me show you around.'

Sandra led Col and Andrew around the supermarket. They inspected fruit pyramids, neatness of shelve packing, use-by dates, and watched the checkout chicks for speed and customer service. Sandra showed them the deli, grateful her staff had managed to clean it up to standard—spotless sink with all utensils out of away (a miracle), chicken oven looking normal, and containers in the counter overflowing with produce. She nodded with a serious I'm-in-charge facial expression at her deli chicks, her eyes glaring. If they stuffed up while the Big Boys were there, she'd have them for dinner.

She caught Rachel's eye and turned her gaze to the chicken oven expecting her to follow. She looked again at Rachel, who'd picked up her silent message to watch the oven and wandered towards it. She could not afford to have Col or Andrew open the oven and find the cold, bleached chickens. To her relief Rachel looked through the glass door, fiddled with the broken timer and wiped her hands on her apron in one swipe as if she'd successfully completed a task.

'About another ten minutes until the chickens are cooked,' Rachel said to Justin and Valentina, catching Sandra's eye. Sandra didn't show approval too often. She didn't want her staff getting cocky. But she could feel her lip upturn at Rachel's improvisation.

'Well, Sandra,' Col began. 'We have no reason to suggest you're not meeting targets and keeping up with the demands of food exchange here in the deli. But... '

She held her breath.

'Red shoes?' He flashed his gaze at Valentina who was busy at the sink.

Damn it! She should have made Valentina change her shoes. 'I can explain,' she began, wondering what lie she could spin.

'No need,' Col gave a kindly look. 'She reminds me of my mother and her quirky ways. No telling them sometimes,' he smiled.

'Well, yes, we do what we can,' she said, trying to look like she cared.

The Big Boys shook her hand and disappeared up the aisle towards Bader's office. Sandra surveyed the deli, her pride and joy. Employee of the Year and Bader's job were in the bag. She beamed at the thought. She also beamed at the thought of her email, which had obviously done its job. Sure, she didn't want to go around destroying people's careers like he'd done to her. This was an exception. He defamed her first with his email.

She wondered if the Big Boys would talk to Lillian again. She called across the deli. 'Keep an eye on this place, I'm ducking out for a bit.' *Ducking up to watch Bader get chucked out of his office.* She grinned to herself.

Lillian was busy selling cigarettes to an unshaven guy in work overalls and a high-vis vest. She grabbed his cigarettes, plonked them on the counter, and rotated the packet to highlight the graphic photo on the back. He looked unimpressed.

Sandra butted in. 'How come Bades didn't take the Big Boys around the store?'

'Well since you had to take them around, I'll tell you,' Lillian said, as if she was doing Sandra a favour. 'Mr. Bader said he was going for a walk. He left with Garth. Odd huh? Those two together.' She gave the customer his receipt. 'When the Big Boys arrived, I called Mr. Bader. He didn't even answer his phone!'

'Did you leave him a message?'

'Yes, said there were some men from Head Office to see him. No reply. Anyway, with those two men standing here looking at me for answers, I figured you knew this place better than anyone.' Sandra nodded, taking in Lillian's compliment. 'So, I called you. But he's back now.'

Sandra hadn't expected this. 'Back?'

'Yes, and when I told him the two men were waiting in his office, he looked like I'd told him he was about to have a root canal. The colour faded from his face before my eyes.'

Sandra hit the counter with her hand, staring in the direction of Bader's office. 'He's in his office?'

'Do you think he's in trouble?' Lillian looked concerned.

'If he's not in trouble with them, he is with me.' Sandra wanted to take Bader's swivel chair and shove it into the industrial bin. Bader and Garth were creating a boys' club. She picked out a Woman's Weekly from the magazine rack, pretending to read while she waited for the Big Boys to leave his office.

A few minutes later, they strutted from Bader's office and out the exit, both on their phones, probably replying to important emails or checking their stocks. They didn't spend long in Bader's office. Something wasn't right.

She stood in Bader's doorway trying to decide if it was safe for her to enter.

'Seem to be bursting a blood vessel, Sandra?' He said coldly.

'Where were you?' She kept a safe distance, shoving her hands in her pockets. She didn't trust her temper. 'I had to show them around the store.' She examined his face, which seemed unsettlingly confident. Shouldn't he be packing up his office or better, be out the door already?

'Yes, well I had a previous engagement,' he glared at her. 'I just received considerable praise for being one of Goodsworth's most efficient store managers.'

'You're lying.'

'Now Sandra, why do I need to lie when it's true?'

Sandra turned her eyes to his computer. How could the Big Boys not know about the emails *he* sent? 'That's a load of crap. You've never even made Employee of the Year, not once.' She glared down at his comb-over.

'Face it Sandra, you'll never be sitting here.' He tapped his desk with both hands. 'So, stop trying. And after you're dismissed, it's Valentina next. Once you're both gone, I might have a chance of improving the intelligence in the deli.' He tapped at his keyboard.

Sandra couldn't fight the urge anymore. She walked up to his desk and slammed the computer lid on his fingers. 'Listen here, dick weed.'

Bader prized his hands from the compacted computer and rubbed them. 'Your rebellious streak isn't serving you, Sandra. Once again—you're forgetting I'm boss, and you're on a warning.'

'Warning?' She picked up his Smarties jar. She could not understand how her emails had been dismissed. She glared at Bader as she pulled open her apron pocket and emptied the contents of the jar. Patting her pocket, she gloated at him.

Bader pushed the button on his phone. 'Lillian, get Troy from security up here now.'

'Can't fight your own battles Badey?'

'Your temper and jealousy are interfering with your judgment. I suggest you get out of my office before Troy lifts you out of here.'

Sandra had to admit Troy, the 180cm tall and one-hundred-and-ten-kilogram ponytail giant, who trained for body building competitions, was an unwelcoming prospect. Last time she got caught in an office with him he didn't draw breath for ten minutes. Describing in detail his latest weekend competition wins and showing her a ream of photos of his glowing, competition-bronzed body. She turned to face the corridor.

'I'm not leaving because of him. I'm leaving because I've had enough of looking at your face. And next time I speak to corporate I'm asking them why Garth has to check those quality control bloody boxes. And let me tell you, it's odd,' she waved her finger at him, 'one week he's all over those boxes as if his life depends on it, and then the next week we have boxes that smell to high bloody heaven for me to dispose of. Where's quality control in that?'

Sandra stormed back into the deli swearing under her breath. She surveyed the shining splash back and loaded trays of food in the counter. She'd gone all out to make the deli glow for the Big Boys. And now, instead of feeling upbeat and proud, she was still chasing Bader and his scheming little arse.

Chapter Nineteen

Sandra kept her life to herself. Apart from meeting Katie at checkouts, no one needed to know the daily goss of her life. She rolled her eyes at the thought of Monica, who had about a sniff of a shift every couple of months unpacking goods onto the shelves where she'd complain about how much she worked. When she was on shift, the monologue of her life would ramble like a fallen roll of toilet paper—unfolding forever. Sandra had no tolerance for Monica's soft-spoken voice. She could barely listen to her end each sentence with the last syllable lingering, for that genteel effect. The workplace was work. Not a therapy room.

Monica would come over to the deli uninvited to moan about how hard her life was: the house extension was taking too long; her husband couldn't decide what colour to pave the driveway, pave the pool, or paint the friggin' house. She complained how she had to work to pay private school fees for her only son. Sandra would think about Nat, certain Monica's *hard life* would make his feet float off the ground. Nat, who had a wife and child, was renting, and couldn't see how on two incomes he could ever get a deposit for a place in Sydney.

It wasn't just the Monicas that annoyed her. It was that staff had forgotten Goodsworth. No one cared about the brand, the business, and making the store sing. Tired from the day from hell, she left early for her futsal game, leaving the morons (she thought this to herself) to pack up the deli.

Opening the door of her car, parked at the far end of the car park, she wondered what she was doing wrong. If the Big Boys weren't going to sack Bader after those emails, they were never going to get rid of him. She was doomed to be working under pin head. Doomed.

She turned the ignition, revved, and drove away, calling Katie.

'You what?' Katie gasped. 'What if you got caught?'

'Bader's not smart enough for that. He's a cheat and a liar.'

'What did you write?'

Sandra relayed the details of her emails. Katie kept gasping. Then after another pause, laughed.

Sandra didn't laugh.

'Okay hun, have a good game. And forget that place, for once. Slow cooked beef on the pot when you get home.'

Sandra hung up.

Katie got her. From the moment they met in the lunchroom when Sandra told her to move her arse so someone else could make a tea, Katie eyed her and told her to shut the hell up.

Katie was short, like Sandra. Her hair was wild and curly, 'good for a bird's nest,' Sandra once told her. Katie had worked in the mining industry in Western Australia—fly-in fly-out—for ten years. After buying her unit in Manly, she decided it was time to settle and work with people.

'Supermarket's where it's at for socialising, Sands.' Katie said on their first date to Luna Park, where Sandra loved to sit on the Ferris Wheel and take in Sydney Harbour at night. 'All of society walk through the doors of the grocery store. The groceries are not the variety, the people are.'

Sandra loved that Katie saw the supermarket like she did. Important. Although, she didn't care for the people side. She cared for the business opportunity side. Once a manager, you managed so much!

Sandra, a stickler for rules—certain ones not pertaining to treatment of Bader or staff—made the decision that one of them had to leave Goodsworth if they wanted to date each other. Katie happily got a job at the big box retailer Big W, as a Sales Floor Team Member. Six months later they moved in together. Three months later Bader trashed her car and took the prime role, Goodsworth Store Manager.

She parked her car at the Warringah Recreation Centre in North Manly. Her futsal girls were there warming up. The sounds of their voices calling out to each other, kicking, and cheering, was music to her ears. It was a hot evening. A slight breeze eased the sting of the heat. It felt good to be outside in the fresh air. The smell of freshly cut grass was strong and comforting. Sandra had once thought about becoming an arborist so she could work outdoors. But after a few weeks at Goodsworth—and the realisation she'd be working in rain, hail, or hot sunshine as an arborist, which didn't overly appeal—she was sold. Her career path was in the supermarket.

She shut her car door and headed across the grass to the game. *At least Bader can't bother me here.* 'Okay, bitches, let's play this game!' she yelled.

Chapter Twenty

Rachel dropped the bleached chickens into a large garbage bag, relieved they were finally going to the industrial bin where they belonged. Tying up the tag she noticed Garth lingering at the cheese display, watching her. She gave him a quick smile and resumed her task.

'Still staring,' Justin teased as he collected his customer's ricotta cheese.

Ignoring Justin, she shut the oven door, secretly pleased Garth was staring. It had to mean he was into her, and checkouts a surety.

Garth swanned into the deli. 'Non-sellers.' He didn't so much ask, but stated, glancing at the garbage bags. 'Unlike Sandra's prize-winning deli to not sell its birds.'

'One of those days I guess.' She brushed him off, hoping he wouldn't talk about them any further.

'Hey Gazman, want one for dinner?' Justin butted in. 'For you, free.'

Garth peeled his eyes off Rachel and eyed Justin. 'Non-selling chickens are usually for the chicken salad.'

'We already have too much chicken salad,' Rachel said, trying to look busy so Garth would leave. She still had blue hair under her hair net and a brown-stained shirt, not her best look.

He moseyed over to the counter. 'Chicken salad's empty.'

Rachel waved her hand suggesting to Garth it was under control. 'It's been really busy. Shoppers have gone crazy for chicken salad today.' *Who cares anyway? Maybe he was trying to find an excuse to hang around her.*

'So, you're tossing out the chickens?' Garth tugged the garbage bag, then teasingly let the plastic slip from his fingers. 'And not keeping them for salads like protocol?'

'Of course,' Rachel said quickly, wishing Justin or Valentina would jump in and say something and not leave this awkward conversation to her. 'I was actually just collecting the bags and—'

'Putting them in the coolroom?' Garth's eyes narrowed.

'Yes.' Rachel grabbed the garbage bag. 'That's exactly where I was taking them. Just resting them here until—'

'Sandra tells us what to do with them. Satisfied?' Justin pitched in from the counter. Rachel smiled nervously. She took hold of the garbage bag that had barely touched the floor and dragged it towards the coolroom.

Without another glance in Rachel's direction Garth left.

'Don't even say it Justin,' Rachel said, reemerging from the coolroom.

She wished Garth had shown more interest in her than the chickens. Maybe it was his way of flirting. After all, he was watching her from the cheese display, and he'd come over to talk. Hopefully she'd played it cool enough.

'This place is exhausting. And we haven't even talked about the trophies yet,' she said to Justin, thinking about the waggish glance he shot her earlier when Sandra had pulled out her trophies.

'Do you think she sterilised them before she adorned our counters with them?' he laughed. 'But whatever floats her boat.'

She smiled at Justin's comment. The trophies gleamed on the counter beneath the large poster of Sandra, her stern face staring down from the stainless-steel wall. Sandra's boat floated very uniquely.

At nine o'clock, all the deli food was placed in the coolroom. Rachel helped Valentina wipe down the benches while Justin made sure all the produce in the coolroom was sealed, and the digital scale and ticket machine were off.

As they walked out of the deli, Justin a few steps in front, Valentina grabbed Rachel by the arm. 'My dear, thank you for the magazines. I'll be reading them tonight.' Rachel, who was exhausted and eager to leave, smiled politely and tried to extract herself from Valentina's grip. 'You know, I get lonely at night times. When I get home Alvaro is always asleep on the couch with the television on. Snores like a foghorn. And worse, he wears only his singlet and undies. His big belly, hanging out.

Says it's too hot. I say put on the air conditioner. He tells me he's saving money. I tell him underwear on the couch is not romantic, you know.

Rachel bit back a laugh, but Valentina wasn't finished.

'He had the operation on his scrotum you know.'

Rachel blinked. "His… what?"

Justin turned around and raised his eyebrows cheekily.

'They tried to straighten it so he could breathe better. It didn't work.'

Rachel clutched Martha, horrified. 'Wait—his scrotum helped him breathe?'

Valentina frowned, confused. 'Or maybe sternum?'

Justin choked. 'Val. You mean septum. In his nose.' He pointed to his face, trying not to laugh.

'Oh yes! That one. Scrotum, sternum, septum—all the same, no?'

Justin laughed with Rachel. 'Trust me, Val. Not the same.' He turned to Rachel, 'Hungry?'

'Starving,' she said, unsure if this was a rhetorical question or an invitation to eat with him.

'Thought so. I know a place. Have a good night V,' he said as he walked purposefully down the aisle, picking up a bottle of water without stopping.

'Better run Val but enjoy your reading tonight! See you tomorrow,' Rachel rushed, interrupting Valentina's rant.

Justin paused at Trudy's checkout to pay for his water. Rachel almost felt a tinge of jealousy as he chatted with Trudy. She was attractive to look at. With glowing dark brown hair, her foundation still in place—even at the end of her shift (albeit a little thick), and her eyebrows neat, thick, and most likely tattooed on. As Rachel walked up next to Justin, Trudy smiled politely, taking in her hair net. Rachel felt undone—like a seven-year-old who'd just had an accident in public.

'I'll meet you out the front,' Rachel said to Justin, forcing a polite smile back at Trudy.

While she waited for Justin to finish his laughing with the obviously hilarious Trudy, she applied lip gloss, realising she hadn't put it on all day. This job was seriously lowering her standards.

Justin signaled for her to follow him. 'Come on Bluey,' he said as she caught up with him.

Rachel gave him a playful punch in the arm. 'I'm far too tired and sensitive to joke about my hair tonight.'

'Well, you wear it well, Rach,' he said as he took a swig from his water.

Was he flirting with her? No way. They were just work buddies who'd survived the trenches today. She didn't think of Justin that way. Besides he wasn't hot like Garth. He was more the unconventional good-looking guy. She'd noticed today that a lot of women shoppers seemed to initiate conversation with him, or were on a first name basis, tossing banter across the counter. Maybe it was just his height that attracted women to him. He did have such great charisma, which, she had to admit, was attractive.

'Do you fancy Pho Mi?' he asked.

'Fancy you?' Had he read her mind? Her face flushed.

'Ha, well no, yes?' He laughed. 'Fancy pho? Food? Want to get something to eat? The Vietnamese place here does a great pho.'

Oh of course! 'Of course.' She felt stupid. 'I was just being silly with that fancy you stuff.' *Digging a hole Rach? Change the subject.* 'How was Valentina nearly sending her customer to sleep with her recipe.' Now she was making it obvious she was feeling awkward. 'I'm starving,' she said as Justin held open the restaurant's glass door.

The Vietnamese woman plonked two small glasses on the table and talked loudly about the busy mall at Christmas, sloshing water into their glasses. Her face was shiny from the clammy warmth of the café, and when she smiled, her teeth sat in a squashed jaggered array. She felt cosy, like someone who would make a delicious pho.

'What will you have?' she said, barely allowing them time to look at their menus.

'Chicken pho for you Rach?' Justin joked.

She pretended to gag. 'Just the veggie pho please.'

'Make that two,' said Justin. 'And a Chardonnay please.'

'One for me too, please.' She needed a drink.

The woman took their menus and wiped their table with her cloth before stuffing it into her back pocket. She called out their order and collected more menus, glasses, and a water jug, moving on spritely to the next waiting table.

'That was some day,' Justin said.

'I've never worked so hard in my life!' She rested her head on her fist.

The woman returned with their drinks.

'Cheers, to the deli.' Justin toasted.

She raised her glass. 'To not poisoning our customers!'

Laughing they took a sip of their wine. 'Food never takes long here. And just as well. As soon as I walk in here the smell makes it hard to wait.'

'Do you eat a lot here?' she asked, thinking what an uninteresting question she'd just asked.

He nodded.

The waitress put their large, oversized bowls of pho down in front of them, carrying out a conversation in Vietnamese with the table adjacent to theirs. She laughed with the other customer and told Justin and Rachel to enjoy their meal.

Rachel took out her utensils from the paper wrap and stuck the spoon into her bowl pulling out a large piece of bok choy. She didn't care it the broth and noodles made a sloppy run down her chin and back into the bowl, or that she needed to use her napkin after every slurp. The soup, full of hearty vegetables, was just what she needed. She'd just about given up on trying to look remotely attractive after the last 24 hours she'd had.

'So, tell me, was that the craziest day you've ever had here?'

Justin eyed her seriously. 'To be honest, probably not,' he said as he then started regaling funny stories from his four years of working in the deli. He told her Sandra was flexible when it came to taking time off for auditions and acting gigs. Rachel was surprised to hear this. He reassured her Sandra had a soft side. She just hadn't seen it yet.

Justin made her laugh with deli stories. Her favourite, when Sandra, a few years ago, cut her hand on the slicer and stapled the skin together so she could be around when the Big Boys came by. She wasn't going to miss making an impression.

'I cannot believe she did that.'

'True story.' His eyes twinkled.

Justin was so easy to be around. He asked what her latest streaming binge was (*Selling Sunset*), how she had her coffee (full milk cap), and what she did for fun (mostly hanging out with Liz and going to the beach). If she didn't know any better, it would've felt like a first date. That is, if they didn't work together, she didn't have blue hair with a hair net, and coffee stains down their white shirts.

She dabbed her mouth with her napkin commenting how good the food was and tipped the last sip of wine into her mouth. After finishing their meal, she pulled out the cash for her payment. She needed to get home. She felt tired and tomorrow was going to be another big day on her feet. Also, she didn't want to give Justin any ideas that she was interested in him. Friends don't linger.

She rubbed her arms feeling the slight chill of the air conditioning blowing on her. She always felt colder when she was tired. She rummaged in her bag for her cardigan and realised she'd left it in the coolroom when Garth came by the deli earlier that day. She'd been distracted trying to listen to him and Justin's conversation (if that's what she could call it) and completely forgot to put it on. She'd placed it on the stepladder, which was no doubt where it still lay.

'I left my cardigan in the coolroom.'

'You grab it while I wait here and pay.'

She smiled back at him. Not sure why he wanted to wait for her, but it felt good, thoughtful. 'Okay. Here's my money. Back in a mini.' She picked up her bag and headed to the supermarket with a spring in her step.

The supermarket was dim, only cleaners and box packers roving the aisles. Mega Mart at the end of the mall would stay open another two hours. She ducked into the deli. The coolroom door stood slightly ajar. Hadn't it been shut when they left? Then again, the day had been a blur.

Her cardigan lay on the stepladder. As she reached for it she thought she heard someone in the deli. Suddenly the coolroom door slammed shut.

'Justin, this isn't funny.' She banged on the door. 'Going too far now.' Panic clawed at her chest. She instantly hated him for the prank. 'Justin,' she yelled, fumbling with her cardigan. She hated closed spaces, let alone a fridge. 'Justin, open the door. Justin!' she screamed, pounding the steel. What was going on? Did the door just close on its own? It had been ajar all day, not once did it close by itself. She shouted again, but this time for 'help,' as she pummeled her hands against the door. 'Open the fucking door.'

Chapter Twenty One

Sandra sprinted around the synthetic sporting field. After a day ruminating about Bader and Garth, and the stressful visit by the Big Boys, her adrenalin was pumping. She flew around the turf with agile coordination, kicking, scoring, and yelling tactical moves and words of encouragement to her team. Unlike the deli, the girls here were her sporting sisters—dependable, admired for their grit, determination, and athleticism. She slammed a ball into the net, feeling a release from the tension of work. Work for her, clown day for her deli staff. But it wasn't the deli staff causing her tension, at least not now Rhonda was gone, it was Bader and Garth who were making her shoulders tense and her jaw locked at night.

Sav, who played forward, ran past, giving Sandra a firm high five with a hoot. Sandra loved it. She was the team's best player and highest scorer. She was tactically skilled. For ten years she'd been playing with this team of five players and two reserves. She had the leg power and high-level shooting and passing ability of her soccer idol, Sam Kerr. Her fifth goal of the night sent her tearing up the field with her shirt over her head, screaming. She was on fire.

As usual, Mario was at the game with his cousin Vince, who was there to cheer on his girlfriend. It was, she thought, a shame she was in Sandra's team. Mario was there nearly every game. Being Mr. Obvious, he was clearly hoping to meet someone. But after two years of being ignored by the women, he still hadn't taken the hint.After the game, Sandra sat on the bleachers to untie her shoes.

'Good game, Sands.' Mario strode towards her.

'Yeah, not bad.' She didn't look up.

'Vinnie's girl's a real scorer hey?'

'She hasn't kicked a goal all season.' Sandra sat on the bleachers to untie her shoes.

Mario nodded as if to himself, then fixed his gaze on her. 'I heard Bader's thinking of—'

'Thinking of what?' She snapped. Did Mario have to ruin her futsal buzz with pinhead's name?

'Well, I went up for my meeting with Bades today, you know, the one straight after yours.'

Sandra knew what he meant. Usually she staggered out of those meetings with a headache, growling something curt, while Mario breezed past with his stock line: It could be worse, Garth could be manager. Lately, that sounded less like a joke and more like a nightmare.

'Him and Garth were in there arguing,' Mario said.

He had her full attention. 'Go on.'

'I hid behind the palm, not the dead one with the note, *Dead please dispose of*, but the fake one, so I could listen.' He sat beside her on the timber bleachers.

She nodded. She knew the one.

'It was weird. Still got me baffled.'

Sandra didn't think it would take much to confuse Mario, but she wanted him to hurry up and tell her what he'd heard.

'They argued about some blonde chick called Renee who Garth wanted in the deli. Weird huh? They've already hired a blonde chick.'

'I know you're not the sharpest pencil in the tin, Mario,' she said. 'Renee's Rachel. Bader never remembers new employees' names.' Mario looked like he'd had a light bulb moment. 'What else did you hear?' Sandra asked.

He pushed out his lower lip. Sandra considered him to look unusually thoughtful. 'Well Sands, it's strange. I heard your job is on the line. You're going to be fired.'

Sandra's brow creased. Hadn't Garth and Bader finished talking about her and Rachel when she'd listened to them, which was just before Mario's meeting? Didn't those clowns have something else to focus on—such as work? Mario had a big mouth. If Mario blabbed, she'd lose respect—and power.

'Mario, remember the morning when Spiro's fingers came off in the mincer?'

'Yeah, bad morning that was.' He shook his head.

'And you remember the amount of blood spewing from Spiro's hand when he removed it from the mincer. You didn't chuck the mince.'

Mario looked startled. 'You came by the Butchery to tell off Spiro for taking your ham hocks and styrofoaming them. You distracted him,' he said defensively.

'Just because your order hadn't come in didn't give Spiro a reason to take my stock.'

'Yeah, well you telling him off mid mincing cost him his fingers.'

'Yes, pity old Spiro. Those three fingers made him five hundred grand,' she said sarcastically. 'Point is Mario, I filmed it on my phone. Spiro with his two fingered hand shooting blood all over the floor, you running around like a headless chook, and the mincer on full throttle in the background. Thing is, I filmed you loading that mince onto the Styrofoam trays. And don't tell me you didn't know where Spiro's fingers were,' she said sharply.

'We were behind budget,' Mario defended. 'Besides, it ain't no different to what's in it already.'

'Head honchos won't buy that. Sometimes we ain't very ethically inclined when our jobs are on the line. If you tell any of those idiots in the deli about what you heard in Bader's office, I'll tell Glen Smyth about Spiro's finger.'

Mario frowned. 'Bit unnecessary, don't you think?'

Sandra sighed, she didn't like threatening Mario, even though he annoyed the hell out of her most of the time. 'I have footage, but I don't want to use it.'

Mario looked serious. 'Understand.'

'You can't say anything to Justin and Rachel about Bader wanting to sack me. Getting my drift?'

'Yeah. 'Course.'

'Good 'cause I'm sure getting yours.'

Mario adjusted his stance. 'Beckham aftershave. Gift from me mum.'

'Not that drift, Mario.' Sandra wrinkled her nose. 'So, we have an agreement? You keep your mouth shut or I'm gonna kick your arse from here to Katoomba.'

'Yeah sure,' he frowned, subtly smelling his arm pit. Quickly dismissing her threat, he called after her as she walked to her car. 'Good scoring tonight, Sands!'

She gave him the thumbs up, taking the compliment, and hoping Mario would keep his mouth shut. Sure, she'd seen him mince Spiro's finger, but she wasn't morbid enough to film it. Besides, she couldn't get her phone out quickly enough. Fortunately, Mario wasn't switched on enough to ask to see the footage. How he managed to get his meat in the Styrofoam containers each morning and meet budget was beyond her.

She parked her car in the communal apartment car park and headed up the three flights of stairs, deep in thought about their conversation. *How did Bader become best buds with Garth? Why would he share the power of Goodsworth with that loser? What explanation did Bader give to the Big Boys to explain the emails she'd sent?* Her brain was about to explode.

She thought about the quality control boxes checked by Garth. What was it about those boxes? Were those buffoons causing her chickens to be off, so she looked incompetent? She needed to find out what the two boneheads were up to, and fast.

She opened the door to her apartment. Katie waved at her from the couch where she sat watching *Law and Order.*

'Well babe,' Sandra groaned. 'It's been another fabulous day.'

Chapter Twenty Two

Rachel banged on the coolroom door, even though she knew no one would hear—not even the ineffectual hulk of a security guard, Troy. She leant against the door, tears streaking down her face. She'd been in the coolroom for two hours. Soon, she'd become hypothermic. Not exactly the glamorous exit she'd envisioned for herself—trapped in a coolroom, dressed like a rejected extra from a supermarket commercial.

She'd learned about hypothermia back in Year 5, when the class studied Antarctica. The symptoms came back like a cruel memory test: tiredness and confusion, slowed breathing and speech, loss of feeling or movement and—if you kept going long enough—cardiac arrest. She yelled again. Her breath was foggy, the cold stung her nose. She prayed someone, a cleaner, delivery guy, or night filler, would hear her. If she didn't get out soon, she'd die. Which, frankly, wasn't on her to-do list today.

She wrapped her arms tighter around her body aiming for more warmth, wishing her cardigan wasn't so flimsy and she hadn't left her hoodie under the counter. She scanned the dimly lit coolroom, hoping to find something that could keep her warm. There was certainly no shortage of antipasto, raw poultry pieces and fish. She'd gagged several times already.

If she was in Antarctica, she'd build an igloo. That was it. Survival 101. She looked up at the boxes on the stainless-steel racks. With her hands painful from the cold, she pulled down the boxes and the large green garbage bags that were lying on the shelf. With cold, numb fingers, she built an igloo from the boxes, then wrapped herself in garbage bags. Despite the cold and the fact she'd probably still die, she felt proud at her ingenuity.

All this, because she'd come back for her cardigan. A cardigan! And Justin? Why hadn't he noticed she'd vanished? Surely he must have wondered where she'd gone. If she lived through this, she'd quit Goodsworth for good and tell Justin exactly what she thought of him. This place was insane.

She must have dozed, because the sound at the door startled her awake. The lock clicked. Pain stabbing her muscles, she could barely move. The dim light of the deli crept under the gaps in her cardboard fortress. Footsteps crunched closer. Was she being rescued? Or had someone locked her in here and now they were coming back to take her somewhere else? She'd heard about this: *never let a kidnapper take you to the second location.*

'Rachel?'

'Ju...Justin?' she recognised his voice.

Justin's face appeared, peering through the crooked igloo wall, his expression caught between horror and amusement at the sight of her wrapped in garbage bags.

'Woah. I've seen everything now.' He reached for her hand. 'You're freezing. Okay the green garbage bag look is going to be hard to walk in.' He bent, slid an arm under her legs—wrapped so tightly it was hard to tell where her knees began—and lifted her in a cradle carry.

'I... I... I... w... w... ent t... to g... get... ' She gave up, her voice failing. It hardly mattered. The shriek of the store alarm and police sirens were enough to make her wonder, *Is that all because of me?*

'H... how'd you g... get in?' she whispered.

'Same way we're getting out.' He hoisted her up in her arms.

She thought she'd feel embarrassed to be carried by Justin. But she didn't care. Relief that she was out of the coolroom and alive washed through her.

The sixty-year-old floor-to-ceiling window, which faced onto the car park, was now shattered and glistening across the supermarket entrance. Several police cars idled outside. Black skid marks traced from the gaping hole to the flower display, where Justin's motorbike lay sideways, wedged in a bucket of carnations.

A police officer shouted to his team as they piled from their vehicles. 'These guys look professional. Prepare for arms.'

Rachel was cognisant enough to know that Justin, carrying what must look like a green sack of potatoes, hardly looked professional. She was about to suggest they call out something to make sure they didn't get shot. She didn't have to.

'Well, I'll be buggered,' the officer muttered. Then, barked, 'Stand down, everyone, stand down!'

Chapter Twenty Three

Sandra was asleep when her phone rang at 1:45 a.m. 'Who the hell is this?' she answered, then sat bolt upright.

'Troy…What?…The coolroom? No—I'll be right there,' she said abruptly.

'Everything alright?' Katie asked sleepily.

'I'm gonna lose my job over this,' she muttered, yanking her hoodie over her PJs. 'I have Rachel locked in the coolroom and Justin breaking windows and turnstiles to rescue her. They think they live in bloody Disneyland.'

The supermarket was lit up. Swirling police lights flashed, while officers stood with serious expressions around the broken glass where the large window used to be.

'A bloody circus.' She stared at the entrance, then at the fire engine, tow truck and ambulance. 'Oh this, I can't wait to hear,' she said, slamming the car door.

Justin, holding an ice pack to his head, looked up at her. 'Hey, Sands.'

'Don't you "Sands" me. You responsible for this mess?' She pointed at his mangled bike in the flower stand.

'You the manager here?' The paramedic interrupted, directing his question at Sandra.

'Deli manager,' Sandra stressed her importance.

'Yeah, right. Well, this should be a good story for the store,' he snorted. 'She owes you one, mate.' He looked at Justin. 'Wouldn't have lasted the night in that fridge.'

The paramedic climbed into the ambulance where Rachel lay on the stretcher, shrouded in a foil blanket. Sandra nodded at Rachel trying to show a small amount of sympathy, which felt unfamiliar. Who needed sympathy in this world? As far as she was concerned most people brought on their own undoing and problems. If Rachel used her brain she wouldn't have got locked in the coolroom. If Bader got his act together and fixed the wretched door his window wouldn't be smashed. And if Justin called security instead of trying to be the hero, then none of this mess would've happened and she wouldn't be standing here in her PJ's at this unearthly hour. She kept her fake semi-kind expression. Deep down, she wanted to give Rachel and Justin one hell of a piece of her mind—the kind usually reserved for telemarketers and ex-girlfriends.

As the ambulance drove away, Bader's car sped up to the entrance. He slammed his door and paced towards her.

'Of all the ridiculous manifestations of behaviour I've seen, this takes the cake.' He pointed his finger at her. 'At Christmas time too. Corporate will want an inquiry into this now, won't they. Evidence you can't manage your staff, Sandra.'

'Yeah, well I've been asking you to fix the coolroom door for a year. So, Bades, this is your problem now.'

Bader pushed his glasses up his nose. 'You need to put your request in email.' He turned his attention to the broken window. 'How could this happen?' he cried, staring at the gaping hole. Clenching his fists and jaw, he went to inspect the supermarket.

Sandra kicked a small shard of glass. 'I ought to sack you both,' she said to Justin. 'But you did good rescuing Rachel.' What was this, niceness, which was oozing out of her?

'Thanks, Sands,' Justin lowered the ice pack from his head.

'Besides, I like what you did, almost given him a heart attack,' she said bluntly. 'She shook her head. 'Tell me: how'd she get locked in there, and why the hell didn't you get security?'

Justin rubbed his chin sheepishly. 'Yeah, funny that. I hunted for security, but no one was around. Still aren't.'

Justin was right. Troy, or one of his henchmen, were nowhere to be seen. Bader couldn't even control his security guards. She stared at the smashed window. Troy not being around actually worked in her favour.

Now Bader, the incompetent fool, would have to explain to corporate why Troy wasn't on his shift. 'Nowhere in sight, huh?'

'Nup. I panicked.' Justin flicked a hand in the direction of the debris.

'I can see that.' Sandra loved the one hell of an almighty mess. She turned to face Justin, forcing herself to look composed instead of thrilled at Bader's dilemma. 'How'd you know she was there? She must've been in there for—'

'Just over four hours,' he said. 'We were eating pho and she went back for her cardigan, which she'd left in the coolroom. When she didn't return, I left, assuming she'd gone home.'

'You didn't check?'

'Who would think?'

'True.' Sandra shook her head thinking Rachel was fast becoming one of her most unpredictable workers.

'And then when I got home, I did some thinking, and realised I hadn't checked to see if her car was still there. So, I messaged her. Then called, then—'

'You got on your bike to check?' Sandra didn't care for all the details.

'Yep.'

'And this is the result,' she said, watching Bader talking to the police, his hands making a continuous path over his comb-over. This mess would at least take his attention off her for a while. She wasn't a spiritual person, but as she watched Bader stumble over his words, wipe his head, and look repeatedly at the hole in the building, she raised her eyes to the sky and mentally thanked the heavens.

The police officer who'd been checking the scene wandered over and suggested firmly that Justin call them next time he thought he needed to break and enter to rescue someone. Justin nodded respectfully. The officer took a statement from Justin and Sandra, each concurring that the coolroom lock had been broken for a year and Sandra had been asking the store manager to fix it.

'You have health and safety checks here?' he asked.

Sandra tilted her head, thinking about this question. 'For food and hygiene, for sure. When it comes to maintenance, our boss isn't so diligent. Finger off the pulse on this one.' She tried to suppress a smile. Corporate would be all over Bader when they got the police report.

'Just, mate, can I give you a lift? I'm figuring you don't have a way to get home,' Sandra offered. They looked where the police tape was wrapped around his bike. A sunflower resting gently on the wheel.

'That'd be great,' Justin said.

As they headed towards her car, Bader's voice echoed from inside the store—whining, complaining, yelling. Sandra grinned. With the smashed window debacle and the Christmas party in a few days, Bader's week was only about to get worse.

Chapter Twenty Four

Nurse Maggie rattled on about her two 'brainless' teenage boys and how her husband who, by her account, couldn't boil an egg without triggering the smoke alarm. While she vented, she checked Rachel's blood pressure, inserted the drip into her arm, and wrote down her vitals onto the chart at the end of her bed. Rachel watched the warmed saline run through the clear tube into her veins where it warmed her blood. Nurse Maggie's endless spiel was a welcomed distraction. Strangely, along with the people talking, the pattering of feet, cubical curtains drawn open and closed, and utensils clattering, the sounds of the Emergency Department had a kind of comforting feeling. Chaos had never sounded so safe.

Maggie didn't stop for air as she recounted her shift. Rachel heard about the guy who came in with a slashed face 'probably a drug deal gone bad,' Maggie muttered, her mouth twisting as if she knew more than she was saying. Then came the surfer with a gash along his chest after colliding with his board, the woman who loudly passed a kidney stone, and and the twelve-year-old she gave ketamine for a fractured arm, who screamed, 'Fuckin' lit! Drugs are awesome!' before his parents beamed, 'He's adorable.' Maggie shook her head. 'Cute, my ass. I just created a monster.'

Rachel was still laughing when Ian's pale face poked through the curtain. 'I was so worried,' he said, crushing her in a hug. 'And what have you done with your hair?' he asked, surprised. 'When did you have time… no don't bother. I don't want to know.' He sat on the edge of her bed and asked her to tell him how she found herself locked in the coolroom.

By the time she was given her own room it was almost morning.

'I can't believe it!' Liz swept into the room. 'Look at you.' She waved her hand at Rachel lying in bed wearing a hospital gown with the drip in her arm, her heart rate monitored on the screen beside her. 'You bloody scared me, bitch!' She planted a kiss on Rachel's cheek before thrusting a Maccas bag into her lap. 'Hospital food's garbage. I brought you the whole menu.'

Ian rose to hug Liz. 'Can you believe there's no safety switch in that coolroom?'

'Crazy,' Liz shook her head, already unpacking Egg McMuffins, hash browns, and hotcakes like she was laying out treasure. 'So how'd it happen?' she said, nestling herself comfortably on the bed.

Rachel's mouth watered at the smell of Maccas. She opened the bag, now realising how hungry she was. She stuffed down a hash brown, followed by the hot cakes drizzled in syrup and butter, and told them the dramatic story, leaving no detail out. Liz picked at a McMuffin looking horrified.

'You need to reconsider this deli job,' Ian said, 'and Liz, did you have anything to do with her hair?'

'What hair?' Liz gave a wry smile.

Ian looked at them both. 'You girls never cease to horrify me.'

'Okay then, who's the hero who found you? No one destroys a window for just anyone you know.' Liz eyed Rachel, suggesting something was going on between her and 'Mr. Wonderful,' which she jokingly called him.

Rachel ignored her comment and Ian's raised eyebrows. 'He's a guy from the deli who figured I was there because we… well he just figured.'

She couldn't be bothered going through the details of their pho dinner and the fact that Justin seemed to be a genuinely decent guy. Liz would force her to over analyse it even though it was nothing but friends. During the early hours of the morning, when she couldn't sleep, she'd checked her phone and saw several messages from him asking if she was coming back to the restaurant.

The first message was chilled: *Hey Rach, still in the centre?*

The second message she guessed he would have been annoyed.: *Guess you went home. See you tomorrow.*

Then about an hour later she had his missed call and voice message. "Hey Rach, just checking you made it home okay. I wasn't sure if you were coming back and ah, just checking, all good. See you tomorrow."

Funny, but she kept replaying his message. It kind of felt good to know someone was checking in on her, wondering where she was.

'You're going to need acupuncture for this,' Liz said, flicking through her phone. 'I'll send you my guys details.'

'I'm fine really,' Rachel insisted.

'You've had a near-death experience. You don't want to develop PTSD.'

Rachel slumped back into her pillow. She didn't want to hear Liz rant on about near-death experiences. After all, she wanted to say, most people probably have them, and they don't even know it. She thought about the time she almost opened her car door as a bus whizzed by inches away. 'I don't need to see an acupuncturist.'

Most effective treatment for PTSD is acupuncture and massage. True. I read it. There, sent.' Liz put down her phone and studied Rachel. 'That deli guys a hero don't you think? What's his name?' She searched for him on Instagram. 'Don't worry, found him. Cute.' She winked at Rachel, dropping her phone on the bed, and taking a hash brown.

Ian looked thoughtful. 'I need to thank… what's his name?'

'Justin.'

'Justin.' Liz and Ian said together. Ian with a serious pondering expression. Liz with a *tell me more about this guy*, look.

'And after I thank him, I'm going to write Goodsworth a letter of complaint. In fact, I'm going to sue,' Ian said, the frown returning.

Rachel felt relieved he was moving off the topic of Justin, even though she knew he wouldn't sue anyone, not even a company. He just wasn't the type to create conflict or seek justice, unlike Liz, who said if Ian didn't, she definitely would.

The squeaky wheels of the morning meals trolley stopped at her door. The tea lady, wearing a similar hair net to her own, briskly lifted the meal tray off the trolley and walked into the room, placing the tray in front of Rachel. She smiled briefly. 'Enjoy.' Rachel thanked her and lifted the stainless-steel lid off the dish, revealing cold set porridge. She was glad for her Maccas feast.

'I'm fine,' she told them, peeling the paper lid from the orange juice. 'And I know Bad… Mr. Bader, that's the manager, will make sure the lock is fixed, and I'm treated well.' She doubted Bader would do anything, but she didn't want Ian to worry. She could tell by his sustained frown and shake of his head and, 'We'll see,' comment that he wasn't convinced.

'Ah, so tell me more about this Justin?' Liz persisted.

'He's just someone I work with.'

'Someone who's old… married… single?' Liz fished.

'A guy who works in the deli and wants to be an actor.' There, that should get Liz off her case.

'Knock, knock.' Justin hovered by the frame, hesitant, a bunch of flowers in his hand. 'Hey, Rach. Can I come in?'

Rachel froze, the McMuffin halfway to her mouth. 'Justin! She wanted to dive under the covers. She looked a mess.

Liz, never one to miss a cue, turned with a grin. 'Oh, so this is the famous Justin. Huh.'

What was he doing here? Here, meeting her best friend and dad. Once she would have felt annoyed at a work colleague rocking up invading her private world, oddly, she didn't feel this with Justin. As he smiled at them all and started to make small talk, she found herself feeling okay, after all, hadn't he carried her and seen her sobbing wet face.

Justin shot Rachel a look; equal parts awkward, apologetic, yet still confident. 'I just wanted to see if you were okay. Thought these might cheer you up.' He handed her a bunch of peonies. 'The florist downstairs opens surprisingly early.'

'Oh, thanks.' *Was he going to lean down and give her a kiss? And did she want him to?*

'You're a real hero, Justin,' said Liz.

'Hero?' He smiled looking back at Rachel.

No kiss on the check. Oddly, she felt disappointed. And she wished Liz would shut up.

'Nice to meet you, Justin.' Ian introduced himself. 'We owe you a huge thank you. How did you guess Rach was there?' Ian said animatedly, like he was standing in front of royalty. He was relieved she was alive and Justin, standing next to him, was the reason why.

Justin shook Ian's hand and started to answer his question, while Rachel subtly smoothed her hair and blew into the palm of her hand to check her breath. Stale, but not bad.

Justin continued his story. 'After work we had Vietnamese—'

'—You had dinner?' Liz interrupted, turning her head to eye Rachel.

Justin paused, checking Rachel's expression.

Why couldn't he just explain about Bader's dodgy lock. Why mention dinner? As she thought about this, she realised it made sense to explain they'd been hanging out and she'd suddenly disappeared. Why else would he question where she was? What she wanted to keep private—dinner with Justin—was now public. It was impossible separating work and private life.

'After a big day we were hungry. Anyway, the most important detail is Justin figured out where I was and I'm super grateful. Really.'

'So, dinner then, because it was dinner, right?' Liz persisted.

Ian panned the room with his eyes and commented how nice and new the hospital was, 'Only open a few years.'

Justin turned to look out the window. 'Nice view.'

Rachel mouthed to Liz, *Stop it!*

'Awful thought of what could have happened to Rachel if you hadn't saved her,' Ian finally said.

'Just lucky I was there I guess,' Justin said. 'How you feeling Rach?' He sounded sincere.

Rachel straightened herself higher in her bed. 'Oh, I'm fine. Just enjoying my first meal outside the freezer.' There was awkward laughter.

'Thank you for the flowers by the way. They're lovely.' They were. *Now Rach keep the conversation light and short so Justin can leave.* 'We'd better let you get to work.' She eyed Liz. 'Really appreciate you dropping by.'

Justin didn't budge. He turned to chat with Ian, who asked him about his bike, and apologised on Rachel's behalf that it was now at the mechanics.

'Well, thanks again for the flowers. Seriously thoughtful.' *Maybe he'll go now.*

'Okay, enough talk about flowers,' Liz said. 'I need to get to work. Call you later,' she hugged Rachel and whispered, 'for more goss.'

Rachel watched her leave. Ian followed, excusing himself to get a coffee.

She felt weird sitting in the narrow hospital bed with Justin. She wished he'd gone with them, or Ian had stayed. She'd told him they could get coffee together when she was discharged. Ian told her he'd be happy to get another one with her later. She smoothed the blanket across her thighs, hoping the doctor on duty would come in soon and tell her she could go home.

'So, what's the damage?' Justin joked as he studied the monitor next to her bed.

'You tell me.' She rested the flowers on the bed.

'Hmm, pulse 66, blood pressure 110 over 70, and problematic fungal blue hair.' He sat on the edge of her bed.

She sensed he was completely comfortable in his own skin. He smiled at her, not an ounce of awkwardness.

'Can't believe you got locked in there,' he said.

During the early hours of the morning, she'd contemplated her movements when she went back to get her cardigan. She was certain she'd heard a noise at the coolroom door but hadn't seen anything. She really couldn't be sure how the door closed. 'Do you think the police believed our story? They seemed kind of unimpressed. I guess CCTV footage will have it recorded,' she said.

'I doubt Bader had a camera outside the coolroom. Goodsworth is a bit stingy when it comes to upgrades—in case you hadn't noticed. Mostly just a camera at the entrance of the store and a few around the aisles and checkouts.' He looked thoughtful. 'You thinking of quitting?'

She remembered she was going to quit if she ever got out alive. 'No, I need the money.' *And hopefully checkouts is now going to happen.* 'How's your bike?'

'Towed. Easy fix. I'll have it back in a week.'

'Sorry.' Rachel knew he'd have to pay on his insurance.

'It's nothing, don't worry about it.'

'How was Sandra when I left?' she asked.

'Worried about you. Kept saying how relieved she was I found you.'

'Really?' She didn't believe him.

'Nah, she was pretty pissed I'd ridden my bike into the store. Weirdly she became uncharacteristically chipper when Bader showed up and almost had a stroke at the sight of his precious entrance.'

'Well, she'd be thanking you then.'

'Yep.' He laughed.

'All they care about is their dumb power struggle over that stupid place. And Bader didn't ask how I was, right? Oh, hold on, he doesn't even know who I am. Did he call me Renee?'

'You were lucky he didn't call you something else,' he joked. 'Imagine if I'd guessed wrong and you weren't in the coolroom? Bader would charge me with something for sure.'

'I hope he realises if he put me at checkouts, where I wanted, then his window would still be intact.' She then said thoughtfully, 'I'm grateful you took the risk. Thank you. Bet no one's been locked in the coolroom before?' She tried to dismiss the uncomfortable reality.

Justin nodded and told her the details of how he'd paid the bill and then waited fifteen minutes for her to come back. He walked past Goodsworth, but the front security grill was down, and the store was locked. He figured since she'd taken her bag, she must've gone home. 'I forgot to check if your car was in the car park,' he said shaking his head.

'What made you think I was in the coolroom?'

I tried to contact you—'

'—but I didn't reply.'

He raked his hands through his hair like a man auditioning for a shampoo commercial. 'I couldn't figure out why you ghosted my messages. Or why you suddenly left.'

'Must've seemed weird,' she said thinking how he must have worried enough to come and find her. She loved listening to how he circled the car park on his bike, saw her car and figured she must be in the deli, locked in the coolroom. And without thinking of the consequences, he rode through the window. If they weren't just friends, she'd love to tell people about her Romeo saving her life. Although maybe Romeo was not a good example. He hardly saved Juliette.

'A bit.' His smile lit up his eyes.

'Bader will definitely fix the lock now,' Rachel said.

'Have you seen that place?'

She thought about the turnstiles. 'He's never going to fix it.' She laughed. 'And you didn't think to ask the security guard for help? Like the reason for going through the window. Not that I'm not grateful.'

'If I could find Troy, or anyone else, maybe the store might look a little different, yeah,' he said.

'It's weird none of them were around.'

'Up for the Christmas party?' Justin asked.

She remembered Lillian mentioning this event to Bader on the day she arrived. 'When is it?'

'Friday after our shift. In the lunchroom.'

'Maybe,' she said. 'You?'

'I usually pop in for a bit. There's free food and drinks.'

'You had me at free,' she joked, just as her phone rang. 'I don't know the number. I'll leave it.'

'Nah, get it. Might be some local reporter wanting to interview you.

Pretty good story for them,' he said, waving at her phone suggesting she pick it up.

Looking back on that moment, she wondered why she had to ruin the time with Justin by taking the call. It had been days since her incident and since she'd been to work and seen Justin, who now probably never wanted to see her again.

Sitting in the cafe at South Curl Curl she drank her coffee, watching surfers set their boards on a wave, gliding into shore. Grey nomads occupied outside tables, comparing hip replacements. Barefoot swimmers came by for takeaway, and young mums strolled past with prams. She loved coming here, it was calming, an escape from retail and all the things she should do. As she stared out at the surf, or tried to read her book, her mind kept drifting back to the moment Justin lost his cool.

At his encouragement she'd swiped her stupid phone.

'Renee. Baby. Heard about your accident.'

Garth?

This was terrible timing. His voice blasted through her phone. Rachel shrugged at Justin, trying to act neutral, like she wasn't excited he'd rung. She mouthed, 'He's just being nice.' Justin flicked up his hand, the universal sign for none of my business. He hopped off the end of the bed and went to stare out the window like a man auditioning for a 'Brooding Male Lead.' Would it have killed him to leave the room?

'Garth,' she tried to sound chill.

'Free for dinner tomorrow?' He didn't waste time.

'Oh, um… .' This was unexpected. Did Bader give him her number? That was unethical for sure. Did she really mind? If she had dinner with him, maybe she could persuade him to move her to checkouts, instantly. Her hair was booked to be coloured tomorrow. The timing was perfect. She turned away from Justin, pressing the phone firmly to her ear and whispering, 'tomorrow's fine, and, ah, I get called Renee a lot, but it's Rachel.'

'I'll pick you up. Text me your address then, Re…Rach.' He hung up.

'Garth huh?'

She dropped her phone onto the bed cover like it was contaminated. 'No.' She gave him a look suggesting she had no idea what he was talking about.

'Renee? Dinner tomorrow?'

'You listened to my call?'

'His voice isn't exactly soft.' He sounded annoyed. 'You know what dinner with Garth means.'

'I'm not like that,' she snapped.

'No, but he is.'

Awkwardly she picked up her phone and checked her messages, dismissing his presence.

'Can't you see what a dick he is?'

'Are you insinuating I'm naive?' She pulled herself higher in the bed, folding the sheet neatly up over her waist. Why couldn't he leave it? Pretend he hadn't heard. She felt vulnerable, sitting between hospital sheets with a thin cotton blanket, mascara smudged under her eyes, and her blue hair like a birds nest, while he was pissed off.

'Why would you say yes to a guy who can't even remember your name?'

'It's just dinner.'

He raised his eyebrows.

'This has nothing to do with you. I don't understand why you're getting upset about this. I don't need your truculent criticism of Garth.' She wished he could go back to being thoughtful and interested in her.

'I'm not upset. It's Garth we're talking about. Garth, who thinks *Fifty Shades of Grey* is a documentary.' He reached to grab his jacket from the chair. 'Enjoy your date, Rach,' he said flatly.

She stared out at the ocean. Two surfers caught the same wave, barely missing each other. *Life is like that,* she thought. *Just when you think your wave is coming in, someone else goes and drops in, and ruins the ride.* She wished like crazy she'd let Garth's call go through to voicemail.

Chapter Twenty Five

When Rachel called Sandra to let her know she was taking sick leave, as per doctors orders, her response was typical.

'It's the Christmas period. We don't take sick leave. But since you almost died…'

Rachel had hoped for sympathy, a little understanding, a, "Sure, of course, wouldn't expect you back so soon, glad you're okay." With Sandra, it seemed you took what you got. The sick leave was the only good thing to come out of her coolroom drama.

Sandra was really getting under her skin. Rachel reminded herself, almost hourly, that Sandra was just her boss, and at the end of each day, as she walked out of the supermarket, she didn't have to think about her until the next day. Somehow, thoughts of her were becoming more and more entrenched. It was unfair the way Sandra picked on her. The way she was always, it seemed, out of the deli. And the way she could eat the deli food, with her daily morning salami sandwich, but no one else could.

She needed to get her act together. She still lived at home, even though she'd been thinking of moving out for the past two years. How many times had she strolled past the interiors shop eyeing off the plush cushions for her apartment? They'd be nice if she had an apartment. She didn't own anything aside from her old car, which had almost been given to her. The twenty something guy with a goatee and long blond hair, had looked pleased he could sell it for a grand and not tow it to the tip. It seemed no one her age owned much these days aside from clothes. And hers were either all over her bedroom floor or in the car.

Her mind darted to the two police officers with their guns in holsters, attachments on their uniforms, and authoritative faces, who turned up at her door at seven in the morning. As she sat on the couch in her dressing gown trying to wake up, she felt angry that Goodsworth had let this happen to her. Bader needed a certificate in *How to Prioritse Workplace Repairs*. Did Goodsworth even have a computer log-on ticket system for repairs? Goodsworth's operation was first class 1970's.

The interrogation by the police heightened her fears. The older officer, who looked near retirement, sat close to her, taking notes, his hand shaking, the scent of alcohol catching her attention from time to time. The younger officer, in her twenties, short and stocky, with a loud voice, kept darting her eyes at Rachel's blue hair, or did she imagine that?

It was possible, they explained, that Rachel had disturbed someone in the deli who was stealing stuff. A one-off panic by some idiot who'd shut the door hoping this would give them time to get out of the supermarket before she could catch them.

She nodded, thinking this made sense. Maybe they hadn't meant to harm her.

'Most coolrooms have safety latches,' said the older officer. He rose from the couch, hitting his small notepad with the back of his hand, as if annoyed at the supermarket's negligence.

'We'll make sure that lock gets fixed,' said the younger officer. 'What supermarket doesn't fix safety locks?' She frowned.

If they came to Goodsworth and met Bader, they'd see what sort of supermarket doesn't fix locks.

Ian made cups of tea, reassuring her the police would do their job and catch the culprit. He even offered to pay for her hair to be professionally coloured. And he read her the draft he had prepared to email Mr. Bader. She told him it wouldn't make any difference. Bader didn't care. But Ian was going to give, 'that Mr. Bader, a piece of my mind for not having proper CCTV footage or fixing the lock.' She felt grateful but told him to wait until after she secured the job at checkouts.

Her hair appointment was at two o'clock. How synchronic it was she had sick leave the day she'd planned to do her hair, and the day Garth was taking her out on a date. Maybe date was a bit strong. Catch- up? Dinner? Yes, it was just dinner.

She sent Liz a message, asking to borrow her new Zimmerman dress. An image of Justin's pissed off face crossed her mind. He'd brought her flowers, came to visit her in hospital, and ridden his bike through a glass window for her. Did she wish it was Justin taking her out tonight?

Chapter Twenty Six

She stood in front of the mirror critically assessing how she looked in Liz's dress.

'You don't think this is too much, do you?' She tugged at the dress, her voice laced with nervous excitement.

'The Zim? Nah. You look great,' Liz said, sitting on Rachel's bed eating chips. 'Garth will think so too… I'm surprised it's not Justin taking you out, though.'

'Garth is seriously good-looking Liz.'

'What's his personality like?'

'Who cares?' Rachel dismissed the question, recalling the hair colourist's earlier comment.

'You are soooo lucky,' Jackie the colourist had gushed as she slapped the bleach through Rachel's hair. 'Garth's like the hottest guy in the mall. I bet he has an amaze rig.'

Jackie was right. Garth was hot, and with his pecs, no doubt his abs were ripped too.

She studied her reflection The dress was perfect. She remembered how Garth looked at her in Bader's office, the first day. Hopefully she'd catch that look tonight.

A car horn tooted outside.

'Is the guy in the Mustang GT tooting for you?' Ian frowned, looking out the window.

Rachel dashed to peer out the window. Garth, sat in his orange Mustang on the other side of the road, tooting his horn and chewing gum.

'Okay. Well, see you later guys,' she said quickly.

'He could at the very least text you if he's too lazy to come and knock on the door,' Ian looked unimpressed.

'Red flag Rach. You sure about him?' Liz raised an eye-brow. 'Tooting? Looks a dick, no offense.'

She sighed. 'Offended.'

'Sorry.' Liz sent her an air kiss.

'Latest model.' Ian muttered, still fixated on the car.

Rachel grabbed her bag from the couch. *They'll see he's okay when they get to know him.*

'Be home before he turns into a pumpkin,' Liz teased. And then as if to encourage Rachel, because she could tell she needed it, she said, 'You look great.'

'Don't stay out late, you're still recovering.' A hint of worry lined Ian's brow.

'Text if you need me,' Liz echoed.

'I won't need you,' Rachel said, a little too confidently. As the door closed, a sliver of doubt flickered across her face.

Garth blasted the horn, scrolling through his phone and chomping on his gum like a man possessed. Rachel tapped the side window. He looked up and grinned, flashing his pearly whites, his sunnies on his forehead. Smiling at him, she opened the door and slid into the smooth leather seat, silently admiring his car. It was her first time in a sports car. She thought about her own car—the old rust-bucket barely holding together, ready for the scrap heap. He could never see her car. Absolutely never.

With his elbow resting casually on the car door, he planted his foot on the accelerator. 'You like pizza?' he asked.

'I do,' she said, slightly disappointed he hadn't commented on how she looked. His own style? A white crushed T and a black leather jacket. Classic. 'It's not what we're having,' he laughed.

'Oh.' She didn't get it.

The car shot forward, pinning her to the seat.

'There's this cool Mexican in Manly. Mexi Max. Know it?' Garth asked.

'I do.' She'd been to Mexi Max a few times with girlfriends. 'Mexi Max? Of course,' she said, trying to sound casual. She'd been there a few times.

It was a trendy spot, a bit more upscale than the usual taqueria. Hopefully, her hundred and twenty would cover her half.

Garth parked his car directly outside the restaurant. With his dark sunnies, smooth sauntering walk, and Mustang GT, he looked like someone people thought they should know. Actor? Influencer? Kid with a trust fund? Or perhaps a developer? This seemed to be the latter guess as people gave up looking at him and returned to their meals and conversations. Garth didn't wait to be seated. Striding confidently to a corner table, claiming the seat with the view.

'Armani.' He placed his jacket on the back of the chair, carefully wiping his hand over the width of the shoulders, suggesting its value.

'Hmm.' She pretended to look impressed, sitting in the chair facing the wall, trying to ignore the sense that he purposely took the better seat. It was a small detail, she told herself. *Stop. It's just a chair. Why am I even bothered?*

Garth waved to the waiter to take their order. The waiter, dressed in a black T-shirt and black jeans with a designer stubble, rested his hands on his hips. 'So, what'll it be?' He was one of those waiters who remembered an order rather than wrote it down.

'We'll have beef tortillas and tamales,' Garth said without looking at the menu.

Garth knew the menu. He came here often. Was it with other girls? By the way the waiter looked at Rachel in a kind of sympathetic way, she guessed it was.

'Actually, I'll have chicken enchilada,' Rachel said to the waiter.

'Girl with her own mind.' Garth looked impressed.

'Hope so, hate to have someone else's,' she pretended to joke. 'And I'll have a corona with lime.'

'Something different then,' the waiter said, giving her a wink.

Was he giving her hints? Signals? She smiled back at the waiter; conscious she was being a bit too sensitive. Of course, Garth, Mr. Hot, was out there dating. In fact, it was a compliment she was here with him. *Relax. Enjoy yourself.* She coached herself.

'Make that two.' Garth handed the guy his menu without even so much as a sideways glance of thanks.

Rachel handed the guy her menu. 'Thank you,' she said with a smile.

Garth leaned back in his chair. Maybe now he was taking in how nice she looked in the dress she was wearing, and her hair ash blonde again. After a long pause and no comment on her looks, not even to be polite, she ignored the disappointed feeling and decided to ask him questions. He didn't hesitate to tell her how long he'd been working at Goodworth and when he became in charge of checkouts. He moved his body constantly as he talked, while checking his phone, seeming a bit agitated. *Maybe he's nervous.* This would excuse his walking into the restaurant first, not complimenting her, and his lame jokes.

The waiter smiled slightly at her as he placed her meal. His expression turned to dismissiveness as he placed Garth's abruptly. She stuck her fork into her enchilada. The filling with chicken and sour cream oozed onto her plate. She lifted a bite sized piece onto her fork, glad Garth had brought her to the dimly lit restaurant with a lamp on the table, a full bar along the adjacent wall, cocktail jazz playing, and delicious food. Garth had good taste. She started to relax. After all, here she was on a date with hot Garth, looking hot, in a classy restaurant. Not the pub, where most of the losers she'd dated had taken her. Liz was wrong about him. So was Justin.

Garth asked for a second corona having downed the first before the food arrived. He picked up the pace of his conversation and began to tell her more jokes and stories about staff in the deli. She listened as he talked through every mouthful and surveyed the restaurant. Several times he picked up his phone for an incoming message and tapped one back. 'Loser night fillers from work. Can't do their job,' he complained, then launched into a series of unfunny jokes, laughing loudly, his mouth full of tortilla.

Rachel took a sip of her beer, trying to find his jokes funny, while telling herself that she could tolerate him talking through his mouthfuls.

She was finding it hard. She turned her head to look out the window, her eyes falling on his orange Mustang. She took a long swig of her beer.

Garth followed her gaze. 'You're wondering how I can afford that beast right?'

'Ah, no,' she lied, placing her beer on the table, and taking another bite of her enchilada, while also thinking about his expensive Breitling watch. Initially she thought it was a fake, but as she glanced at its quality she was now wondering if it was real.

Garth leaned forward, as if letting her in on a secret. 'I live at home. Don't pay board.' He shoved his tortilla in his mouth. 'It's a badge. But hey,' his expression changed. 'I'm a manager, earning good money. Gonna have my own apartment soon. You'll see.'

You'll see? She pushed her food around with her fork. Garth, was alluding to something between them.

'Babe, what do you like doing? You know, in your free time?'

His question was unexpected but a nice change from him talking about himself through his mouthfuls and laughing at his own jokes. She dabbed her mouth with her napkin, 'Well, I—'

'Is that my friend's kid sister over there at the bar?' Garth interrupted. 'No, don't look,' he said. 'She's had cancer. Don't want her to think we're talking about her. I'll just go over and say a quick hello.' He rested his napkin next to his plate and walked over to his friend's sister.

Rachel stabbed her enchilada with her fork, eyeing the time on her watch. She turned around, watching Garth sit next to his friend's sister and another girl, at the bar. She didn't want the girl who had been sick to feel she was staring, so she turned back to face the wall and ate the last few mouthfuls of her enchilada, turning to look out the window, the light of the evening sun settling on Garth's Mustang. Fifteen minutes later, having finished eating, scrolled through her news feeds, and downed her drink, Garth returned.

'Best Mexican hey?' He pulled out his chair and sat. 'Haven't seen her since the news of her cancer.' His eyes darted back to the girl at the bar. Rachel turned to follow his glance. He placed his hand on hers. 'Bet you were wondering when I was going to ask you out? Had you in my sight since day one.' He squeezed her hand. 'Bet you hate working in the deli hey?'

'It's okay.' *Really?* She surprised herself with her answer.

He leant forward, resting his arms on the table. 'I can make checkouts happen.'

She forced a smile. Thinking about the girl at the bar and why he didn't want to introduce her.

'After all it must be hard working with those tragics. Sandra's a ball breaker, and Valentina waddles around the deli like a duck with a fat arse. What about the awesome hair net she wears every day,' he laughed, sipping his beer, catching Rachel's eye. 'Don't get me wrong. It looks good on you.' He pointed his beer in an unconvincing toast to her hair.

'I think Val's pretty amazing. She's moved countries, speaks more than one language, and worked full-time while she brought up her kids. Better than anything I've ever done.'

'Yeah, well she's past her use-by. As for Mario, see him at checkouts a lot lately. Drools over Charlene as if he's in with a shot. What an idiot, don't you think?'

'I don't really have an opinion on him.'

'Good, good. Don't want chicks with opinions.' He laughed. Then changed his expression quickly. 'Nah just kidding. Big feminist.'

'Oh,' Rachel faked a laugh, trying to hide her confusion.

'I'll tell you what to think about Mario.' Garth pointed his finger at her in an instructional manner. 'He's a try hard. Sucks up Bader's arse and goes on about being 2IC of the butchery one day. My arse that's gonna happen. He can't organise himself out of an Ikea store.'

'Not many people can,' Rachel tried to act more upbeat.

'I can get Bader to move you to checkouts in a snap, if you want it.' He lifted his beer to his lips, and tilted his head gulping his drink, studying Rachel. 'Deli on your resume looks weak. Checkouts on the other hand… front of house… trusted with more responsibility. I can do it for you.' He ran his eyes down to her breasts. 'For certain.'

'An offer too good to refuse,' she said, feeling uncomfortable by the way he seemed to be undressing her with his eyes. The image of Justin and his bike helmet tucked under his arm popped into her mind. She could see his face, smiling at her as he stirred her—about everything. He was never mean. She wished it was Justin sitting opposite. 'You have actually been promising me checkouts for a while now.'

'True, true.' He tapped the table. 'Been working on Bader. Guy's hard to move.' He looked into her eyes. 'Let's get the bill.' Before she could answer he waved at the waiter. 'Hey dude, the bill.' He patted his pockets. 'Ah, left my wallet at home. Bad habit putting it on the bench before I leave. Do you mind? Soz. I'll take a piss while you pay.' He rose from the table.

Rachel picked up the bill to check the amount. She didn't want him to think she was stingy. But she did wonder why he didn't have Apple Pay or similar on his phone? Or at the very least offer to transfer the amount. She guessed it would even out on their next date. People with money either forgot or never knew how those who live from pay cheque to pay cheque can't afford to be out of pocket.

There were two extra red wines listed on the bill. She glanced back at the bar. The drop-dead gorgeous nightmare with flawless skin and long dark eyelashes framing her eyes, and who looked the epitome of good health, was drinking a red. Rachel hopped out of her seat and walked towards her. Her jeans, so tight they looked painted on, her top, sheer, and low cut, and her unnaturally large breasts were exploding out of her bra. And if Rachel wore those stilettoes, she'd turn an ankle with one step. She felt almost dowdy in her Zimmerman dress.

'Excuse me,' she said, moving her fringe with the side of her hand, trying to contain her composure and not feel too inadequate around these leggy supermodels. 'I'm Garth's friend… ' she hesitated; she hated doing this? 'He mentioned you're his friend's sister. Sorry to hear you've been sick.'

'Hey, hon. Sick? What kind of sick?' She looked so confident.

'Garth, your brother's friend, came over to see you, said you had cancer.'

'Hon, I don't have a brother, and clearly I don't have cancer,' she gave Rachel an empathic look.

'And you're his friend, who's dog died and he's taking you out to cheer you up,' said the other girl.

Dog? Died!

The girls gave her a commiserating look.

'He bought us a drink and asked for my number,' said the non-cancer patient girl, who looked like she could run ten marathons.

Rachel wanted to thump him.

'Interesting guy,' the slender drop-dead gorgeous nightmare said kindly.

'Sure is.' Rachel felt embarrassed. But smiled and laughed, trying to hide there was a problem. She sat back at the table, this time in Garth's seat, looking out across the room.

He sashayed back, checking the girls at the bar, who didn't look his way.

'Paid?' he asked, standing.

'Not yet.'

He sat down awkwardly, as if trying to work out why she'd changed seats and hadn't paid.

The realisation Garth was a conceited, cheating dick was shattering, although strangely, no surprise. But why could he not wrangle in his narcissistic urge just for one restaurant meal? There had been red flags all the way, but she'd ignored them. She wanted to slap herself that she even imagined them as the 'It couple' of the supermarket. Or better still, slap him.

'I ordered us another drink,' she said, her voice carefully neutral.

'Oh, I'm driving.'

'You don't care about that sort of stuff, do you?'

He looked uncertain. 'No, but… '

'I ordered you a cocktail, the Blue Balls.'

He smiled awkwardly. She reached across the table and took his hand, giggling, at nothing. Garth seemed to like this sort of mindless giggling and goggling at him, so she upped the ante. She wanted to see how much of a dick he really was. 'Tell me more about that beast out there,' she referenced his orange Mustang through the window.

The designer stubble waiter placed the cocktails in front of them, looking at Rachel with warmth in his eyes, as if to note the change of seating. She picked up her glass and theatrically pursed her lips around the straw, Garth narrowed his eyes seductively.

She wanted to tip her drink right down his pants.

'You know Garth,' she enjoyed the satisfaction he couldn't look around the restaurant anymore, 'you're a bit of a self-assured hubris.' She had no doubt he wouldn't know what she meant.

'I'd agree if I knew what you just said,' he snorted, drinking his cocktail through the straw.

'I'll interpret it for you.' He leaned closer, his face expectant for good news. 'You're a womanising arsehole.'

Garth darted a nervous side glance at the guy and girl about their age, sitting next to them, who had suddenly stopped talking to each other. He reached to grab Rachel's hand as if trying to make it appear all was fine, but knocked over his cocktail, which ran down the edge of the table onto his pants.

'Shit. Now fucking look at my pants.' He stood up brushing his pants with his dirty crumpled napkin still left on the table.

Rachel stood up and grabbed her bag. 'Oh, and since you don't like women to have opinions, how do you feel about emotions, because that's what you're about to get. And don't think I believe for one minute you don't have your wallet or can't at least pay on your phone.'

Garth rushed up behind her as she began to walk away. 'You don't have to make a fucking scene,' he said under his breath.

'Since I'm supposedly your friend get your hand off my back.'

The waiter gave Garth a curt look as he took his hand off her back and pulled a couple of hundred-dollar bills from his back pocket and threw them on the counter. Then trying to look cool, he held his Armani jacket over his shoulder.

As Rachel stepped out of the restaurant, she caught a glimpse at another couple, who'd been laughing together and were now reaching out to hold each other's hands. God she was an idiot to think this could be her and Garth.

'Look, I'm sorry,' Garth said, coming out of the restaurant and lighting up a cigarette. 'Let me drive you home.'

'I'll get an Uber,' she said, calling Liz.

'You're gonna regret this,' he snarled, snubbing his cigarette butt under his shoe, pushing it into the gutter.

'I doubt it,' Rachel said to herself as she watched his car speed away. She knew he was right though. He'd ask Bader to sack her. Not only was it goodbye checkouts, but it was also goodbye employment. Why did she have to go out with him?

Fifteen minutes later, Liz pulled up in her car with the passenger window down. 'Oh hon,' she said through the window. 'I told you he was a dick.'

Chapter Twenty Seven

Sandra gloated at the red police tape sectioning off the turnstile and flower area, and the thick covering of plastic shrouding the hollow window. *This must be giving old Bades a heart attack*, she thought pleasingly.

She listened intently with Jen and Wilma, while Lillian explained how she'd heard Bader's management of the staff had been brought into question by Head Office.

'Marj from Head Office tell you that?' Sandra asked. Lillian's friendship with Marjorie and the inside information she got made her jealous.

Lillian nodded. 'Apparently, they're going to send someone from HR to see if he's okay. Think they're concerned he's losing his marbles.'

Sandra rolled her eyes. 'Marbles? He didn't have any to lose in the first place. Besides he's not that old.' Bader, as far as she knew, was only forty-six. But with his dark rings, heavy creases under his eyes, and the beginnings of saggy jowls, he looked more like sixty.

'Well, if they get rid of him, you might get his job Sandra.' Jen looked at her proudly. 'You deserve it.'

Sandra knew the hens trusted her to look after them and do the job well. 'What else did Marj say?' she said quickly, dismissing Jen outwardly, but inwardly feeling grateful for her vote of confidence.

'Marjorie said Mr. Smyth was furious about the front window, in the festive season too,' Lillian reported.

'Was he really?' Sandra stared at the plastic on the window, thinking this was awesome news.

'And the window won't be repaired now until after the new year.' Lillian turned to Sandra, concerned. 'You don't think Mr. Bader will get the sack, do you? I mean, I'd love you to have his job, but, well, he is trying to buy a new car you know.'

Sandra couldn't care less if he was going to buy a new pacemaker. She wanted to know how he got himself out of the clever mess she so aptly tried to put him in.

'Lills, if Bades can't do his job properly then that's his problem. Now, get him on the blower and tell him Troy's at the loading dock with a problem he needs old Bades to fix,' she scoffed to herself. *Like that will ever happen.*

The hens looked at her, curious.

'That's why I came up here to talk to you wasn't it?' she said curtly. 'Tell him it's urgent.'

Looking slightly bewildered, Lillian picked up the phone and dialed. As soon as Sandra saw Bader walk towards the loading dock, she dashed up to his office and read the email she'd previously crafted.

To: Glen Smyth
From: Ferdinand Bader
Subject: Re: Up yours!

Glen,
I've been seriously disappointed in your leadership of the Goodsworth stores. You offer zero support, sit on your staunch arse and think it's okay the turnstile is still an archaic feature in our store. And what about self-serve check-outs? When's that going happen? Glen, you're doing a crap job navel gazing on your throne. I demand new turnstiles, a pay rise, and Garth gets the chop. He's a loser wanna-be and a waste of space. A little like yourself.

Season's Greetings
Ferdinand Bader
Store Manager
Goodsworth

Quickly she clicked on his inbox in anticipation of Glen's response. It had to be scathing. There, marked *Important*, was his reply.

> *To: Ferdinand Bader*
> *From: Glen Smyth*
> *Subject: Please explain!*
>
> *Ferdinand,*
> *I am very surprised and deeply concerned at your email and requests!!! We are hoping you have an exceptionally good explanation for this email. If not, you will be required to report to Head Office for review of your employment. I will be calling management today to have a chat.*
>
> *Glen Smyth*
> *Regional Manager*
> *Goodsworth*

Bingo! It was just as she hoped, Glen was outraged. So, what did Bader say to squirm his arse out of her cleverly crafted plan? She opened another sent email to Glen.

> *To: Glen Smyth*
> *From: Ferdinand Bader*
> *Subject: Re: Please explain!*
>
> *Dear Glen,*
> *I am so deeply sorry for the horrific email you received. Fortunately, I have been able to discover how this has happened. A cleaner, suffering from delusional schizophrenia, thought*

I was trying to kill him. This led him to hacking into my account to write the obscene email. I terminated the cleaner's contract immediately.
Once again, I sincerely apologise for the cleaner's behavior.

Regards
Ferdinand Bader
Store Manager
Goodsworth

She read on. Glen's reply email went as follows.

To: Ferdinand Bader
From: Glen Smyth
Subject: Hacked emails

Ferdinand,
Thank you for the explanation in response to the unwelcome email I received. I now understand your email account was most unfortunately hacked.
Please, if this happens again, notify technical support immediately. I suggest you update your IOS security.
On another serious note, the way you addressed Marjorie O' Donald my PA, was extremely unprofessional and abusive. Col Manning and Andrew Moore, the regional managers, will be talking to you about this when they visit your store. This, Bader, is a written warning of your misconduct. I will await Col and Andrew's review of your store and of your mental state before raising this with you again.

Glen Smyth

Regional Manager
Goodsworth

How did he wrangle his way out of this? Her anger spiked. She felt outraged. She noticed another email.

To: Glen Smyth
From: Ferdinand Bader
Subject: Deli Manager

Dear Glen,
I am putting in writing that on the evening when the young Miss Renee Wilson unfortunately found herself locked in the coolroom, I witnessed Sandra Saunders to be the last in the deli at the time of Renee's alleged disappearance. I have good reason to believe her jealousy over this young Renee's excellent work ethic and management skills would be motivation for such an act as to lock her in the coolroom.
I look forward to hearing from you.

Sincerely
Ferdinand Bader
Store Manager,
Goodsworth

Her eyes widened. This was why Marjorie had rung her and asked her where she was that night. She could hardly believe Bader would sink this low, although he had stashed her car with groceries. So actually, she could believe it. *Passive aggressive bastard. Well, Badey, I'll show you passive aggressive!*

Chapter Twenty Eight

Liz made sure Rachel knew what an idiot she'd been going out with wanker Garth.

'What were you thinking, going out with that self-infatuated, egocentric narcissist?' she'd asked her sitting at the bar on the wharf in Manly.

Rachel stirred her Aperol Spritz with her straw. 'I apply for like a million jobs and the only one I get is the deli—a job I don't even want. And I take it. And Miss Desperate here,' she pointed to herself, 'goes out with dicks like Garth so he can get me transferred to checkouts.'

'Seriously?' Liz looked unimpressed.

'Yes. Sandra won't help because she's a bully, and Bader,' she scoffed, 'is about as present as a politician at a protest march. And because of that place, I almost become the frozen meat in the deli.'

Liz laughed, 'Great news article headline: *Deli Chick Becomes Dead Meat.*

'Liiizz.' Rachel frowned.

Liz was no fool. She eyed Rachel. 'You're telling me you were using Mr. Hot Stuff Narcissist to get you a job at checkouts?'

'When you put it that way, it sounds bad.' Her mind wandered back to their first brief meeting. 'I thought he was hot… '

'And he is, that's a given.'

'And he paid me attention.' She thought about his surprise drop-bys at the deli and how interested he seemed. 'I mean really Liz, he had nothing to gain by dating me, right? Other than the fact he was interested in me.'

'And sex.'

Rachel wondered what would have happened if he hadn't bought the drop-dead bombshell a red wine?

'Hate to say it Rach, but his looks marred your judgment. Good looks are wasted on narcissists. What about Justin babes?'

'I'm not interested in him. He's more the… '

'Substance kind?'

Liz was right. Justin was nothing like Garth in personality, looks, or behaviour. He was funny, intelligent, and considerate. That mischievous glint in his eyes, that way he just didn't give a damn what people thought—except about the white king chickens. Poisoning customers was, she supposed, a fair reason to care.

No eggshell-walking and no wandering eyes.

'You should quit. That place is a crazy house. Except for Justin, who, I decided not to pursue, because I think he has eyes for you.'

Rachel eyed Liz. 'No, he doesn't.'

'He rode through a window for you.'

'Because he's a friend. Or was.'

'Friends don't ride through windows.'

Liz had a point. They laughed at his crazy selfless act. It was amazing, they agreed, he didn't cut himself.

'How am I going to face Garth at work?'

'Think about his blue stained pants,' Liz laughed.

Rachel choked. 'Karma.' Even though this was funny, she still had to face Sandra micromanaging her. Then there was Justin. How could she work in the small cubicle with him for an entire shift? She needed to quit. But earlier in the day Mario sent her a text to remind her of the Christmas party in the lunchroom for the following night.

'You're going right?' Liz asked.

'No way.'

'Hon, if you ask me, this is the perfect place to get back into work life—if that's what you call it.'

'Justin will be there.'

It was true. He'd be there. It was tradition. And he'd asked her if she was going.

'You know what?'

'What?' Liz looked curious.

'You're right. Stuff Garth. Why let him, and Justin with his angst at me, stop me from going.'

Liz smiled. 'You never know what might happen at a Supermarket Christmas party.'

****

The doors of Goodsworth were halfway down, preparing for closing. Worker-bee stackers dumped boxes in the aisles and lobbed produce onto shelves with the care of a luggage handler. Rachel inhaled slowly as she made her way to the lunchroom.

She hadn't expected this many staff to turn up. Lillian waved at her, beaming. She'd gone all out decorating the room. The same tinsel and red and silver shiny balls, which hung across the supermarket ceiling, were replicated in abundance.

Merry Christmas signs plastered the walls. The chairs were stacked in one corner and the lunchroom tables, covered in red plastic tablecloths, were joined together to form one long table. Christmas cake, mince tarts, peanuts, dips and biscuits, cheeses, red grapes, strawberries and melons, chips, and small sausage rolls, and party pies filled the table. Rachel picked up a cup of sparkling wine and silently toasted her survival.

'Thank God you got out alive,' Lillian said, hugging her.

Sandra picked up a sausage roll and shoved it in her mouth scanning the room. 'Will you look at that,' she scoffed, directing her attention to the tiny, gift-wrapped boxes and bargain-bin wine stashed under the spindly plastic Christmas tree.

'Bader said since there wasn't a Santa this year, we could blow the budget on gifts instead,' Lillian announced proudly, as though this was a masterstroke in corporate generosity.

'Is that so?' Sandra eyed the gifts. 'No names?'

'All the women get chocolate and the men wine.' Lillian looked like she could spring from her shoes with excitement.

'Who said women have to get chocolates? Sexist rubbish.' Sandra walked over to the Christmas tree and took a bottle of wine. She smirked at Rachel as she placed her gift on the chair next to where they were standing.

Rachel sipped her drink, agreeing with Sandra but also thinking how ungrateful she could be. 'Chocolates are a nice gesture.' *And so is saying something kind after someone gets locked in a coolroom!*

'A nice gesture would be a bonus. I've been here long enough to get one. Bet bloody Bades gets one. And, ah, glad to see you've recovered Rachel. Sure, the sick leave helped with that.' Sandra's face was deadpan. Rachel wasn't certain if she was sarcastic or not.

Valentina, her plate full of an assortment of nibbles, bounced over to Rachel. 'Oh, Rachel dear. It's good to see you. A terrible disaster to happen to you. We were so worried. The food is good,' Valentina said, surveying the table and moving on from talking any more about Rachel and the coolroom.

'What happened with Santa last year?' Rachel asked.

'Let's just say he picked the wrong female to pull his lecherous hand moving act on,' Sandra replied.

Valentina frowned. 'You nearly pulled his chin off.'

'How was I to know his beard was the real deal?' Sandra went to get a beer.

'She yanked his beard.' Valentina squinched her eyes at the memory.

'Must've been quite a scene.' Rachel wished she'd seen it.

'Ah hum,' Valentina nodded. 'Lillian panicked and got the Glen 20, which she had under the table—hygienic reasons.' Valentina shrugged at this idea. 'She sprays it at Sandra 'til she lets go of the beard.' She bit into her party pie. 'I think a gift is a much better idea.'

George Michael's *Last Christmas* played through the speakers. Wilma, Jen, and Lillian cackled and danced with each other. She wondered where Mario and Justin were. And Trudy, Charlene and Lucy weren't there either.

Nat waved from where he stood with a few of the guys from produce. She was relieved Garth was nowhere to be seen. But she knew when she did see Mr. White Veneers again, it would be incredibly awkward.

'Deep in thought,' said Sandra, taking a sip of beer.

'Thinking about what to eat.' She reached for another strawberry.

Sandra took a long sip. 'These things are painful, but I come for the free feed. Idiot Bader has no imagination. This dumb tradition has been going on for years. Mega Mart doesn't waste revenue on Christmas nibbles,' she swished her drink like a wine critic before swallowing. Rachel spat her moldy strawberry back onto her napkin. 'When I manage this store, I'll do it differently. Goodsworth loses hundreds for this one pointless evening.

'If you manage this store, get rid of hairnets,' Rachel joked.

Sandra didn't crack a smile.

Bader shuffled into the lunchroom, as if it pained him. His slouched body and lagging gait replaced his brisk stride. He picked up some cheese and crackers and stood examining the lunchroom whiteboard. 'Why hasn't anyone updated the rosters this week?' he grumbled.

'Because they're online,' one of the teenage holiday grocers piped up. He couldn't have been older than fourteen, but Rachel admired his spunk—or naivety.

'Well, there's supposed to be a timetable on this whiteboard as well,' Bader looked caught off guard. 'Some people don't look at it online do they Valentina?' His tone was superior, deflecting his embarrassment.

Sandra downed her beer. 'That dweeb needs to be told off.'

'It's quite okay. He is right. I don't read the online version.' Valentina seemed unperturbed.

'Not for that,' she said to Valentina. 'For trying to pin the front entrance mess on me.'

'He did that?' Rachel asked, surprised.

'He's a stupid man.' Valentina ate her cake and shook her head.

Rachel looked curious. 'How do you know he tried to blame it on you?'

'Got a call from Marj, Glen Smyth's PA, asking me about the night you were locked in. Said Bader emailed Glen telling him I was the last one to leave the deli. Suggesting I locked you in.'

'What? Why would you do that? I mean not that you did, but what motive would they conspire you had to—'

'Knock you off?'

'I was going for more of an accidental type of lock in.' *Could everyone please stop suggesting I almost died.* 'Why would Bader blame you?'

'Because he's an insecure child. Anyway, I had an alibi. Valentina vouched I left early for my futsal game.'

Valentina smiled and nodded.

'And besides, I think they know it's bullshit. Marj and I go way back. She used to work here in the store. She rang to warn me about his accusation.' She glared across at him. 'Anyone for another drink?'

Rachel declined. Sandra reached for a VB at the end of the table.

Bader picked at a piece of fruit cake from the table. 'Enjoying the food, I see.' He eyed Valentina's full plate with fruit cake, a mince pie, and two party pies.

'Delicious.' Valentina ignored his sarcasm.

He turned to Rachel. She wondered if he might ask about her wellbeing, but instead he stumbled over his words as he said, 'Enjoy the party then. There's some chocolates under the tree for you, ah, ladies,' and walked away.

'Bades not so fast.' Sandra returned to the group with two VBs in hand. 'Merry Christmas.'

Bader scoffed at the beer Sandra extended to him, then glanced surreptitiously at Rachel. With a tut of his tongue, as if trying to make out he was the good guy, he snatched the bottle from Sandra's hand. 'I hardly call it merry.' He moved off, checking the food on the table.

With a fisheye look, Sandra followed him, curiously. Rachel watched them, at the other end of the table, their faces full of contempt for each other. She excused herself from Valentina who was happy to wander over to the hens and join in their chit chat. Placing a sausage roll on her plate, Rachel moved where she could listen to Sandra and Bader.

'I trust after the window fiasco you're looking for employment elsewhere Sandra.'

'Yep. Looking at your job.'

'I'd give up then as that's never going to happen,' he scoffed, moving up and down on the balls of his feet. 'Let me remind you in case you didn't hear,' he coughed, attempting to clear his throat. 'Your days at Goodsworth are numbered. You'll be out before you know it.' He sculled his drink, wiped his mouth with the back of his hand, and threw his bottle at the bin—missing—then headed into the supermarket.

Rachel absentmindedly bit into the lukewarm sausage roll, wondering why Bader would threaten Sandra (and why she was eating a lukewarm sausage roll)? The management in this place had serious issues. Did any of them get along?

She decided the power struggles weren't her problem. Tomorrow she'd tell Sandra she was quitting. She could hardly wait.

As she said her goodbyes, Mario swaggered into the room, beaming like a proud rooster, Charlene hanging off his arm.

'Beau'ful, you're alive!' He crushed Rachel in a hug. 'Can't believe it!'

'Thanks, Mario. Close call.'

'Bet your boyfriend's happy.' He reached past her for pigs in blankets.

'Oh—you know—we broke up.'

'Ohmigods babe. That sucks.' His cheeks full of blanketed pig. He pulled her in for another hug. Mario really needed to learn the basics of deodorant.

Charlene made her way over to Mario and Rachel, eyeing them as they embraced. Her thick nails curled around her plastic cup of Chardonnay.

'Charls babes, try these pigs!' Mario said enthusiastically.

Charlene took a pig and turned to Rachel, her face a little less stern.

'Fuck darl, you coulda died. Like, so full on.'

'Thanks.' People in this place were blunt.

'We've been freaking out about the psycho who did it.'

'It's just a faulty door,' Rachel dismissed her.

'We don't think so. Glad you're okay.' She wrapped her arm through Mario's.

Charlene's comment was uncharacteristically warm. But Rachel would take it.

'Babe, coming out for drinks after this? It's tradish. Trudes, Luce, Just, Nat, partners, a few grocer boys, the good guys, all coming,' Mario said.

'I'll see,' she said, leaving them to their conversation, which Mario had directed to his late last century Holden Torana and new subwoofers that he bragged, 'shot music around his car like a concert.'

She headed out of the lunchroom towards the deli. Something niggled at her about the coolroom. She wanted to check that lock for herself.

Chapter Twenty Nine

She didn't expect to see Garth disappear into the coolroom. Strangely, he was carrying a black duffle bag. She ducked behind the cheese display, so he couldn't see her. When he came back out, his duffle bag was bulging. What did he have in there? Antipasto? And if he did have food in his bag, why would he be stealing it? He wasn't struggling financially.

A voice from behind broke her thoughts. 'How's Garth?'

'Justin?' She nearly jumped.

'Strange place to hide.'

'Oh, I… did you see—'

He had the familiar twinkle in his eye, as if he found her behaviour amusing. 'Avoiding someone?'

'Garth was passing. Didn't want him to spot me,' she muttered, pretending to fuss with the coolroom door.

Justin waited on the other side of the counter, drinking his kombucha. 'Saw Garth leave with his black duffle bag. Never can work out why he brings his gym gear to work. So… how was the date?'

The lock was the same—broken, easy to get locked in.

'Oh, you know. We're just friends.'

'Garth doesn't do friends with chicks, Rach, and friends don't hide.'

'If you must know. He's not my type.' She felt her face flush.

'Isn't he though?' he teased.

'No,' she didn't want to discuss him. 'And I'm quitting. Tomorrow.'

'Good for you.'

She felt a pang of disappointment that he didn't protest this idea, or comment it was a shame, and that he'd miss her. 'Yeah, good for me.'

The sound of disco music started to blare loudly through the store. Laughter radiated from the checkouts. Realising something out of the ordinary was going on, they hurried to the entrance.

In full high-key, Mario was dancing up on checkout three. However, it was Bader, grooving next to him, on checkout four, that was the true surprise. Strips of tinsel were wrapped around his head. His white shirt hung freely. His pants were flung across the register, which Nat kindly went to get and rested across his arm while trying to persuade Bader to come down. The staff looked on. Some giggling with each other. Others were concerned, discussing whether he'd lost his mind.

'He must've met budget.' She heard the fourteen-year-old-looking staffer comment.

Phones were out. Sandra snapped away like paparazzi.

'It's completely out of character for him,' Lillian fretted.

'Can't handle his drink,' Sandra said.

'A few drinks wouldn't do this,' Rachel calculated. 'And not this quick.' She thought about the beer Sandra handed him in the lunchroom. 'How many did he have?'

Sandra tucked her phone away. 'Meds plus wine. Irresponsible.'

Did Rachel see Sandra smirk to herself?

She pressed Lillian. 'Disco music?'

'I put it on. Liven the mood a bit,' Sandra said flippantly, strolling over to Nat where he stood anxiously watching Bader.

'Sandra seems to be enjoying this?' Rachel noted.

'Sandra and Mr. Bader never see eye to eye unfortunately,' Lillian frowned. 'He's been under a lot of stress lately. Maybe Sandra's right. Meds do react with alcohol. Because this behaviour,' she pointed at Bader grinding on the register, 'cannot be driven by stress alone.'

Rachel agreed. She looked across at Wilma and Jen, who cackled together, enjoying the show.

Valentina joined Lillian, concerned, 'The little man has gone too far.'

Rachel watched Mario (in control of having fun) and Bader with his tie now wrapped around his head and his belly showing through his unbuttoned shirt (completely out of control). 'This is going to be streaming through everyone's socials. I feel sorry for him.'

Justin rubbed his hand under his chin. 'Nah, Mario'll love the attention.'

'Not him,' Rachel gave him a backhand slap on his chest in jest. 'Bader. He's going to regret this tomorrow.'

Justin nodded as they watched Bader copy Mario's attempt at the splits. Neither were successful.

Mario jumped off the checkout and jiggered up to Justin and Rachel. 'Jeeze, this is great, isn't it?' he puffed. 'Who'd a thought Bader had all this piss and vinegar in him?' He wiped the sweat off his brow and looked in Charlene's direction. 'Hey Charls,' he yelled, strutting over to where she stood with Trudy.

Bader swayed on the checkout. Nat tried to coax him down. Troy scrolled through his phone, unperturbed. She'd had enough of Troy's slack attitude. If he did his job properly, she wouldn't have been locked in the coolroom, Justin could have asked for help at the entrance without bowling through the window, and Bader wouldn't be dancing on checkouts and streaming through staff news feeds. He looked up from his phone as if she'd disturbed him from his favourite television show. 'Troy, I think Bader needs you to do something.' She moved her eyes in Bader's direction.

'Might be enough huh?'

'Ya think?' She was so over the incompetence right now.

Troy called over the music, 'Hey everyone, keep it down. A ten'—he held his hand at head level—'to a five.' He lowered his hand to chest level. Then gave Rachel a thumbs up and continued checking his phone.

'Well, that was helpful?' she said to Justin in a mock tone.

'I've never seen the dude do his job,' Justin said. 'Probably watching his latest stunts online. He has fifty thousand Instagram followers you know.'

She didn't know. And didn't care.

She could see Nat standing at the edge of the checkout still trying to coax Bader down. 'I'll get him home safely,' she heard him say to Lillian. He deserved a promotion. He was loyal and obliging to his managers. Even to

Sandra, who he knew pulled fruit from the bottom of his pyramids daily. He never complained.

Mario, with his arm perched across Charlene's shoulder, asked if they were ready to head off for drinks. Rachel hesitated. If Justin was going to go it would give her a chance to smooth things over. She waited for his response.

'Sure,' he said. 'I'll come for one. Coming Rach?'

That made it easy. 'Sure, I was going home but why not.' She tried to sound chilled.

Mario looked chuffed. Without waiting further, he steered Charlene towards the exit and led her to his car.

'Want a lift?' She asked Justin, knowing he'd caught the bus to work since his bike was still being repaired, and knowing he wouldn't judge her car.

'Sure.' He smiled.

They walked, without much conversation, into the balmy night air. She looked across at Justin, who looked in his own world of thoughts.

'Crazy night huh?' he said.

'Crazy. Is this… '

'Common? Yep.'

She laughed.

Oh, what would transpire tomorrow? The images of Bader on the checkout half undressed would be viral. She thought about the awkward supermarket manager who, when he delivered Rachel to the deli, had smirked at Sandra as if he had one over her. Well, the tables had turned. And maybe that's what Sandra had been counting on.

Mario strutted his best Elvis jigger to his 1978 Torana. He opened the door for Charlene. 'Welcome to the love machine, babe.'

Rachel and Justin laughed as they heard Charlene complain, 'What? You 'spect me to sit in that?'

Mario coaxed her into the car. 'Babe, I'll fix the hole in the floor next. And no doughies, promise.'

Chapter Thirty

The bar on the wharf was abuzz with people having Christmas work drinks, friend catchups, and amicable dates—unlike hers and Garth's. The bar opened onto the main street with the harbour pier at the rear. Rachel walked with Justin to the back deck crammed with people enjoying the summer evening, the smell of sea spray heavy in the air. Mario and Charlene, already sitting at a table with four stools in the corner, waved them over. Fairy lights sparkled overhead.

She messaged Liz: *Work drinks with Justin.*

Liz buzzed back with a bunch of emojis.

The comparison of Garth to Justin was black and white. Garth walked ahead of her. Justin waited for her to enter first. Garth talked about himself and made bad jokes. Justin listened and made her laugh. Garth checked out other women when she was with him. She'd only seen Justin survey the scene, and immerse himself in group conversation, while spending, what she thought, more time talking and looking at her.

Before Rachel and Justin had time to sit down Charlene complained about Mario's car. 'Have you seen Maz's car? There isn't even a passenger floor.' Charlene gestured with her hands as she spoke, moving them apart as if to show a gaping hole. 'Blasted air up me toosh the whole trip.'

Rachel laughed. She could tell Charlene didn't really care.

'Best car ever. Got it with bonus subwoofers and sheepskin car seat covers.' Mario looked unfased. 'What'll you drink, babe?'

'Justin, let me get you a drink for saving my life.' Rachel placed her bag on the stool. 'Beer, wine, vodka?'

'Beer.' Justin smiled, accepting her offer.

Charlene snatched a fifty from Mario's hand before he could stand. 'What do you want?'

Justin gave Rachel a wink. It said so much more than words. What did it say? Thanks for the drink? Great being here? She edged through the crowd smiling to herself at his wink. A guy politely drew back to give her way. As she passed, Rachel caught his eye, he winked at her with interest, which she received with a smile. Two winks in a minute. The night was off to a good start.

'Trude's gonna be pissed. Thinks Justin's into her,' Charlene said, winding her way through people to get to the bar. 'Trude's no match for Justs. She thinks those fake boobs of hers will do it,' she said unimpressed. 'Maz's cool right. I've known he's had the hots for me for ages. Darls, ya gotta drip feed 'em. You come across too easy, they'll treat you like they own you.' She scooped up her drinks. 'Meet you back at the table, babe.'

Rachel took a minute to collect her thoughts. How quickly the direction of the evening changed. As the bartender handed her the two beers with their oversized limes, he asked how her night was.

She reached for the beers. 'Good thanks.' *In fact, it's great.*

Sipping beers, laughing at the brutal reality Bader would face tomorrow, the night was starting out awesome. She loved the way Justin threw his head forward, the laughter falling out of him—unguarded, magnetic—as Mario made joke after joke at Bader's expense.

She surprised herself that she was feeling so calm, here with Justin. Mario and Charlene were looking more like a couple, his arm never far from her shoulder, or her hand from his knee. She almost felt a ping of jealousy when he pulled Charlene close and gave her a peck on her head. She'd never had a guy so endearingly and spontaneously do that to her. As if noticing her watching Mario and Charlene, Justin made a random comment about how warm the evening was. She smiled, agreed, thinking how undeniably cute he was.

The other "cool kids," like Mario had suggested, turned up, cramming into a table nearby. Trudy was there. Rachel made an extra effort to laugh at Mario's jokes, happy to make Trudy jealous that she was sitting next to Justin. She hadn't expected Garth to rock up, even if he was with Lucy, who everyone knew was enraptured with him. She gawked at him, as he peeled off his Armani jacket like it was a catwalk, resting it on his stool.

'Who invited that dick?' Mario asked.

'Probs Luce,' Charlene said. 'She has a massive crush on him. Secretly I think he's got a crush on Trudes, but she's got a crush on Justin, in case you didn't know,' she said flippantly to Justin who shrugged his shoulders and smiled suggesting he did and didn't care. 'But she also has the hots for Tezza from the loading dock. Girls got options.' Charlene tilted her beer bottle in Justin direction.

'Not me. Tezza it is,' he joked. 'And this might be Lucy's lucky day,' he said, and then as if remembering that Rachel had obviously been interested in Garth, he added, 'He's fucking a tossa.'

'A tossa,' Mario echoed, raising his beer.

Rachel clinked her bottle with theirs, showing her open dislike for the guy who only last night she'd looked over at him in his car and thought he was the hottest thing on two legs. How wrong she'd been.

Charlene leaned in. 'Trudes spilled about your date with Garth. Luce was fuming. Apparently he only gives her quickies at the loading dock.'.

Rachel winced. 'Really?'

Charlene smirked. 'No go then, babes?'

'Nup.' She tried to sound breezy. How had she not seen this? She avoided Justin's sudden glance. She felt embarrassed. Justin was probably sitting there thinking she didn't know her own mind. Sometimes she did wonder.

As if trying to change the tone, Justin pulled out his phone. 'Check this out.' He showed them the supermarket Facebook page and the video of Mario and Bader dancing. Charlene broke into fits of laughter, while Mario stood up and moved his hands to the sky in a dance move. Rachel glanced at the views. 'A thousand!'

'Sandra put this up.' Justin tapped like. 'We all agree that place is a nut house, right?'

She was having fun. Her thoughts shifting from Garth's rejection to feeling like one of the gang, as Mario put it. As she lifted her beer to her mouth a sudden crash at the table next to them, made her pause mid drink.

Garth. Of course. Cornered by a stocky thug with a shaved head and more teeth missing than present. No one could glean what he said, as he mumbled some code talk to the whimpering Garth, who took the punch to the nose with a scream. 'You broke my nose, you shit.'

The guy picked Garth up by his collar, kicked him in the sides several times, punched his face again, and then smashing a glass on the table he held it up in front of Garth. 'This is just a warning.' He ran the broken glass down Garth's face and shoved him onto the table before bolting.

Everyone on the deck seemed to freeze. Rachel had never seen a fight before. 'Is he alright… ' she started to say as Justin and Mario rushed over to help him.

Blood oozed from his nose and cuts seeped open on his face. Justin handed him a bunch of napkins. A small crowd gathered, looking on.

'Garth,' gasped Lucy. 'Your face. Oh god, and nose?' she cried.

Charlene screamed in distress. Rachel's stomach flipped—she hated the sight of blood.

'Mate, you look bad. We need to call an ambulance,' Justin said.

Garth snatched the napkins and held them against his nose. 'Piss off deli dick.' The blood seeped onto his linen shirt. 'Fuck!' He looked at his shirt, and the blood oozing through the napkins and fainted, hitting his head on the table as he went down.

Lucy screamed and crumbled to her knees shouting at him and everyone else to do something. Charlene picked up her bubbles and sipped as Trudy rushed over, as if for protection. The two of them watched on with a hysteria running commentary. Mario held his stomach and doubled over at the wharf railing. Bar staff had gathered and were shouting at each other to call an ambulance. Others were filming on their phones.

Justin walked back to Rachel where she stood next to her stool, stunned at what she was seeing. He looked down at her, grabbed her around the waist and pulled her into him. 'I don't know about you, but right now I couldn't give a stuff about Garth.' They both momentarily darted a glance at Garth with a couple of guys forcing more napkins on him.

'Same,' Rachel said, surprised but thrilled at Justin's assertive move.

He pulled her tighter. She was focused on giving him the *kiss me look*. As his face closed in on the tiny gap between them, they closed their eyes, their lips touching lightly at first, then the pressure increased. As Rachel lifted her arms around Justin's neck and he pulled her as close as he could, their kiss moved into a passionate embrace. They forgot about Garth, who moaned in agony. They couldn't hear Lucy, who cried that Garth's face would be ruined forever. They were oblivious to staffers rushing at him with wet towels. And they had no idea Mario barfed over the wharf, while Charlene asked if it was the sight of Garth's serrated face, to which he barfed even more.

The ambulance came and tended to his face. Garth yelled for his Armani jacket, which Lucy obediently grabbed. He moaned and groaned as he left the venue. With Lucy, click clacking in her high heels after him, twisting her ankle as she hurried. The music blared while the crowd returned to what they were doing before Garth got his head kicked in.

'Well,' said Rachel, as she came up for air, 'Someone had to give it to him.'

Chapter Thirty One

It was seven in the morning when Bader stole into Goodsworth, looking slightly disheveled, wearing sunglasses, a take-away coffee in hand.

'Late today, Bades?' Sandra called from where she stood chatting with Lillian. 'Too much to drink last night?'

'What are you talking about?' he said sheepishly, fiddling with the lid of his coffee.

Sandra waved her hand across her face. 'Whew, no one light a match.'

'I would think you need to watch yourself, Sandra.' He tried to sound authoritative, walking staunchly towards his office.

Sandra smirked. 'Enjoy the day.' *I know I will.* Sandra almost felt sorry for him. Almost.

'He certainly isn't himself lately,' Lillian said, concerned. 'Maybe Marjorie's right. He is losing his marbles.'

'Seems to be the same incompetent fossil to me.' Sandra stared at the plastic sheet covering the hole in the wall. The edges flapped from the warm gusts of wind blowing through the gaps.

Lillian frowned. 'No, I mean, he's more on edge. Have you seen how many tablets he's taking? Hannah from the chemist told me he's taking Zoton for his reflux. And now diazepam. She says it's anxiety. And Sandra,' she looked aghast, 'you posted his dance on Facebook.'

Sandra nodded. She'd been watching the views and likes on the private store Facebook page grow like an eventful day on the stock market. Admittedly it was mainly used by the older women in the store to post inspirational messages. Shares of the post were exploding. 'Yep. Two thousand likes already.'

'I think you should take it down,' Lillian suggested. 'It could cause problems.'

'Lills, Bades has probably already seen it. Besides, behaviour has consequences,' she said, deciding she was going to pay him a visit.

Bader slammed his top drawer shut as she entered his office. 'We don't have a meeting, Sandra.' He threw a white tablet into his mouth and swallowed without water. With his crimson, bloodshot eyes, Sandra considered one tablet—whatever it was—would not be enough.

'I need to know you're going to fix the lock on my coolroom door.' She used this as an excuse to start a conversation.

'I've told you before Sandra, these things take time.' He barely looked at her.

'What happened to 'round-the-clock-security? And how come the only security these days is Troy, who spends half his time on Tinder swiping right.'

'Make a meeting Sandra.' He rubbed his face with his hands. 'Now I have work to do... Garth!' Bader looked aghast.

Garth had a menacing look as he walked into Bader's office. One side of his face was lined with cuts neatly held together with tiny stitches. Sandra stared, shocked, and always curious by a bit of gore. What had this dipshit done to garner such a brutal beating though?

'You're l... late,' Bader stammered, as if trying to process Garth's rearranged face.

'Didn't think you noticed my coming and goings,' he snarled, pretending there was nothing wrong with his appearance.

Sandra cocked her head, pondering his face, and wondering why Bader didn't address the elephant in the room. 'What happened to your face?' she asked.

'I tripped and landed on some broken glass,' he said, as if this would completely explain the topography of his face.

'Sure,' Sandra said, not believing him.

Bader cleared his throat. 'Garth, I was telling Sandra we don't have a scheduled meeting and neither do you—'

'I hear you're upping the security,' he snapped.

Bader wiped his head nervously. 'Well now—'

'A staff member locked in the coolroom and your front window destruction would not have happened if we'd had more security and my lock was fixed now, would it?' Sandra eyed Garth's face. How many stitches did he have? Was he in pain? It looked painful.

'You need to teach that blonde chick to be smarter than that Sandra.' Garth sneered.

'Smarter? That girl is smarter than you boof heads put together. Striptease over there,' she referenced Bader with her hand, who looked questioningly back at her, 'and you with a glassed face looking at me like you've lost a contact lens. I hardly think this is intelligence.'

Sandra thought about the destruction of Bader's office at the hands of Garth. The potting mix smudge marks on the wall behind him were hard to ignore. The Smarties jar had been reloaded. Garth glared at her. For a moment she wondered if he would repeat his outburst. Both plants had been removed from Bader's office. The filling up of the Smartie jar was a risk. Bader looked at Garth and then the jar. Perhaps the same thoughts crossed his mind.

'What are you doing about my off chickens?' she asked.

'Ask your staff,' Garth snarled.

'My staff has nothing to do with those bloody chickens.'

Garth gave a fake cough.

'You did say Rhonda was to blame,' Bader said seriously, his voice rising in a questioning tone.

Sandra felt momentarily flustered. She turned to look at Garth, Prince Prick, who had his eye on Bader, gloating at his comment.

'I hear you got this job through a friend?' She watched a small droplet of spit leave her mouth and land on Garth's arm. He didn't notice. She wished it had landed on his face.

'Not a friend, a referee,' he said.

'Wonder what your referee would think of you turning up to work with your looks down the tube.'

Garth opened his mouth to respond as Troy appeared at the door, wearing his aviators, smiling broadly. His face and body, sprayed that morning with fake tan ready for his body building competition in two days' time, was particularly orange and glowing.

'Bader,' he said, upbeat.

'Troy, can't you see I'm in the middle of a meeting.' He wiped his comb-over.

Ignoring Bader's comment, Troy stepped right into his office. He lifted his aviators off his eyes and studied Garth's face. 'Sick! Heard about your face, but woah—it's worse than Lucy said. Came off second best, hey. Too bad.' He slapped Garth on the back.

Garth pushed his hand away and moved to the side of Bader's desk. 'We're in a private meeting.' He snapped.

'Ah, yeah, but who really has meetings 'round here right.' Troy looked at Bader. 'What sup?' He settled into the office chair, oblivious to the tension in the room. 'Lillian said you called for me.'

'Ah yes, now Troy.' Bader glanced nervously at Garth. 'It seems I miscalculated… Head Office wants to—'

'Bades,' Garth interrupted. 'Clive at Head Office said Troy alone would be fine, remember?'

Clive! That was the name she'd heard the other day when Garth and Bader were arguing. He was the pain in the arse who told Bader to hire Garth, the inferior grocer boy who demanded the sacking of Stephanie and Mohammad so he could grease his way up the Goodsworth ladder. She could barely stand looking at the two buffoons.

'Well idiots, we can clearly see what happens when Troy's managing security alone. No offence or nothin' Troy,' she said.

'None taken.' Troy shrugged.

'Clive knows what he's doing,' Garth snapped.

'Clive who?' Sandra pushed.

Troy clicked his finger and pointed it at Garth. 'Clive, that's the guy who comes to see you at the end of your shift. Met him a few times. Bit of a cool distant bugger. Nice suits though.'

'Shut up Troy,' Garth snapped.

Bader sighed, succumbing to what now was becoming a meeting. 'Clive works at Head Office.'

'He told you to hire Garth, didn't he?' Sandra placed her fists on Bader's desk. 'No one in their right mind would hire Garth.' She eyed him. 'I'm right, aren't I?'

The phone on the desk rang. The digital screen lit up. It was Anita from HR. Bader waved for everyone to leave. No one moved. He sighed, picking up his phone, and pushing the receiver close to his ear. Sandra strained to hear Anita, who fortunately had a loud voice. She confirmed the date of the window repair would be after Christmas, and that someone would be out in the next few days to ascertain his well-being. 'Psychological well-being Mr. Bader,' Anita reinforced.

Anita's call sounded promising. Bader's office would soon be hers. Once she put the final touches on Bader's dismissal, she'd need to make sure Garth, the slimy turd, didn't weasel his way to getting his job. That would be hell. She watched Bader replace the receiver, sweat glistening on his brow. She stared at his piddly half-day professional development certificates hanging on the wall behind his desk pondering how good her Employee of the Year certificates would look there. His were from short courses, hers were peer awards. She was the winner.

Bader tapped his fingers gingerly on his desk and cleared his throat. His left eye twitched. 'Sandra, get your deli chicks under control. Check the deli and coolroom before you leave from now on. Garth,' he continued, trying to sound assertive. 'I am in charge, not you or Clive. Troy, as of tomorrow there will be three security guards. I will work out shifts shortly. Now everyone there's no meeting so get out of my office!'

At that moment Mario swung around the doorway. 'Baaadaaar,' he drew out his name for dramatic effect. 'Have you seen yourself on Tik

Tok yet? You're a bloody sensation. The video of you and your epic dance moves is trending. Friggin' thirty thousand views man!'

Later, when Sandra recalled that moment with Lillian, Wilma, and Jen, she told them how this time she really thought Bader was going to have a stroke. Mario shoved his phone in Bader's face and talked him through the moves as if Bader would think this was something to salivate with proudness over. Troy instantly looked on his own phone, while Garth picked up his Smarties jar and tipped them over his desk calling him a "fucking nutcase." All the time Bader bit into the curve of his hand and silently screamed. Sandra had quietly walked out of his office, hoping to escape being his chief suspect. 'Girls,' she said to the hens, 'that's what happens when you can't keep your pants on.'

Chapter Thirty Two

'Good night?' Ian walked into the kitchen and pulled up the blind.

She closed her eyes at the sharpness of the sunlight. It was nine o'clock in the morning. Her head pounded. But Mr. Peterson next door, who always seemed to mow the lawn early when she had a hangover, was at it again. She took her cup of coffee to the dining room table and flicked through the *Sydney Morning Herald* to find the entertainment section.

'See you came in late,' he said, opening the fridge.

'Ah huh.'

It was after two in the morning when the Uber dropped her home, and Justin had walked her to the door to say goodnight. And with such a night, it was impossible not to lie awake thinking about it all.

The paramedics came to the bar and taped up Garth's face and nose. The police arrived to get his statement, but he had already left. Rachel didn't pay much attention. After Justin's passionate embrace and long kiss, he looked at her, their lips touching, and asked, 'Want to dance?' And, taking her hand, he led her to the dance floor where, holding her close, they danced until Mario interrupted with whisky highballs.

Mario, in charge of all the fun, recovered from his barfing, kept them going with frequent refills. After a few whisky highballs, none of them cared where Garth was. And Mario had so many great stories about the supermarket. The one about the finger in the mincer she found hard to believe. 'He exaggerates,' Charlene said, her words slurring. Later, Justin told her it was a legit accident that everyone knows about but pretends they don't.

Who would've thought, her and Justin? Maybe now, with a workplace relationship, she really did need to quit. Nah, no one in that place cared about those sorts of things.

Ian lifted the orange juice from the door of the fridge. He studied the bottle as he spoke. 'Ready for work? Oh, shame, I bought orange juice with pulp?'

'I like pulp.'

'Never could like it.' He walked over to the bench and pulled out the tea strainer and rested it on a glass. 'Working today?' He poured in the juice.

'No, day off.' She planned on picking her car up from Manly, where she'd left it, to head to the beach for a swim.

Ian lifted his favorite 1970's brown pottery mug, which he'd inherited from his mother, from the draining board and reached into the matching pottery container for a coffee pod, while he drank his juice. 'Only one coffee pod left. I'm off cycling, need at least two shots to get me going.'

She placed her finger through the handle of her mug thinking she needed another coffee. Ian's shutting of the cupboard and the sound of the coffee machine felt louder than normal.

'Rach honey can you get me a box of pods when you're at work? Arabic.'

'Yep.' She eyed the shirt he was wearing. 'New?' she said, flicking over the page on the paper.

'Ah yes. What do you think? I can return it. David Jones.'

'It's fine.'

'What's wrong with it?' He knew her well.

'It's fine for the house.'

'Well, that's not why I bought it.'

'What, you bought it to do the garden?' She stirred.

'No, I have a… '

Rachel narrowed her eyes. 'Date?'

'In fact, I do.'

'Sorry dad, before we get to the shirt, a date? Like how? I mean I'm happy for you, but who? You never said anything about anyone. It's not Michelle, is it? I'm happy for you by the way. If it's not Michelle,' she reiterated.

Ian smiled. 'Her name's Cheryl. I think you would like her. I met her—'

'Cycling?' This was about the only place Ian could meet someone—unless, 'Online?'

He smiled awkwardly. 'Cycling.'

'Dad, I'm so pleased for you, seriously. However, if you want to impress her, don't wear that shirt. On special, right?' She didn't wait for a response. 'You can't go wrong with a linen shirt.'

'I should have taken you shopping with me in the first place.'

She smiled. 'No, you just need to trust your judgement and not go for the sales stand.' She turned her attention to the newspaper, but she couldn't concentrate. Justin was filling her mind.

She'd had an inkling he liked her the day his coffee went all over their shirts. Admittedly, she'd liked being against him. The way his arms instinctively went to wrap around her, but stopped, and rested on her arms. She could tell he wanted to hug her. And in the moment of their bump, after surprise left his face, she felt like he'd truly noticed her.

Her phone buzzed. A text from Liz: *How was last night?*

At the same time, Ian asked, 'So where were you last night? Got in late?'

'Dad, I'm not fifteen.' Her brow creased as she typed out a text to Liz: *Awesome. Call soon.*

Ian placed the juice back in the fridge. 'Never too old for a parent to worry.'

His blue eyes looked kind. She smiled at him, aware she was being towy. 'Worry or nosy.' She gave him a smile. 'Anyway, it was a work Christmas party. You know how they are.'

'How's the guy in the Mustang?' he asked.

'Don't worry, nothing there,' she said, straight-faced.

'Not worried,' he said. 'I'm seriously relieved!'

'Yeah, he was a di… ' she paused. Her dad wasn't a fan of profanity, even if it was just the dick word. 'Um, Dad, do you mind dropping me at my car at Manly?'

'Was wondering when you were going to ask. Saw, I mean heard, the Uber,' he said with a smile. 'I'll get my keys and put the shirt in the bag to return.' As he walked down the hall he yelled back. 'Rach, honey it's only six days until Christmas, can you pick up a frozen turkey?'

She thought of Valentina's offer. 'Actually, Dad, we could go somewhere for Christmas this year,' she yelled back, walking down the hall to wait at the entrance.

'I don't think I'd enjoy a restaurant meal.' She could hear him changing his shirt.

'We've been invited to Christmas lunch at a work colleague's house.' She liked the sound of *work colleague*. 'She insisted. Said we could both go. It's a great idea.' Even though Sandra was going to be there, it was better than just the two of them trying to pretend they were having a nice dinner, the absence of her mum magnified.

'How much do you really want to go?'

She could hear him picking up his car keys.

'I think it might be nice.'

'Let me think about it,' he said. 'Right now, let's get you to your car, and I better sort out this shirt. The things you do to impress. I'm not sure going out with this person is a good idea.' He headed through the front door.

'It's a good idea, Dad,' she said, shutting the front door behind them. 'In fact, it's a great idea.'

Chapter Thirty Three

The next day, wearing her new white shirt, Rachel looked forward to sneaking into the coolroom for pashes with Justin. She smiled to herself at the idea as she slammed her car door and locked it manually from the outside with her car key. A reminder she needed to save up for a new car before this one conked on a main road.

She spotted Garth having a ciggie, his face looking like a bloated-seeping tomato. His nose taped, dark bruises emerging under his eyes. *Why didn't he take a sickie?* she thought. It wasn't like he'd be missed.

She had to admit, even with his cut-up face he was still strikingly good-looking. He glared at her as he slowly let the smoke ease through his lips. She lifted her middle finger, her face giving him the best fuck-off look she could muster. Nothing was going to ruin her day.

Now, one week before Christmas, the familiar sound of carols wafted throughout the supermarket, matched by overzealous displays of fruit pyramids, pop-up gourmet food exhibits, and bulging shelves with excess produce for the festive season. Rachel was late as usual, but she didn't care.

She waved to Nat, setting up an orange pyramid with headphones on. Had he seen Bader's dance moves trending on TikTok and didn't want to chat about it? Bader had to be the talk of the supermarket.

She avoided looking at the overnight replenishment of tinsel-lathered vacuumed-sealed quarter pigs. Valentina scrubbed the trays at the backbench. Sandra was out of the deli, as usual. Rachel placed her bag under the counter and glanced around to see Justin.

'It's going to be busy,' Valentina said, squeezing the wet paper towel in her hand and watching the water drip into the sink. 'Christmas is only a week away, and Sandra's away. She's never away. Plus, the new quality control box is here. Garth's already checked it. My gwad, his face.' She gave a horrified expression. 'How'd he get those cuts? He wants to hope they don't scar. I have my doubts. Anyway, he tells me, "Don't use the chickens in the quality control box." Do we ever?'

'Not that I know of.'

'You know,' she paused to look at Rachel. 'I don't understand where the bleached chooks went. You put them in garbage bags and the coolroom, right? But they disappeared.'

'Maybe Sandra chucked them. Did you ask her?'

'No. She'd just blame us.'

'True. It was most likely her. I wouldn't worry.'

'Then what about yesterday's quality control box? This morning, when I went to the coolroom, the box was open, and all the chickens are gone. Then we get this new delivery, already. And by some strange delivery guy, with a scar down his face and missing teeth. Gave me creeps, the way his dead eyes glared at me.' She gave Rachel a serious expression before launching into her next thought. 'I see someone likes you.' She raised her eyebrows.

Rachel was trying to process her narrative on the chickens and strange man, but Valentina's last comment distracted her. She liked the fact Valentina could see Justin liked her. He must have looked at her a certain way. How had she not seen it?

Valentina dawdled to the counter, hitting the ticket machine and taking her customer's order. 'I met Alvaro in Ecuador when we were in our early twenties. Six months later, we were married.'

Rachel served a flustered father, his children hanging off the trolley, nagging for ice cream.

'When we met, he was the handsome prince. After we marry, eh, he goes and turns into a lazy pig,' she gave a wicked laugh. 'And,' she tapped Rachel's arm, 'he never sees what I do: the birthday cards, gifts to the family, washing his clothes, cooking, cleaning, sweeping the patio, cleaning the toilet—every week for twenty years. The invisible chores, like a cleaning fairy. What does he do? Goes to Bunnings, has a sausage sizzle, and work in the garden. Rachel, I tell you that story because Mario, the stupid boy, is like this.'

'Mario?' she scoffed.

'What you need Rachel, is the handsome prince who won't change into the lazy pig. They're hard to find.' She threw the smoked ham onto the scales with passion.

Hang on, did Valentina mean Mario liked her? She tweaked her shower cap, then picked up the tongs and fiddled with the sausages. Oh, who cared? Maybe it was just as well she didn't know about her and Justin, who, she could tell, was totally into her. When it was 10:30 that morning and Justin still hadn't turned up for his shift, she started to worry. Maybe he had second thoughts and took a sickie to avoid her.

Her phone buzzed: *Have my break in 5. Free for coffee and goss?*

She felt disappointed it was Charlene and not Justin.

Be at your checkout in 5. She hit send.

'Val, I'm just going to get a coffee. Do you want one?'

Valentina shook her head. 'Hurry, it busy and no one here but me,' then muttered under her breath, 'as usual.'

Garth was at checkouts, arguing with Lucy while simultaneously yelling at a grocer boy for dropping the box of magazines at the end of the checkout, even though he was stacking them in the rack. As Charlene and Rachel walked by, he muttered, 'whores' under his breath. Rachel wanted to punch him right in his swollen nose.

'Ignore him, Rach. He's beggin' for a fight,' Charlene said as she scowled at Garth. 'Hopefully Lucy's finally seen the light. He tried it on me too when I started. I saw right through the bastard.'

Rachel wished she could have seen through him too. Was she as hopeless as Lucy in character judgement? Was she that desperate? Only it had been to get to checkouts, she reminded herself. Even that was a bad reason.

'And why come to work looking like a cat fight happened on ya face? Right?' Charlene continued.

'Weird,' Rachel said, thinking how even his messed-up face couldn't keep him from obsessing over the chicken box in the deli. 'He's weird.'

'Freak,' Charlene agreed. 'Okay, we haven't talked about the friggin' obvious: Bader on TikTok—trending.' Charlene bragged about how she shared the video from Sandra's post, and then moved on to her Instagram story of Mario dancing on the checkout. 'I know he's no Harry Styles, but Mario's really grown on me. He's hot when he wears his sunnies on his head. Seen his hairy chest?'

'No.' And she didn't want to.

'Last night was an intoxicating mix of violence, injury, and mayhem—heard that on Love Island once.'

The Italian barista, who looked like he belonged more on the Riviera than a humble suburban shopping centre handed her coffee. 'Ciao, Rachel,' he said warmly. She smiled as she read the comment scrawled on the lid of her coffee cup. *Happy day.*

'It's a good day, no?'

'Yeah, I think so,' she said, giving him a smile, hoping it was a good day after all.

Charlene cleared her throat, gaining Rachel's attention. 'Hey, what about Maz's car? Like, he thinks I'm gonna put up with that heap for long. Told him if he wanna hot babe like me, he's gonna hafta fix the floor asap. Draft up me toosh is pushin' it. His Beckham aftershave shows he's got class. And he's second in charge of the Butchery, 'bout to be manager any month now. Poor Rog.'

Rumour had it that Roger's slipped disc would bring his retirement forward—the rumour started by Mario, of course.

'You know he chundered over Garth's beating?' Charlene continued. 'I said Maz, you wear blood on your apron. You know what he says? The bloody apron is like an artwork but watching Garth get beaten looked terrifying. And he hates the sight of human blood. He's a sensitive, modern man, Rach.' Charlene smiled.

Charlene took her coffee and looked at the writing on the lid of her cup. 'Hmm, *Breathe*,' she read. 'Okay, so I talk fast.'

The barista grinned.

'And,' Charlene continued, lowering her voice like she was about to reveal state secrets, 'I saw Justin leave work on his motorbike with… your worst nightmare.'

'Garth?' Rachel joked.

'No silly. This chick, with big tits, who seemed pretty friendly. And it wasn't Lucy.' She looked at Rachel, her lips falling to the side in sincerity. 'It was a few weeks ago. Let's hope it's over.'

'Ah, yeah, let's.' *Shit! Of course he'd be dating.* No matter what he'd told her. But it was a few weeks ago. Today is today. The present. But a niggling worried feeling started to tug at her.

Back in the deli, Justin still wasn't there. She checked her messages. Maybe he took a sickie because of his hangover. She was beginning to wish she had too, the antipasto made her stomach turn. What if he was having second thoughts and didn't want to face her? How stupid could she be trying to date another guy at Goodsworth? If he'd changed his mind, or worse, it was a one-night heat of the moment pash, of course she'd have to leave. She arrived last. It would just be too difficult to stay. And besides, checkouts was now out of the question. Her heart sank, just when she thought things were getting better in her love life and work. Now, it was possible, both were heading down the drain again. Why were guys so complicated?

Chapter Thirty Four

Sandra stood outside Mega Mart in her jeans, oversized T-shirt, and sports cap. She'd called in sick, hoping that her absence from work would make her less likely to get the blame for the new emails she was about to send.

She sighed, taking in the expansive entrance while her mind stewed over her plan to sneak into Bader's office and send Glen Smyth, what she hoped was her last fake email. How dare Bader lie she was to blame for Rachel being locked in the coolroom. And how dare he plot with Garth to get rid of her. With the Big Boys ignoring her previous emails, she had to up her game.

On occasion, she'd wander through Mega Mart, taking notes of the various new features and the modern, state-of-the-art installments throughout the customer-luring store. She'd read in the newspaper that this Mega Mart was the blueprint rollout for all its stores set to be remodeled around the country. Of course, they'd blueprint one in their tiny shopping centre. Goodsworth was no competition, and the Mega Mart head honchos knew it. This new store was pissing all over Goodsworth.

Her eyes glazed in envy at the refrigerated pick-up cabinets where customers could conveniently collect their online orders on their way home from work. She was jealous of the expanded floor space, making room for a larger meat and seafood selection. She looked in the glass encased flat bread oven, noting the bakery had a custom, made-to-order, cake offering, which claimed to be the biggest in the nation.

The tension in her body rose, not only was she envious, but she was also furious that this store had implemented ideas she had for Goodsworth. She'd been foolish enough to tell Mac Sprink about her ideas. 'Emphasise the entrance,' she'd told him, 'With those new pick-up lockers and convenience meals. And add ethnicity. Variety's where it's at. Can't only cater for the Devon and cream bun devourers.'

Sprink, being the mindless blockhead he was, distracted by Karen from The Coffee Hub, didn't listen. Even though she complained to Bader about the store and the changes they needed to make, there was no way she was going to tell him about her ideas. She took notes on her phone: *local produce engaging local community, flame roasted chickens.* She stole past the delicatessen, pulling down her cap so Dimitri the manager wouldn't recognise her. She'd seen him strolling through Goodsworth, smirking at the inadequacy of her deli. She pushed aside the disdain she had for him and tapped out the ideas she could see before her. *Cut-to-order meat through online ordering. Coffee-making.* What she'd give to make herself a daily coffee or four. Imagine the coin she'd save. The staff at Mega Mart wore caps, no hair nets, they smiled and smiled, asking how the customer's day was. Yeah, well that one would never fly at her deli.

The olive island heightened her envy. Genius. She watched a customer scoop out their own selection of the various slippery little buggers. She observed the staff. There were six behind the counter, one making coffee, another loading in flame-roasted chickens, another tidying the cheeses, and the remainder smiling cheerfully at their customers.

'Extra shot cappuccino,' she ordered, shoving her phone in her back pocket. Holding her not-too-hot, not-burnt, lightly frothed, perfectly sprinkled-with-chocolate cappuccino, she strolled back through the broad entrance free of turnstiles, buzzing with self-serve checkouts.

She sipped her cappuccino imagining sitting in Bader's high back leather swivel chair, commanding his office, planning changes across the store. She'd start with flame-roasted chickens, get rid of the turnstiles, and add more self-service checkouts. Mega Mart was a supermarket on steroids. Sandra would bring Goodsworth up to competition. First, she needed to get rid of Bader. She didn't know if it was the caffeine or the thoughts of Bader's dismissal that made her feel so good. She thought about it as she drank her coffee, deciding it was his ousting.

Lillian sat at the service desk reading the latest gossip from a magazine article. 'You're not in uniform?' She looked concerned at Sandra in her oversized T-shirt and cap.

'I'm doing some offsite work. Big Boys want me to ah, do some investigation.'

'Oh?' Lillian looked confused.

'At Mega Mart. Undercover checking, you know,' she said, hoping this would be enough to get Lillian off her case.

'Sounds exciting,' Lillian looked pleased for her.

'Yeah, well Lills, I need you to get old Badey on the blower and tell him the frozen food fridge is on the blink. He needs to check its condition before the food defrosts. Troy passed on the message to me.' Lillian never checked what she told her.

'It is? Oh, that's a big problem. The Christmas period too.' She picked up the receiver and dialed his number.

Sandra listened, hoping Bader would buy it. The frozen food aisle was the furthest from his office, hopefully this would give her enough time to carry out her plan.

'He's coming.' Lillian replaced the receiver.

Sandra checked her watch, mindful of how long she would have in Bader's office. She felt annoyed with him, that she always had to sink to his level. She wouldn't have grabbed him by the shirt or let the air out of his tires if he hadn't planted the groceries in her car. She wouldn't be defaming his character if he wasn't trying to sack her and blame Rachel's accident on her. But she knew how upline management worked. No one would listen to her, not even Glen Smyth, despite being the nicest man she'd ever met. They would see her issues with Bader as a personal conflict and make them have mediation. She wouldn't tolerate that!

If her plan worked, there was every chance Bader's job could become hers.

She looked at Lillian. 'Remember, I'm not here today.'

'I'll remember,' Lillian replied, curious.

Pretending to examine a packet of tea from the edge of aisle two, Sandra watched Bader walk towards the frozen foods, then hurried to his office. She sat in his swivel chair, running her hands down the sides of the armrest, taking a moment to envision herself taking over the top job. With that, she promptly opened his laptop and composed another letter to Glen Smyth. Before sending it, she logged into her Gmail account, opening the email with the selection of photos of Bader from the night before. She uploaded the best ten—his near-naked attempt at the splits on the counter was almost as good as the bin-puking.

The night before she'd ordered Nat to go home, saying she would look after Bader. Nat had hesitated, but it didn't take much to change his mind. She told him she was going to put his name forward for promotion, he was such a loyal employee. She'd make sure Bader would know he'd tried to help, but that she'd suggested he go home to his family, after his long day unstacking and loading fruit and veggies. Nat, taking the bait, looked grateful and left.

When the staff were gone, and Troy was out the front talking to Trudy and her friend Tezza, a thirty-five-year-old part-timer from the loading dock, Sandra snuck down the corridor to Bader's office, where she found him puking into his bin. Secretly, she snapped photos.

She reread her email. 'Sorry Badey. You gave me no choice,' she said, feeling a faint sense of guilt. 'And besides, if I don't get rid of you first, you'll get rid of me.' And with that, she hit send.

Chapter Thirty Five

Rachel leaned against the sink, mulling over her future while she played with her latex glove. Garth strutted past the deli, acting like he was the author and owner of cool. How could he pretend he hadn't had his face beaten to a pulp? His strange behaviour was now becoming a welcomed distraction from obsessing over Justin and his disappearance.

As Garth disappeared around the aisle, her mind flashed back to when she'd seen him in the shaving aisle chatting with some guy. She'd gone to get some tampons because she never had any on her—ever—and there was Garth, standing near the pads, talking to some bruiser. He handed him a plastic package, about the size of his hand, before turning around and seeing her. Quickly, she pretended to inspect the tampons.

'Hey, babe,' he'd called down the aisle in his smoothest voice. 'Shopping?'

Bruiser, looking startled and awkward, grabbed a box of pads off the shelf and left.

'Oh, ah, yeah.' She clasped her hands over the tampons.

'One of those days, huh?' he winked.

She felt so stupid the way she'd giggled like a schoolgirl at the class hunk. How had she not been more suspicious of this scene? She was so consumed in Garth liking her that she'd missed what was objectively a pretty dodgy interaction. She snapped herself back to reality. Bruiser; she'd seen him again. Wasn't he the guy from the pub last night? The one who'd slashed Garth's face?

It was starting to become obvious. She wondered why no one else was putting this together. No one working in a supermarket can afford a Mustang GT, a Breitling watch, gloss white veneers, and a three-bedroom apartment in Manly all at the same time, especially on an award wage. It had to be drugs. Is that why that dickhead's in charge of the quality control stupid chickens?

'The quality control box is off again, right?' she asked Valentina.

'Correct.' She gave an affirmative nod.

Rachel glanced at the counter. 'We're low on ham hocks. I'll grab some more.'

Up until now, she had avoided the coolroom since it had almost become her tomb. But now she was on a mission. She pushed the stepladder against the coolroom shelf and climbed up. There was the quality control box, sitting at the top. What did quality control even mean? Weren't all the boxes of produce checked to make sure they were fresh? How had no one asked these questions?

She lifted down Garth's 'special box', resting it carefully on the top of the ladder. She was no expert in chickens, but as far as she was concerned, they didn't smell off. Wishing she'd taken a minute to get some gloves, she ignored the sick feeling as she opened the cavity of the raw chicken and looked inside.

'Holy hell,' she yelped.

'Need help?' Valentina poked her head through the door.

'Oh, no, no, all good. Just getting the hocks,' she said, the chicken slipping from her fingers. 'Garth didn't seal the box properly. Typical.'

'He a stupid boy,' Valentina said.

Stupid? Understatement, she thought, pulling out the plastic package, which was slightly smaller than her hand. *He's a fucking dealer.*

Valentina didn't see her snatch the scissors and tape from the back bench and rush back into the coolroom. Her hands shook as she snipped the plastic packet enough to see the white powder inside. *Fuck*!

'What now?' she heard Valentina say.

A male voice, unpleasant and curt responded. 'I can come here whenever I want, useless old bat.'

It was Garth. She had to move fast.

'Hopeless,' Garth said to her, as he stepped into the coolroom, an olive squishing under his foot.

'Ouch,' she said sarcastically, relieved she managed to shove the box back onto the shelf and push the ladder away. In her haste, she knocked the scissors and tape off the ladder, and when she tried to grab them, she bumped the olive container, sending everything crashing to the floor.

'Thought you're in charge of checkouts.' She darted a glance at the scissors and tape on the ground.

'Gotta check the quality control chickens bitch.'

She stared at his face, pieced together like a broken vase. The only reason he came to work was to get the drugs. Anyone else would be hiding their face for weeks. 'Go on then.'

He stepped onto the first rung of the ladder. Quickly she reached down to pick up the scissors and tape and slipped them into her apron pocket. 'Anyway, why doesn't Sandra check them? It's weird. You're weird.'

'You don't know shit about how a store's run. Deli shit.' He stepped off the ladder. 'You're nothing but a dumb deli chick who's never going to go anywhere.' He twisted his watch around his wrist. 'Where's your boyfriend today, huh?'

She stared at his messed-up face. That perfect face, straight white teeth, hot bod, and on fleek appearance had sucked her in. Now all she could see was an abusive narcissist. She felt sorry for his face. 'Looks are only skin deep you know.'

'What's that supposed to mean?'

'Don't worry, that one needed an IQ of at least 100 to figure the riddle,' she said sarcastically. 'Go ahead. Check your stupid box. Guess a plastic surgeon will fix your face.'

He looked at her like this was a good idea.

'I mean it's not like you can't afford it right?'

He looked awkward, waiting for her to leave.

She glanced up at the box pretending she didn't know he'd already checked the chickens that morning. 'You going to check them?'

He frowned, lifting his phone from his back pocket as if checking a message. 'K got business to tend to.' He pointed his finger at her. 'Clean this mess up.'

She could hear his voice grow fainter as he told off Valentina while storming out of the deli. 'Made more than one sale today, Val? Time to retire don't you think?'

As she pumped three squirts of soap onto her hands, prizing the tiny chicken pieces from her fingernails, while running them under hot water, she wondered what to do. She'd seen the movies. You didn't know who you could trust when it came to drugs. Even the cops were sometimes involved. Valentina had too big a mouth to let her in on it, and Sandra, well, she'd disappeared again. Garth would return for his drugs most likely at the end of the day. She needed to hide them so he couldn't take them. How could she prove the drugs were his? He had to be caught red handed.

She wiped her hands, staring at the chicken oven. She had an idea.

Minutes later she called to Valentina, who was holding ransom another customer, as she held their package in her hand, sharing a recipe idea.

'Val, back in a sec.'

Valentina sighed. 'When we have this long queue?'

Rachel hardly thought three customers made for a long queue. 'Got my period, unprepared, so I need to—'

'Buy some protection.' Valentina went to her bag. 'I'm always prepared. Can you believe it, fifty-two and no menopause? It's why I have good skin—collagen.' She handed Rachel a slim long cosmetic bag. 'Supermax pads, for first day big flow. Use what you need.' She patted her hand.

Rachel took the bag and thanked her for the *surfboards*.

'If Garth comes back, tell him Lillian's looking for him.'

'She is?'

'Do you want him around here without Sandra, Justin or me?'

'I'll tell him Lillian's looking for him,' she nodded.

Rachel's mind was spinning. Where was Justin? She could do with his help right now.

Chapter Thirty Six

She knocked at Bader's closed door, wondering how she would succinctly explain the drugs in the coolroom to him. With no answer she decided to open the door to check if he was there.

'Sandra?' Surprise registered on her face. 'What are you doing here?'

Sandra looked caught off guard.

'What are you doing sitting at Bader's desk?' *Snooping at his computer most likely*. And what on earth was she wearing?

Sandra, equally incredulous, shot back, 'What are you doing opening Bader's door?'

Steam rose from Bader's coffee cup. He couldn't be too far away. Why had he left his office with Sandra? She became acutely aware that she was taller than Sandra. She raised her chin, trying to feel even taller. For the first time since they met, she didn't feel intimidated.

Sandra's sharp gaze landed on the floral cosmetic bag in Rachel's hand. 'And what's that?'

'Oh, nothing,' Rachel blurted, hiding the bag behind her back, the same way she did when the mean girls hovering in the school toilets used to ask her the same thing about her own smaller, less colourful bag holding her first pads when she was thirteen.

Her heart pounded in her ears. Her mouth went dry. What if Sandra was in on this drug deal too? It would make perfect sense. Boss of the deli, a quality control box, Garth to help. Pretending to hate each other. 'I came to tell Bader the next quality control box arrived empty. Nothing in it.' If Sandra was on the deal she'd care about the empty box.

'That's it? That's why you came to Bader's *office*? Bader couldn't give a toss about those boxes. He's doing it to make my life hell. Anyway, why check? Who cares?' She hadn't reacted. She clearly didn't care about the boxes.

Sandra, there's something you should know.'

This piqued Sandra's interest. 'What?'

'I found little plastic wads of white powder in the quality control chickens. I think it's drugs.'

'Drugs?' Sandra's eyes popped. She dropped her clipboard on the desk.

'Yes. And I thought, since you weren't around'—*again*— 'I needed to tell Bader.'

Sandra's face was red. 'In the quality control box? Right under my nose?'

'There are about twenty packets. We need to find Bader and tell him.'

'I just thought they were doing that to fuck with me.' She darted glances around, like someone had hidden cameras in the walls. 'Come on. We can't talk here.'

Rachel's urging Sandra to wait until Bader returned fell on deaf ears. She had no choice but to hurry after her, out of the supermarket and into the female toilets in the mall. Sandra checked under all the toilet cubicles—suspiciously. 'I knew Garth was up to no good,' she fumed. 'Him and his new bromance with Pea-Brain. We can't tell Bader.'

'But Sandra, he needs to know. Police need to be involved!'

Sandra darted glances in several directions as if checking for spies. 'Bades might be in on it. I read their emails. They want to sack me. And why would he let Garth check those stupid boxes? He's got Bades wrapped around his finger.'

'The photos?' She studied Sandra's smug expression. 'Were they for a specific purpose—like ammunition?'

'You could say that,' Sandra gloated. 'Glen at Head Office needed to see what his manager was up to. Besides, it's on Facebook already.'

'And Tik Tok.'

'Do we care? Our little friend tried to pin your near-death experience on me. Not to mention, is possibly up to his eyeballs in this drug deal. Why else would he let Garth oversee those chickens and try to sack me?

Besides, the prick pissed me off. Sent an email to Glen, trying to get rid of me.' She pursed her lips as if trying to digest her actions. 'Makes me even happier now that I sent those photos. Nothing like a picture of an employee gyrating on a checkout with tinsel 'round his head to give cause for sacking. You do what you must to save your job. Glen's gonna nail his balls to his desk.'

Rachel would never have guessed Bader, the odd officious man, could be guilty of such a crime. On the other hand, Garth, no surprise there. She hated to admit it, but Goodsworth was a great cover for a drug syndicate. So many products delivered by a variety of suppliers. The comings and goings would be hard to track. Especially with some of the stoners at the loading dock, Troy who was never present, and Mario who, sure, kicked Garth out of the butchery that one day, but noticed nothing else beside his meat and Charlene—and maybe her for a minute or two.

Sandra washed her hands and pulled a paper towel from the holder, ripping it off with force. 'I'll call Glen Smyth,' she said. 'And Rachel, we can't tell anyone. Not even Justin.'

'Is he in on it?' Rachel hadn't thought about this. It was possible. The guy who seems amazing turns out to be a sociopath and never, for one moment cared but only wanted to use you for their own purpose. Oh hello, that sounded like Garth.

Sandra scoffed. 'Doubt it. But we can't trust anyone,' she said firmly. 'I'll get on to Glen. And Rach, it's time to put your big girl pants on and make sure Garth the dick doesn't get those chooks.' It was the first time she looked at her without a competitive snarl. Sandra inhaled deeply. 'Gotta get a Red Bull first. Rach, this is gonna be epic!'

Rachel could see a faint smile form across Sandra's lips. Or maybe it was adrenalin, because this was all Rachel could feel right now. Spiking like a geyser from New Zealand's Rotorua.

Chapter Thirty Seven

'Did Garth come back?' Rachel asked Valentina, trying to sound calm.

'Not that stupid boy,' Valentina said, shaking her head. 'But Justin finally here.'

Justin emerged from the coolroom carrying a tub of ricotta. 'So… Garth's at work today, huh?'

Rachel, relieved to see Justin, tried to sound casual. 'He was, uh… checking his goods. I mean… box. Wait till you see his face.' Her pulse raced. Two problems were presenting: Justin possibly trying to avoid her, and the drugs in the coolroom.

'Yeah, he looks pretty stitched up. Broken nose too.' Justin gave an easy smile, like he didn't have a care in the world. This, she thought, was a good sign. Still her heart pounded as the adrenalin raced through her body.

'Sometimes you deserve what you get,' she said, figuring Garth's beating was drug related.

'My thoughts exactly,' he smiled. 'How you feeling?' He wiped his fringe, pausing to look at her.

'If you're suggesting I have a hangover? I do. Three Panadols and two coffees helped.' she tried to sound casual. 'Did you leave your script at home again?'

'Had an audition this morning.'

'Oh, you didn't say….'

'I don't talk about them before I go.'

Their eyes met, holding. Rachel felt an almost irresistible pull to lean into him, breathe him in, smell his always-clean hair. She spun toward the ticket machine, hoping she didn't look too eager.

'Everything okay?' he asked, curious.

'Ah… yeah. Very well, actually. Hope the audition went well.'

'Yep, went well.' He reached under the bench. 'Here.'

She blinked at the cap dangling between his latex-gloved fingers. 'What's that… ?' She snatched it and saw her name scrawled in indelible ink. For a second, the drugs were forgotten. 'Is that my cap? Did you take my cap?'

'Yep.'

'What?'

'It's a joke. It's a ritual with new workers.' He moved towards her.

She stepped back and shook the flaccidly hanging cap at him. 'I don't find it funny. I wore this… this stupid shower cap for—'

'Hardly long.'

'One hour would be too long.' She threw her hair net in the bin, annoyed she couldn't find this funny, and that she never looked in the storeroom for a new cap.

Justin quickly changed the subject. 'Did you see Mario's Insta?'

Rachel nodded stiffly. Mario had posted photos of him and Charlene saying, "Out with the hottest babe on the planet," and, "I must've died and gone to heaven." She glared. He needed to fully apologise for letting her look like a complete and utter idiot for wearing the hair net. In front of Trude, Lucy and Charlene too.

She took her customer's order. A man in his mid-fifties with a well-worn T-shirt and faded khaki shorts. He read from his list scribbled on a crinkled wrapper. His fingernails were caked black, his hands rough and sunburnt brown. He caught her glancing at the wrapper. 'Have the memory of a fish,' he joked. Rachel smiled back, Mario coming into view, catching her attention.

'Love birds.' He navigated to the antipasto on the other side of the counter. 'Good night, bro,' he said, going for a high five which Justin politely returned, glancing Rachel's way. 'You guys are hawt together. And Juz man, you said you weren't interested. Changed your tune quick.' He shoveled some feta stuffed olives into his mouth, bits of spittle flinging down his chin.

Rachel glared at Mario. Like a ship hitting a snag in the shallow shores before anchoring, she felt like the smooth mooring about to take place in her love life, suddenly become horribly problematic. Her heart sank.

'You said that?' She glared at Justin in disbelief.

Mario, what are you talking about?' Justin looked confused.

Mario, accidentally biting his tongue while trying to munch through his mouthful of green olives, held up his hand suggesting he couldn't talk.

Rachel handed her customer, with the memory of a fish, his package. 'What do you mean not interested?'

'I didn't—'

'Yeah bro, you did.' Mario grimaced in tongue pain. 'Babe like I was sayin'—'

'Shut up Mario,' Rachel said. She looked across the deli, her mind racing, trying to mentally piece together how quickly Justin could change his mind. 'Not your type?' She tried to compose herself but the more she spoke, the more unraveled, confused and pissed off she felt. 'Does this go with the disappearing cap trick? Shit. I should've guessed. You didn't have an audition this morning, did you? You were going to avoid me, right? I bet you came to work because Sandra kicked your arse over the phone to get in here.'

'It's a full moon, right?' Justin said.

'I'm not crazy,' she defended. 'Thanks for letting me know Mario.'

Justin placed his hands on top of his head and looked up to the ceiling, as if trying to contain his frustration. He eyed Mario. 'Mate, I think you're still a little buzzed from last night. I never said I wasn't interested.'

'Yeah bro, you did. At the counter, remember? We were talking about me and Rach, then me and Charls, and then I asked you if you liked Rach and—'

'He said he wasn't interested,' Rachel finished. *Great. Just wow! Could today get any worse?*

Justin flicked back his fringe. 'Rach, it was your first day. I was getting big mouth Mario here off my case.'

Mario turned back to face the antipasto, dropping in another mouthful of olives, forgetting all about his tongue pain.

'It was just a joke.'

'At my expense,' she blurted.

She lifted out her water bottle from her bag and turned to face the sink, trying to hold in tears. She couldn't bear to hear him say it was a mistake—that he'd changed his mind. And now Garth the narcissistic thug, who'd fooled her into thinking he cared, who strutted around the supermarket like a rooster in a pen, with his face stitched together, still thinking he was awesome, strutted his arse back into the deli as if he owned it. She glanced at her watch. What was taking Sandra so long?

'Ha, what does a group of losers look like?' Garth pushed his way past Rachel, rubbing too close, intimidating her with his stare. 'Customer's waiting, losers.' He mouthed, *Incompetent* to the waiting customer, who tried to look away from Garth's face.

'Bro, you sure youse up to working? Face looks like it was under a snow plough.' Mario licked his fingers as he replaced the tray of olives and reached for some sundried tomatoes.

'Lift another fucking weight Mario,' Garth spat.

'These organic babies take effort.' Mario kissed his biceps. 'Unlike your steroid fakes.' He gestured at Garth's chest.

Garth's nostrils flared, something that must've hurt. He turned back towards the coolroom.

Rachel went to bite her thumb nail but remembered her gloves were on. She took a deep breath. She had to keep her mind on the drugs. She'd worry about Justin later. Sandra would've called Glen Smyth by now. So even if Garth managed to find the drugs, he'd have a hard time getting them out before the police arrived. She imagined Garth with his hands in cuffs behind his back, the police shoving him into the back of their car. Garth wouldn't think he was so special then.

Seconds later, Garth came out of the coolroom, holding the empty box. 'Okay you dumb bitches, where's the chickens?'

'Where *are* the chickens?' Rachel corrected.

He tossed the box at her feet. 'Tell me you fucking bitch. Where are they?'

'Language. We have customers.' Rachel moved away, hitting the ticket button and calling for number forty-five. A tall young man handed her his ticket, and asked for six ling fillets and if everything was okay? She assured him they had it under control. 'He's our one.' The guy ordering the ling fillets looked bewildered. 'Pro-bono, the one we help because, you know, he has a problem—anger management.'

'Oh, of course,' Mr. Ling Fillet said, his face sincere and respectful.

'You know what I'm talking 'bout don't you?' Garth came up close beside her. The stench of stale alcohol and tobacco on his breath hit her left cheek. She held her breath and lifted her hand to her nose. Garth inched closer, the stitched cuts in his face were clotted with blood.

Justin pulled Garth back by the scruff of his shirt. Mr. Ling Fillet watched awkwardly. 'Listen mate,' Justin said, letting go of his shirt. 'I don't know what you're—'

'Why's this box empty?' Garth pointed at the box on the floor, giving Justin a shove.

'Why do you care? Didn't you say they were off?' Rachel teased.

'Actually, we've all messed with the box,' Mario said, winking at Rachel, as if he knew she'd done something and needed his help.

'Yeah, all of us,' Justin joined in.

'Whatever they did, I did too,' Valentina said.

Garth put his face up close in Mario's. 'You don't know what you're up against.'

'Jeez, chill.' Mario pulled back his head. 'Need a menthol. Breath's nasty.'

'You fucking fucks!' Garth stormed out of the deli leaving everyone to stare at each other in disbelief.

Mario shook his head and wished them luck as he headed off for his lunch break. Rachel handed Mr. Ling Fillets his order and tried to reassure him that Garth was going to get help.

'Okay, that was weird.' Justin said, scanning the deli. 'What's going on Rach? Garth's completely lost his shit, and Mario… ' He shook his head, wiping his fringe, looking confused.

She wanted to tell him. Only Sandra had told her not to. 'I'm hungover, that's all,' she sighed. 'Garth's probably reacting to pain killers, endo or something. Probably why he came to work. He can't feel the pain and it's making him more of a psycho than usual.'

Justin didn't look convinced. 'Rach, about the cap stuff… '

At that moment, Sandra returned. Kicking aside the box still lying on the floor ignoring Valentina and Justin's curious expressions at what she was wearing and why she'd come into work. She hinted at Rachel to join her at the oven. *What was it Justin was going to say?* It was hard to focus on everything. Justin would have to wait.

'Only a matter of time before Badey's fate is sealed. Probs choking on his coffee and bagel reading his emails.' She gave Rachel a thumbs up. 'Called Glen. Shocked the bejesus out of him. Couldn't believe it. Said he'd call the upline manager and then work out the plan of attack. You know, call police, who call detectives, who call reporters.' Sandra had on her important look again.

Rachel whispered, matching Sandra's excitement and intensity. 'The chickens are in here.' She tapped the oven.

Sandra's eyes widened. 'Cooking?'

'I turned it off.'

'Good thinking.' Sandra looked at her, impressed. 'Bloody chooks have given me hell.'

'When do you think the police will be here?' Rachel spoke quickly.

'Depends. Glen, ain't exactly the fastest mover.' Her eyes darted to Valentina, suggesting Glen would be just as slow.

Rachel nodded.

Sandra took a deep breath and walked over to the counter to make a sandwich.

'Rach,' Justin touched her arm. She looked uncomfortably at his latex glove that had probably touched antipasto. He pulled his hand away.

'Why didn't you give back my cap earlier? Like the same day?'

'It was meant to be a joke. I forgot.'

'Didn't you notice I was wearing a hair net?'

'No, actually I didn't.' His eyes were warm. 'You're acting ridiculous. You know that?' he said.

Her smile vanished. 'Ridiculous?' *Did he just say I was ridiculous?* 'You're so disingenuous.'

'Do you even know half the meaning of the words you use?'

'Yes. I read. Unlike you who only reads scripts.' She overreacted. 'Who's the girl on your bike? Charlene told me.' She felt like a jealous girlfriend. *Girlfriend?* She'd ruined that possibility. Damn him for taking her cap, being disinterested, saying she was ridiculous, and inferring she was dumb.

'As it happens, she's an old friend from school, who works in the shopping centre and lost her wallet. She saw me and… why I'm even explaining this. It was weeks ago. And why listen to Charlene who thinks carrots grow on trees?' He shook his head. 'Listen, Rach, none of this means anything.'

'It does.'

He looked frustrated. 'Okay, okay,' he walked away, his hands up as if in surrender. 'You know what? You're insecure and indecisive.'

'Insecure and indecisive?' She followed him to where he now stood at the back bench.

'Yep! You accept a job you don't even want and then use Garth to get to checkouts.'

'I don't need to listen to this.' She took off her apron and shoved it under the back bench next to her bag. 'Sandra, I need some fresh air.'

'Two minutes Rach,' Sandra said, holding up two fingers then whispering, 'I need you here to help with Operation G & B.'

Chapter Thirty Eight

She sat on the seat at the edge of the car park breathing in the invisible fumes of carbon monoxide. Over at the loading dock Mario, who held a bag of Maccas take away, chatted to Troy, who was wearing a new tan. She guessed it was in preparation for his body building competition in a few days. He drank his Powerade while he showed Mario something on his phone. She watched as they laughed at the image. *Always busy Troy,* she thought sarcastically.

The heat radiated from the bitumen. It was hot, but she didn't want to be in the supermarket right now. She didn't even care anymore if Sandra did sack her, although they'd formed a kind of alliance, so sacking was probably not going to happen. Every assumption she'd made about the supermarket had been turned upside down. Sandra, wasn't belligerent, she just didn't tolerate incompetence. Bader, had nothing under control in the supermarket. Garth, wasn't into her—he was into his drugs. And Justin, allusive and cool, was faking everything. Troy gave her a short salute wave as he smoked. She waved back at him thinking how Troy was exactly as he always seemed—self absorbed but harmless.

Mario wandered over. 'Beau'ful, your break time too?' He sat down beside her and tended to his Macca's bag. 'Here.' He handed her fries, 'I always get two packs.'

She felt grateful for the warm salty chips. With all the chaos there was no time for a lunch break.

He pulled out his hamburger and sandwiched several fries between the bun and the meat patty while he talked. 'I've tried to teach him.' He took a bite and licked the dripping juice from his fingers. 'Never listens.'

'Mario, he's not interested in me.'

He wiped his mouth with the back of his hand. 'Babe, trust me,' he took another bite of his burger. 'He's got a crush the size of my biceps on you.' He spoke through his mouthful. 'See the way he walks around you? It's the pheromone walk. The walk to keep you hooked.'

'I doubt it. He didn't even try to explain.'

'He rode through a thirty-foot window for you and pashed you all night. That ain't just friends.' Mario swallowed.

'I guess,' Rachel said thoughtfully.

'Look babe, we dudes act clueless sometimes 'cause if we don't then chicks think we're full of ourselves. But if we're all clueless we stuff it up and chicks think we're arseholes, right?'

'Some guys are arseholes—Garth.'

'Yeah, but mostly, we're identical to you chicks. Trying to figure out how to do the dance. You know?'

She looked at him confused.

'The dance, like Charls and me. She brushes me off, so I up the attention. She gets interested, so I back off and act cool. She gets cross at me about my car, so I agree to anything she wants—almost.' He bit into his burger. 'It's a dance babe.' He spoke through his mouthful. 'Justin acts not interested, but he is. You get your hat and hate him, but you don't. When one person is pissed and pullin' away, the other person must figure what move to make so they don't mess it up. Gettin' what I'm saying?'

She nodded. 'Yeah, I think I do.'

'Good. Babe, you can't sit here and do nothin'. He eyed her. 'You here, Justin in there, someone's gotta make the first move. Like me mum always says, "if you want something you gotta take it."'

Rachel stared across the car park. Mario's talk was surprisingly calming.

Mario looked serious. 'There's the dance babe but there's also the Dr Phil attention look.' He modelled a sincere frown while looking intently into her eyes. 'You think I'm listening right? I might be thinking about something else… '

'Like your car?'

'Exactly. Trust me babe, it's an essential relationship tool, which I've told Just.'

'Maybe you should write a relationship book one day.'

He raised his eyebrows at her idea, downing the last mouthful of his burger and licking the juice running down his wrist. Mario had no idea she was joking. Her phone buzzed.

It was Sandra: *Get your arse back here now.*

Lightning flashed across the sky followed by a loud crack of thunder. Several drops of rain fell. 'We should get back inside,' she said, then thought about how much Mario hated Garth. 'Mario,' she could trust him, 'Any minute now the police are going to be here because Garth has been smuggling drugs in the quality control box. I hid it so he wouldn't find it… the drugs… they're in chickens.'

'Bullshit!' he gasped.

'All true. That's why he asked about the box and is behaving crazy—which he is.'

'Bloody hell!' He still looked stunned. 'What are we doing out here. Come on, let's get back inside.' Mario chucked the rubbish in the bin and grinned back at her as she stood up. 'Babe, this is gonna be epic.'

Chapter Thirty Nine

A hurricane had gone through the deli. Chucked containers from the coolroom lay strewn across the deli. Chicken necks, ham hocks, red splattered sundried tomatoes, slippery olives, and tossed unraveled butcher paper decorated the floor. Justin leaned against the front counter, chatting casually to a customer, both entertained by Garth's meltdown.

'Closed me checkout. Didn't wanna miss nothin',' Charlene said, rushing up to Mario, her voice rising with excitement. She pushed in the metal seal on her can of Diet Pepsi, offering it to Mario.

'He's cracked it,' Mario said, taking a swig. 'This gonna help the police nab him for sure. Probs the steroids.'

With his tight shirts and large pecs forcing the friendship with the stretched buttonholes, it wasn't hard to believe he'd be on steroids. She glanced at the knives on the back bench. If he was crazy enough to crack it in front of everyone, who knew what else he might do? As Garth, acting like a crazy man, raced back into the coolroom, Rachel hurried into the deli to hide the knives

Valentina looked distressed. 'Has a fit over one box. One box. He's got no resonance.'

'Resilience,' corrected Rachel, eyeing the coolroom door.

'I always thought he was a psychotic.' Valentina shook her head.

They ducked as a container of bocconcini flew into the deli from the coolroom, hitting the bench, the lid flying off, sending the white balls plummeting and bouncing across the floor like large silent hail. Crouching, she turned to see Justin's frown. She wanted to say something to him—apologise for being so melodramatic. She ducked, avoiding another roll of spare butcher paper, torpedoing through the door. Mario rested his arm on Charlene's shoulder, confident like a prize boxer, who knows his next fight is a certain win. Charlene sipped her Diet Coke, between loud whistles of encouragement at Garth's crazy, as if she was enjoying a music festival.

'Justin, where's Sandra?' *Why wasn't she here?*

'Don't know. She was here a few minutes ago,' he said. 'Almost as soon as she left douchebag turned up.'

'He's only been at this for a few minutes?' She stared at the mess.

'Told youse it's steroids,' Mario looked confident in his appraisal of Garth. 'Gives him fake speed and strength.'

Valentina shook her head in disgust. 'Where's that Troy boy? He should be here to help.'

Rachel agreed, remembering the last place she saw him was in the car park, having a smoke. Before she could rally the troops to find the missing in action Troy, Sandra stormed back into the deli.

'What the bloody hell?' she bellowed, grabbing the butcher paper and smacking it down on the back bench like she was tenderising meat. 'This Garth's handiwork?' She jerked her head, signaling Rachel to follow her over to the chicken oven.

Rachel whispered, 'Where were you?'

'Me? What took you so long?' Sandra whispered back in her demanding tone.

'You're the deli manager. You needed to be here. And why are the police taking so long?'

'Don't know. Went to check with Lillian. Had to tell her what's going on. Didn't want her to pass out when Bades the buffoon gets handcuffed out of here.'

'You told Lillian about the… ' *drugs*, she mouthed.

'Keep your head on. I told her Bader's made a massive mistake and the cops are on their way. Took it well—shoved a donut in her mouth and called out to Jen.'

'She told Jen?'

'She just said Bader's committed a crime and the police are coming.'

'Sandra!' Rachel looked over at the counter where Jen and Wilma stood, with a distressed looking Nat coming up behind them. It didn't take long before half the store was there looking on.

'So, where're we up to with ball-brains? He's scaring my customers,' growled Sandra. 'Mario, go drag thick-head Troy back here before my deli's destroyed.'

'Call him,' Mario shouted back.

'What's his number?' Sandra asked.

No one responded.

Charlene hit Mario's chest with the back of her hand. 'Maz, be a hero.' She gave him a seductive look. 'I'll keep your spot warm.'

Mario kissed Charlene on the head and bolted off to find Troy.

Rachel caught Justin looking her way. He hadn't lifted a finger to fix anything—Garth's mess nor dissing her. But she couldn't waste time on him now. Garth stormed out of the coolroom, looking like a man who'd just lost a million dollars—probably because he had.

'Place is a mess. You dickheads need me to show you how to clean a coolroom,' he bellowed.

'Sure then, you can clean my car when you're done.' Sandra shot back, biting into a slim salami as she scrolled her phone. She leaned toward Rachel, lowering her voice. Lills says our visitors are almost here.'

Relief surged through Rachel, tangled with a wild thrill she couldn't shake. The police were nearly here. Garth wouldn't have a chance to bolt or bury his mess. Everyone had seen his meltdown. Sandra looked assured, biting into her salami and reassuring Valentina that help was on its way. Justin surprisingly began to pick up the paper rolls off the floor. Perhaps he was trying to make amends by being kind of helpful. She eyed Garth, who stood seething, looking like he wanted to kill her.

'Hey, Garth.' She was surprised at how confident she sounded. 'I actually do remember where I put the chickens.'

He snarled at her. 'Where bitch?'

'Here's the thing. They were off, right? And me being the shit deli chick that I am, wacked them in the oven here.' She patted the oven. 'We were low on stock,' she sounded glib.

'Bullshit!' He looked horrified.

Sandra, seizing Rachel's cue, snatched up the tongs and yanked a chicken from the oven. 'Here—' she dropped it onto her shoe and booted it across the deli. The chook smacked Garth square in the face. 'Cooked to your liking.'

'You bloody bitch!' Garth roared, then—catching sight of the gawking onlookers—quickly dabbed his stitched face. He grabbed an empty box and, in a frenzy, began scooping up the drug chickens just as Bader barrelled into the deli, red-faced and puffing, looking one breath away from self-combusting.

'I'm going to kill her!' he bellowed, shaking Sandra's clipboard in one hand, while the other performed several frantic runs over his comb-over. 'You sent those unsolicited emails, didn't you? I have evidence.' He held up her clipboard. White spittle gathered at the corners of his mouth. 'I'll have you sacked for defaming me.' He didn't seem to notice Garth at the oven, wildly chucking the chooks into the box.

'Bades mate, you should've kept your head together,' Sandra shot back, utterly unimpressed.

'You injudicious cow! I should've sacked you when I had the chance!' he spluttered.

'He's going to have a heart attack,' Valentina cried. 'Or kill someone.'

Rachel glanced at the knives on the bench, which she'd forgotten to hide earlier. Quickly, she rushed over and hid them under the bench.

Sandra didn't care if he had open heart surgery in front of her. She was cross and on fire. 'You tried to pin Rachel's coolroom drama on me. I saw your email. False accusation!'

Garth finished packing the chickens into the box. As Bader and Sandra's argument took centre stage, he crept out of the deli with the chickens, as if he was doing a civil service saving the customers from putrid chickens.

Police sirens echoed through the store. Rachel drew in several deep breaths, trying to regulate the wild rush of excitement rising in her body. But after three breaths, she decided it was impossible to instil any sense of calm and regulation. Help was finally here. Garth was about to be arrested. How could she deep breathe through this? She couldn't wait to see the circus. Although, she felt sorry for Bader, the bumptious, desultory supermarket manager, who didn't deserve to be blindsided by Garth.

Bader darted his eyes anxiously towards the entrance. 'What's going on?'

'Why don't you ask Garth,' Sandra told him.

His eyes widened in terror.

'It's called a drug trade Bades.'

Bader wiped his comb-over several times in the wrong direction as the blood drained from his face. 'Drugs?'

'Because of your incompetent management skills, Garth's been trading drugs through my deli.'

Bader wobbled and rested his hand on the counter.

'Losing your pants and puking in your bin, isn't going to fair well with corporate now, is it?' Sandra looked like she'd just been awarded the line umpire's ruling that her futsal ball crossed the line for a winning goal.

Bader pointed his finger at her. 'You, you… you haven't heard the… . the end of this,.' he said, his voice shaky, his pupils enlarged, his left eye twitching. Frantically, he ran towards the milk section, then made a sharp turn along the cheese, yogurt, and pre-packaged hams and raced towards his office.

Lillian's voice interupted the chaos, echoing over the PA. 'Attention staff and customers. We're sorry to announce the store is ah… closing. The police,' her voice quavered, 'are… we need everyone to stay where they are…' She finished, forgetting to turn off her microphone, and telling the hens, who came up to the service desk to see the drama that, 'Garth the drug dealer is going to prison.'

A frantic commotion hit the store as shoppers scooted up to the entrance to watch the unfolding drama. Garth was half-way up the fruit aisle, his box heavy, pulling on his tight shirt forcing a button to pop off and show his chest. The police demanded he stop. Garth told them he had an important errand to deliver and tried to shove past. When they snatched his box and forced him to the ground, everyone in the store could hear Garth shout that they had the wrong guy, and he was just doing his, 'fucking job.'

'Some job,' joked Rachel.

Sandra high fived Rachel. 'Come on Rach, let's go see the misogynist pig get cuffed.'

Rachel nodded, liking that Sandra called her Rach. She started to follow Sandra and Valentina to the front of the store, then paused. In all the commotion she hadn't noticed that Justin was nowhere to be seen. She looked over to the shelf where he placed his bag when he arrived that morning. It was empty. He'd left. Was he taking an early mark thinking with all the craziness that no one would care? She felt strangely uncomfortable. Where was Justin?

Chapter Forty

Heavily armed special force police, wearing dark uniforms and helmets, stormed the store. Bader lingered anxiously near Lillian at the service desk as two detectives strode towards him, his comb-over still brushed in the opposite direction. Reminiscent of the night he'd danced on the checkouts, Rachel cringed at the sight of him humiliated once again with staff gleefully snapping photos.

Moments later, Glen Smyth and a contingent of head honchos entered Goodsworth. Their expressions were grave as they questioned Sandra about the drugs and Bader's emails.

'This is Rachel.' Sandra introduced her to Glen. 'She found the drugs stuffed up the chooks arses and stashed them so boofhead Garth wouldn't get his mitts on them.'

Rachel forced a smile, trying to feel proud, but her mind spun. Where was Justin? Why vanish the moment Garth turned psycho? Her thoughts leapt back to when he'd opened the off chickens—why hadn't he checked properly? Why had he urged them not to tell Sandra? And the coolroom—he knew there were no CCTV cameras. Did he invite her out for pho just to kill time until he could grab the drugs? Did he lock her in the coolroom to keep her out of the way—then stage the grand rescue as a decoy? She felt ashamed she was thinking this was even conceivable. She gazed around trying to find him, not wanting to believe this could be true.

Glen looked impressed, congratulating them for their amazing work. Sandra shook his hand with gusto, jerking her thumb to her poster on the wall, reminding him she'd been Employee of the Year for five years in a row. He seemed to magnify his interest, just to be polite.

She looked over at Bader's terror ridden expression, vehemently denying any involvement with Garth. 'I don't know anything about the drugs. I swear, someone hacked into my account.'

Glen excused himself from talking to Rachel and Sandra. A pragmatic and fair man, he placed his hand on Bader's arm and lead him patiently away to his office. Bader blew into his handkerchief, his voice muffled so that whatever he was saying to Glen was not possible to hear. She hoped Glen would be kind. It was hard not to feel sorry for the ineffectual blundering store manager.

She didn't feel a bit sorry for Garth, who handcuffed was being jostled into the back of a police car, the buttons on his shirt popped, fully exposing his sculptured abs. It was such a shame his physique was wasted on him. As the car pulled away from the curb, Sandra jubilantly waved him off as if he was about to embark on a three-week party cruise.

She scanned the supermarket, hoping to see Justin. Instead, Charlene, Trudy and Lucy chatted excitedly with Tezza and Mario. Troy, wearing his aviators and a serious expression, acted like he was all over it, as he concurred with the police over their take on the events. Lillian, with her hand on her chest, looked aghast as she mulled over the drama with the hens. Nat was there too, his face white. Wilma consoled him about Bader's demise, her arm around his shoulder.

Slowly, staff returned to their positions, while others continued to watch on as the police cornered off the deli for further investigation. Lillian, chatted excitedly on the phone. Mario and Charlene, after telling Rachel how brave she was, snuck out to the loading dock—alone.

'That's what I call a good day's work,' Sandra said, surveying the store from where she stood with Rachel at the service desk. Her hand using the wind-up signal at Lillian. 'On the phone to Marj, gotta hear the goss,' she said to Rachel. 'Hurry up Lills,' she ordered. 'And Rach, can you believe Justin? Right when I'm in the thick of telling Dimitri from Mega Mart about the drugs, he texts me he's leaving. Like timing buddy.'

'Leaving?'

'Something about an acting gig. Took the call when Garth was offloading the chooks.'

So that was where he went. Not a dealer. She wanted to slap her own face for thinking such a thing. 'So, he… he… '

'Text me to tell me, when I went past Bader's office to check how the sniveling little shit was going. Only the door was shut.'

'So, what did he say to you?'

'Bader just kept telling Glen he had nothing to do with it.'

'Not him. Justin.'

'Oh, that's he's quitting.'

'Quitting?'

'Yep. I ought to dock his pay. Quits now when there's gonna be restructuring. I'm used to it. He always comes back when acting gigs dry up.'

Rachel checked her phone. No messages from him. How could he not say goodbye? 'How long ago did you see him?'

'Ten mins.'

She glanced at her watch, calculating how long it would take Justin to leave.

'Back in a minute Sandra,' she said, not waiting for her response.

Rachel sprinted through the mall towards the car park. Steam rose off the hot concrete pavement from the passing shower. She loved the smell of summer rain on the concrete. Lightning cracked across the sky, another storm was on its way. She looked across the car park hoping to find Justin.

'Looking for something, someone?'

She spun around. Justin stood behind her, keys in hand.

'No, I, um.' *What do I say?* 'I was just about to leave. You know, with all the commotion, I don't think the store needs us.'

'Without your bag?'

'Oh, can you believe I forgot it? All the commotion… '

Large drops of rain began to fall. Justin clicked the keys in his hand. The lights on the silver Golf parked nearby flashed. 'Borrowed my mum's car.'

Of course, she remembered his mangled bike. 'Sandra said you got the acting role. Congrats.' She could barely stand herself for thinking he might've be in on the drug deal.

'Thanks. Supporting role. Filming here in Sydney actually.'

Great! But what's he thinking? He certainly wasn't saying goodbye. A good sign. She studied his expression. Maybe Mario was wrong. Maybe he just wanted to leave on good terms so neither of them bagged each other out. 'I was a little bit weird back there. Sorry. I was stressed. It's great news about your gig but I think I already congratulated you and—'

'I kept your cap because I know what Garth's like and I figured, being the shallow creep he is, that he wouldn't be into hairnets.' He flicked his fringe.

'What?'

'Sorry, I should have given it back to you,' he said seriously.

'So, you let me wear the hairnet because of Garth?'

'It was a stupid idea.'

'Yes, if it was a mean prank.' But she loved that he was into her way back when she first started. She wondered, 'I seriously look terrible in the hairnet. Right?'

'No. In fact,' his eyes twinkled, 'you looked cute.'

She snorted, 'Really.'

'Really.'

'Justin… '

'Yeah.'

'I found the drugs in the quality control box. Can you believe they were stuffed in the chickens?' she grimaced. 'Gross.'

Justin blinked. 'Bullshit? That's what was going on? And we didn't see it? Although you did. Awesome detective work. Sandra must love you.'

'Well, she's calling me Rach now,' she laughed.

'Explains the dick's black gym bag…'

She could tell by Justin's pause in conversation he was thinking about the red flags they'd missed. 'Bet you're exhausted. And then I go and dump the cap on you. Sorry Rach. Bad timing.'

'Yeah, bad timing,' she smiled. 'I'm just relieved it's over. So, I told Sandra instead and she said not to tell anyone… but I wanted to tell you.'

He stepped closer, and took her hands.

'I was going to tell Bader, but he wasn't in his office.'

'Makes more sense now. You were weird.'

'I was weird.'

'Very.'

Rain started to fall in large drops. Several fell on their faces.

'It's crazy in there,' she said softly, her heart pounding.

'Really crazy.' He pulled her to his chest.

The rain thickened, thunder cracked overhead. He lifted her chin, brushing her lips with his.

'You know what they say about workplace relationships,' she paused trying to gauge his intent.

'Good thing I won't be working here then,' he said.

She closed her eyes as he kissed her.

Thunder cracked overhead. The rain poured. She couldn't care less.

Chapter Forty One

It was customary for the deli chicks to select a name from a cap for Kris Kringle, which they exchanged on the last shift before Christmas. This year, Sandra, Justin and Rachel were invited to Valentina's for Christmas dinner.

'I've made an execution decision,' Valentina said.

'Executive,' Rachel corrected gently.

'Yes, that one,' Valentina nodded. 'Because of the madness in this place, we're going to give our Kris Kringles at my house on Christmas day.' She selected the Kris Kringle names and let everyone know who they would be buying for. Even Ian and Cheryl were included.

After a week of heat waves, Christmas day was a welcomed 26 degrees. Justin pulled up in his mum's car in front of Valentina's house. His family celebrated on Christmas Eve, so he wouldn't be missed by them today. Rachel hopped out and opened the back door, collecting the Mega Mart poinsettia, Moët, and her handbag from the seat. Justin picked up his gift and flowers. They caught each other's eye and smiled at the sheer pleasantness of it all.

Red and pink roses bordered a red brick path leading straight to the front porch of the 1940's semi-detached clinker brick home. The grass was trim, no weeds in sight, and the smell of roses perfumed the air as they walked up to the entrance.

Rachel pushed the doorbell, which by its traditional ring suggested was as old as the house. Valentina opened the door like she'd been waiting for Vogue photographers to arrive. Freshly colored hair, perfect brows, a low-cut red dress under her apron, and—shock of shocks—black heels instead of the pope-esque red work shoes. Rachel was surprised at how elegant and very attractive Valentina really was.

'My darlings!' Valentina enveloped them in a hug, sniffed the flowers, and declared, 'Justin, you are better news than the Mario boy.'

Justin shot Rachel a look, to which she shrugged, suggesting she'd tell him later about Valentina's assumption about Mario and her—like that would ever happen.

Valentina ushered them briskly into the house telling them Alvaro had been up early with last minute fix ups—mowing the lawn, trimming the hedge along the carport side, and giving the roses a soak. 'Thank god,' she said.

Rachel handed Valentina the poinsettia and the bottle of Moet. 'Figured we have a lot to celebrate.'

'We have indeed,' Valentina beamed. 'The end of Garth. I cannot believe he is in prison. Deserves it... ' She kept talking, walking down the hall towards the back of the house. She whispered to Rachel, 'Justin is your handsome prince.'

Rachel looked back at Justin. Valentina's whispers were not that quiet. He jokingly smirked. She poked out her tongue. He laughed.

They followed Valentina down the hallway, past a gallery of Blanca and Enrique—beach snapshots, school photos, and two large graduation portraits. In their black gowns, caps slightly askew with tassels dangling, they clutched their scrolls like trophies. Rachel remembered how Liz had put her graduation photo in a drawer. She wondered if she had a graduation photo, where she'd put it. She knew where Ian would hang it, on the living room wall. He'd be so proud.

'Enrique and his girlfriend are in the kitchen. I'll introduce you later,' she said, swinging open the door to the covered verandah. 'See the settings on the table?' she nudged Rachel. 'Twelve of us today. A happy gathering.' She handed Alvaro the Moët. 'Alvaro, this is Rachel, the heroine, and Justin, who works with her.' *Heroine.* She caught Justin's raised expression. She could tell there would be a lot of eye-talk between them today.

Alvaro, a stocky man, wore pleated cream pants with a light green polo shirt. Her first impression was a man of taste. She took his lead on a kiss for each cheek while Justin shook his hand firmly. Valentina gave

Alvaro instructions to pour 'the kids' drinks. He gave her a gentle pat on the bum as she turned to rush back to the kitchen.

'Not the lazy pig,' she said quietly to Justin, as Alvaro collected wine glasses from the outside bench.

Justin looked at her inquisitively.

'Nothing,' she said, thinking she'd fill him in later.

Alvaro poured a drink, laughing with them about the antics at the supermarket and the dramatic way Valentina had described the drug hoist. He was different to how she'd imagined him—a disinterested husband with a beer gut. With his tanned olive skin and toned muscles on his lower arms, along with the swept patio, neat lawn without a weed in sight, and the trimmed fruit trees dotting the back fence, she wondered if Valentina had been annoyed with Alvaro when she'd complained about him. If appearances were accurate, he was energetic, warm, and fun.

Rachel glanced at the long table on the verandah, which Alvaro told them he'd extended with flat board from Bunnings. On the white linen sat a vase of vibrant Christmas bush, silver cutlery, white plates with gold trim, tall wine goblets, and napkins folded like origami swans. Rachel raised her eyebrows. Classy.

Taking a sip of her drink, she looked across the yard where the other guests sat on wooden framed canvas chairs sheltering under a large magnolia tree from the sun.

'See your dad's already here with Cheryl,' Justin said, taking her hand.

Rachel was glad she'd insisted Cheryl join them. After all, her own two adult children were spending the day with their father, Shaun the Luxury Sports car dealer, out on his mega yacht. According to Ian, Cheryl was thrilled to be joining them.

Katie was the first to greet her with a warm hug, telling her how much Sandra raved about her. Of course, Sandra denied this strongly, with several cracks at Rachel's incompetence like blue hair, losing her cap, and being 'bloody' hopeless at handling raw meat. 'Necks are her specialty,' she joked. Rachel hadn't seen Sandra out of uniform before—except for the oversized T-shirt and cap, and the PJ-and-hoodie combo—but today, white jeans and a blue shirt made her look like she actually owned a wardrobe.

'Guys, this is Blanca from the Washington D and C,' Sandra joked referencing Valentina.

'Can't seem to get in mum's head it's Washington DC,' Blanca said, giving Rachel a hug. 'Mum's spoken a lot about you Rachel. So glad you both could join us.' She stretched out her arm towards a lean man the same height as her and roughly the same age. 'This is my partner, Nick.'

After greeting Blanca and Nick, Rachel turned to Sandra, who looked surprisingly softer around the edges away from Goodsworth and here with Katie. 'Hear congratulations are in order Sandra,' she deliberately sounded formal.

'Yeah, well done, Sands,' said Justin. 'Great news.'

'Always said I'd get Bader's job. Glen was just about begging me to take the role. Poor Bades, promoted beyond his competence level. Never fairs well.'

Tales of Garth's infamous drug hoist, and Bader's spectacular job loss ricocheted around like ping-pong balls. Rachel sipped her drink, wondering how chaos could be this charming when it involved other people.

'Garth, the drug smuggler. Always knew the guy was up to no good,' Sandra said. She'd been busier than ever mopping up Bader's 'one hell of a mess,' while keeping an ear to the ground to 'catch the goss.'

'I still can't believe an international drug syndicate was operating through the deli!' Rachel exclaimed.

'Right under our noses," Sandra said, sourly. 'Until you came along, Rach.'

Justin gave Rachel a gentle nudge. She glanced at him, letting a small, thoughtful smile play across her lips, and nudged him back just enough to share in the quiet triumph of Sandra's rare, observable kindness.

'Meth too,' Sandra added with a dramatic sigh.

Rachel thought of *The Sydney Morning Herald* headline a few days after Garth's arrest: *Drug Syndicate Operates in Suburban Supermarket.* Forensic police and sniffer dogs had shut down Goodsworth for two days, sniffing everything from the meat counter to the frozen peas.

'Garth deserves to be in prison,' said Katie, having heard every bad story about him.

'And the fact the police had been monitoring shipping container deliveries to Figgles and still hadn't made the link to Goodies.' Sandra shook her head.

'Took Rachel to figure it out,' Justin said, sliding an arm around her and planting a quick peck on her forehead.

'They found over 200 kilos,' said Blanca.

'Prepacked in 200-gram parcels,' added Sandra.

'Secreted under floorboards and metal pallets in shipping containers from South East Asia,' continued Rachel, laughing about how they had all memorised the article.

'Secreted, huh.' Justin gave her an impressed glance.

'Took that word from the article, but it's good.'

'And so was the comment about you and Sandra, that "it was the swift action of two Goodsworth employees, who detected suspicious behaviour by a supermarket employee, Mr. Garth Lincoln."'

'Knew he was no good, the moment he tooted his horn,' Ian said, taking a piece of cheese and a cracker from the platter on the small folding table.

Passionately, Sandra explained how the Feds found hundreds of chicken carcasses stuffed with meth parcels. And she didn't hold back in how upset she was that the reporter called their store "sleepy."

'Riled my blood reading that. Bades drove the store to the ground. Not anymore. I'll see to that. And the flip side of the news article is that we've been busier than ever for this time of year. Kind of famous in a way.'

'To Rachel, Sandra and old Goodies,' Justin toasted.

Everyone raised their glasses. Rachel took a delicate sip of her sparkling, glancing at her dad sitting next to Cheryl. He smiled back, looking impossibly relaxed in his crisp white linen shirt and chinos—Christmas cheer actually visible on his face for the first time in years.

Valentina yelled from the verandah that dinner would be on the table in ten minutes, while Enrique helped Alvaro top up their drinks.

Rachel excused herself to great Enrique and place her Kris Kringle under the Christmas tree in the dining room, which Valentina had pointed out when they arrived. The tall, fake-but-deceivingly-real tree glowed with golden lights, scattering warmth across the room. Its decorations were a chaotic mix from years of family life. She placed her gift under the tree, hoping Valentina, her Kris Kringle recipient, would enjoy the book—*Mastering the Art of French Cooking* by Julia Child.

'Here's mine,' Justin said, coming up behind her, putting an envelope next to hers. 'Gift voucher for Sands. She's hard to buy for,' he said, giving her a kiss. 'Come on, I can hear them at the table.'

Valentina, Nick, Enrique, and his girlfriend Court—a sales assistant with the same obsession for cooking as Valentina—brought the food to the table while Alvaro poured the wine with a flourish. Blanca laughed with Katie and Sandra over more supermarket stories, this time about how her mum was obsessed with handing out recipes to customers.

Platters were passed around, laughter and chatter filling every pause. And if there was a pause, Valentina or Alvaro would leap in with a tiny vignette from their life.

Ian, sitting next to Rachel, clinked her glass spontaneously. 'Thanks, honey, for suggesting we have Christmas here.'

'You're very welcome,' she replied, trying not to beam too hard.

Cheryl, beside him, smiled and guested her glass in a toast.

Before everyone started, Valentina bowed her head and offered a prayer of thanksgiving. At the end of her prayer, she added, 'And thank you that my maraca shaking brings good karma and Sandra is now the supermarket manager.'

As everyone congratulated Sandra again, Rachel watched her glowering in the joy of the moment. The job of her dreams was hers.

There was the clinking of glasses, the scraping of utensils on plates, the sound of cold sparkling wine falling into the tall glasses, and the endless platters of festive fare; turkey, roast pork, baked vegetables followed by fruit pudding and layers of custard, cream, and ice cream. Valentina leaned over and whispered that she'd made a special effort with the traditional dishes, 'knowing how… less than satisfying your Christmases have been since your mum passed.' Rachel dabbed at her mouth, savoring the moment. Warmth spread through her chest—this was Christmas again, real and frenetic and full of joy. She was grateful she'd said yes to Valentina's invitation.

Valentina interrupted the bubble of friendly conversation. 'Everybody, it's time to resign to the dining room to open our Kris Kringles.'

'Mum, I think you mean *retire* to the dining room,' Blanca gently corrected.

'Retire, resign, it all the same to me.'

Chapter Forty Two

Epilogue

A month later, Rachel walked into Bader's old office. Sandra sat behind the desk, which was now neat and sparse. Her *In* and *Out-Trays* were equally proportioned with paperwork, and a large mug, emblazoned with *Keep Calm and Don't Shit Yourself,* held hot coffee.

'New chair?'

Sandra patted the armrests. 'Demanded it as part of my promotion. After all,' she said, 'I'm going to be busy cleaning up Bader's one hell of a mess, so I needed a damn new high-back leather swivel chair for my troubles.'

Rachel smiled, agreeing. With a sideways glance, she took in the office. A new fan in the corner blasted fresh air across the room. The whiteboard, cleanly scrubbed, displayed dates, meeting times, and agendas in neat colourful writing. A new notice board hung to the right of the whiteboard. On it were photos of Sandra with Katie from their last Hawaiian holiday, several cards of congratulations, and Glen Smyth's letter praising her detective-level brilliance in exposing a drug ring. Rachel had received a similar letter, and, like Sandra, five thousand dollars in acknowledgment of their bravery. Against the adjacent wall hung Sandra's six Employee of the Year certificates, framed in black, glaring at her like tiny trophies of glory.

Sandra followed her gaze. 'Got it again. How could I not, after what I did for this store?' She shifted in her chair. 'What we did.'

'You did more than me. You alerted the Big Boys.'

'Yeah, well, as much as I should take all the cred, must be honest, you found the goods. Imagine if Garth, the tossa, had stashed that lot for when he got out of prison? Happens you know. Heard it was Garth who locked you in the coolroom.'

Rachel nodded. The police had called to let her know Garth had been in the coolroom looking for a missing delivery of chickens when she entered. He hid behind the door and shut her in. Obviously, it was better to kill her than get caught with the drugs. And thanks to the CCTV footage at the front of the store, they found he'd taken the garbage bag of tossed white king chickens. What an idiot.

'I'm glad you took the job at checkouts,' Sandra said, folding her hands on the desk like a CEO about to announce layoffs—confident and in charge.

'No dead pigs, cooked chickens, or cold fridges?' she joked.

Sandra didn't laugh.

The newspaper clipping on the notice board caught Rachel's eye. She walked around the desk to read it.

Sandra followed with the turn of her chair. 'Good article, hey?' she said. 'It's about the new CEO of Goodsworth. Says she's an ex-checkout chick,' Sandra stated. 'That's going to be me, Rach,' she said emphatically. 'I'm going all the way.'

Rachel had no doubt she would.

'And Val's been accepted for MasterChef. Can you believe it? Been practising to get on that show for years. And what do you know—one good dish and boom, she's in.'

'Oh, that is so exciting,' she said, thinking how she told Valentina her Christmas dinner was amazing. She felt like she'd be cheating on her mum if she said it was the best she'd ever had—but it was.

Sandra tilted her head, doing her serious HR face. 'Hear you're going to uni? Anything to do with the events here?'

'Pretty much.'

It was several days after Christmas when an envelope arrived by courier to her apartment. With the sender from Goodsworth Supermarket, she guessed it was about the drug deal. Ian was in the kitchen peeling potatoes for dinner, while Cheryl stood beside him oiling and seasoning the roast lamb. Eagerly, they told her to hurry and open the envelope. She read Glen Smyth's letter aloud.

He thanked her for her courage, resilience, and decisiveness. She glanced at Ian, who affirmed the sentiments. 'You always were a bright thinker, Rach,' he said, in the same tone people use when you finally figure out how to reset the Wi-Fi.

It was the gift of five thousand dollars that first made her scream and dance with Cheryl and Ian around the kitchen—and then inspired her to make a choice she'd been putting off—study. Ian was thrilled, mostly because it meant she'd live at home longer and not blow rent money on dodgy share-houses with broken heaters.

Sandra adjusted her position in her chair. 'What are you going to study then?'

'Maybe Business. Surprised?'

'Nup,' she said without expression. 'Always knew you were brighter than you let on. Don't underestimate yourself Rach, be confident, and when you're not, fake it till you are.' She looked serious.

'Thank you for giving me the job at checkouts Sandra.'

'Yeah, well, not gonna lie Rach. I was disappointed you knocked back the Deli Team Leader position.'

It had been a complete surprise to Rachel when Sandra had rung offering her the Deli Team Leader role. 'You know I don't have experience.'

'Rubbish. None of our bonehead managers would've handled Garth and the drug deal debacle the way you did. Kept your head screwed on, made a plan, and did what I told you. Important qualities.'

Qualities. She remembered Bader telling her what qualities he was looking for as a checkout staff member. 'Do you want me to greet the customer's with, "How is your day?"' she asked.

'Are you mad? You see the way customers end up at the checkout? Exhausted. They just want to get home without chit chat. Nup. Ask them nothing. Just get those groceries in the bag as quick as you damn well can.'

Rachel smiled at Sandra, sitting in her chair, confidently in charge. The qualities Sandra admired were loyalty and brains. She could do that.

'You heard about Bader, right?' Sandra shifted in her chair ready to dispel gossip.

'Only that he was asked to leave.'

'Glen found out about some ignoramus at Head Office called Clive who pressured Bades into hiring Garth. Clive was in on the drug deal.'

'Wow,' said Rachel wide eyed. 'Like a conspiracy.'

'Wouldn't go that far. Clive threw old Bades under the bus. Said he'd been cooking the books to show higher revenue. He used this to bribe Bades to hire Garth.'

'Is that true?'

'That Bader cooked the books?'

'Yeah.'

'Bader doesn't know how to keep the books let alone cook them. Nah, Clive was a liar. Threatened Badey that no one would believe him if he snitched. What a fool. I would've reported Clive and shown him who was boss. That's the difference between old Bades and me. He's a pushover. But I've got guts,' she gloated. 'And can you believe this? Yesterday Lills saw old Badey working in Mega Mart—Produce Team Leader.' She wiped her hand across the top of her pocket referencing his name badge. 'Much more his level.'

Sandra was right about his "level." Despite his certificates on the wall, he had minimal people skills. She felt relieved at the news that Bader had another job. It would be sad to think he was unemployed.

'Anyway, back to business. You can take over from Jen on checkout five. Her varicose veins are giving her grief. Why she's still working at sixty-six with legs like a 3D road map is anyone's guess. I've asked Wilma to give you the induction. She's fast and efficient, have you off and running before morning tea break,' she said in her clipped business tone. 'Oh, and finally those Big Boys agreed to more self-service checkouts.

'Bout bloody time!'

After sorting out her weekly work schedule with Sandra, she walked back into the supermarket. The front window was repaired, the flower display had moved next to the service desk, and the Team Leader photos hanging above the entrance had been adjusted.

There at the top of the grid of photos was Sandra, the Supermarket Manager. Her proud grin staring down at the customers and employees alike. Bader and Garth's photos were long gone. Nat the pyramid building fresh food produce employee was there as well. She was glad to see he got the promotion to Checkout Team Leader. After all, besides Sandra, no one was as dedicated to Goodsworth as him. And to her surprise, there was Mario, the title under his photo, Butcher Delicatessen Team Leader.

'Good photo huh.' Mario came up beside her. 'IC of the butchery and deli. Sand's cutting jobs to save costs. Works for me. Twiggies any time I like.' He grinned.

'Congratulations Mario. Pretty awesome to be in charge of both those areas. Nice to see your clean apron by the way.'

'Yeah,' he chortled, wiping his hands over his white apron. 'Did you hear, Charls and me are official. Beau'ful, she's so in love with me. Even comes to the gym. Can't quite get that she wears high heels for workouts. But hey, she looks awesome, so who's complaining.'

Charlene called out to her from checkout three, 'Good to see you back Rach.'

Rachel gave her a little wave. Lillian, who'd greeted her with a hug when she'd arrived, lifted her eyes from her magazine and smiled. Troy, still wearing his aviators, his fake tan worn off, saluted her from the edge of the entrance where he stood, watching what was going on around him, for once. And Jen, at checkout five, relieved to have a break from standing, filled her in on Trudy and Lucy. 'Both dismissed,' she said, her tone serious. 'Not enough checkouts anymore.'

It was true. Where checkout one and two had been, workers in their heavy boots and thick blue work overalls installed three more self-service checkouts. Sandra had sacked Trudy and Lucy and hired her. She smiled to herself. Her job felt even more secure.

Her induction with Wilma over, she pulled out her water bottle and sanitiser and applied her lip-gloss. Her first customer loaded their groceries onto the conveyor belt. She glimpsed at her professionally manicured pink nails as she whisked the groceries under the scanner, which beeped in reply. Her customer thanked her and carried his groceries away. She pumped the hand sanitizer and looked at Justin's message flashing up on her phone.

How's checkouts? Dinner after work? X

She quickly sent a thumbs up to his message and: *Yes to dinner. Finish at 5 X*

Justin messaged*: XX*

Rachel messaged: *XX*

Supermarkets might be chaos, but at least dinner was sorted.

www.ingramcontent.com/pod-product-compliance
Lightning Source LLC
Chambersburg PA
CBHW010435170726
48283CB00011B/3214

* 9 7 8 1 7 6 4 3 6 1 0 0 2 *